HONG KONG COLLAGE
CONTEMPORARY STORIES AND WRITING

Hong Kong Collage
Contemporary Stories and Writing

Edited by
Martha P. Y. Cheung

HONG KONG
OXFORD UNIVERSITY PRESS
OXFORD   NEW YORK
1998

Oxford University Press

Oxford New York
Athens Auckland Bangkok Bogota Bombay
Buenos Aires Calcutta Cape Town Dar es Salaam
Delhi Florence Hong Kong Istanbul Karachi
Kuala Lumpur Madras Madrid Melbourne
Mexico City Nairobi Paris Singapore
Taipei Tokyo Toronto

and associated companies in
Berlin Ibadan

Oxford is a trade mark of Oxford University Press

First published 1998
This impression (lowest digit)
1 3 5 7 9 10 8 6 4 2

Published in the United States
by Oxford University Press, New York

British Library Cataloguing in Publication Data
available

Library of Congress Cataloging-in-Publication Data

Hong Kong collage: contemporary stories and writing/edited by
Martha P. Y. Cheung.
p.   cm.
ISBN 0-19-587483-8 (alk. paper)
1. Chinese literature—20th century—Translations into English.
2. Hong Kong (China)—Literary collections.   I. Cheung, Martha.
PL2658.E1H65   1998   97–50469
895.1'08095125'09045—dc21   CIP

Printed in Hong Kong
Published by Oxford University Press (China) Ltd
18/F Warwick House, Taikoo Place, 979 King's Road,
Quarry Bay, Hong Kong

Acknowledgements

The idea of compiling a collection of Hong Kong fictional works in English translation occurred to me in 1994, when Hong Kong was steeped in anxiety about the future. But it took me a long time to decide on the shape and form I would give to such a collection. During this period, I benefited tremendously from discussions with Dung Kai Cheung, Jamila Ismail, P. K. Leung, and Xiao Si on various possible ways of anthologizing Hong Kong fictional works and on how to present Hong Kong fiction to the English-speaking world at such a historical time. I did not adopt the ideas they had so generously offered me. But being the true friends that they are, they were not only tolerant of my constant change of mind, but were very supportive when I told them what I had finally decided to do. For this, I am extremely grateful.

I would also like to thank the writers for giving me the right to translate their works into English for inclusion in this collection. And of course, the translators, without whose contribution this book would not have been possible. Wong Kim Fan, Esther Kwok, and Lau Ming Pui—my research assistants at various stages of this project—know how grateful I am for their assistance. Still, I would like to say a warm thank you to them here.

A very warm thank you, too, to Jane C. C. Lai, who has always been a dear friend and the sternest and most inspiring critic of my work.

I would also like to acknowledge with gratitude the support from the following institutions: the Hong Kong Baptist University for a research grant to carry out this project, the Hong Kong Arts Development Council for a grant towards the permission fees, translation fees, and publication costs of this collection, and the Centre for Translation of the Hong Kong Baptist University for helping with the preparation of the manuscript.

MARTHA P. Y. CHEUNG
Hong Kong
December 1997

This project is supported by the Hong Kong
Arts Development Council.

Contents

Introduction

The great revelation never came, the great revelation never did come, instead there were little daily miracles, matches struck in the dark.

These words of Virginia Woolf from *To the Lighthouse* capture beautifully the spirit in which this collection has been brought together. The book does not claim to be the great Hong Kong epic that commentators say still has not appeared. It makes no pretence to being the definitive anthology of Hong Kong fictional works that many say Hong Kong lacks. It does not offer the 'great revelation' on Hong Kong that seems to be the aspiration of so many books—fiction and non-fiction alike—which appeared in the run-up to the momentous event of Hong Kong's return to Chinese sovereignty. Instead, it is an attempt, on the part of the editor, to tell her own story of Hong Kong through the mouths of other writers, almost all of whom were born and bred in Hong Kong. It is an unashamedly subjective, defiantly idiosyncratic collection—a collage rather than a representational painting. It speaks to all, especially to those who have no set ideas about Hong Kong.

The collection is unashamedly subjective because these pieces have not been selected for their representative significance—of the different schools, trends, and styles of fictional writing in Hong Kong, though in the course of reading, the reader will no doubt gain an idea of the diversity of style and dynamic vibrancy of the fictional scene in Hong Kong. Neither is the collection meant to reflect the history of the development of fictional writing in Hong Kong. Some of these pieces are not even presented as short stories, rather they take the form of essays (those by P. K. Leung and Xiao Si), or excerpts from novels (those by Xin Yuan and Dung Kai Cheung). But in their different ways, each tells a fascinating story about Hong Kong. And each is included here because, to this particular editor, it has struck a deep chord, captured her moods, expressed what she had wanted to say at particular moments of her life as she felt elated or struck by the forces that were shaping the history of the city in which she lives.

Over the years, a plethora of images has been imposed and superimposed on Hong Kong—by Western writers as well as those from the Mainland. A few of these images have hardened into stereotypes. Hong Kong is the goose that lays the golden egg. Hong Kong is Suzie Wong—infinitely alluring, tempting, and infinitely receptive to the enlightening influence of the benevolent West. Hong Kong is a wayward child, yellow on the outside, white on the inside, brought up under the influence of a ruthless and, at best, indifferent guardian. Hong Kong is the prodigal son about to return to the embrace of his father, who is kind and tolerant enough to allow him carry on with his way of life. To this long-time inhabitant of the city, these images are highly inventive, thought-provoking, and truly amusing; they are also extraordinarily remote, like aliens from another planet, puppets brought to life by different ideological strings.

To come across images that she could recognize and relate to was, to this editor, like meeting a friend on foreign soil. And this is an experience which the pieces included in this collection give her. There is surprise and delight, a momentary tightening of the heart; there is even the inexplicable sense of a minor triumph: a little daily miracle.

What strikes one reader as a little daily miracle might of course be dismissed by another as nothing out of the ordinary and some might find this an idiosyncratic collection. The more so as the pieces are grouped together in a way that might be considered haphazard. The collection is divided into five parts: Prologue, History, Landmarks, People, and Epilogue. But not all the pieces in the 'History' section are necessarily historical; not all the 'Landmarks' are famous sites; the Prologue is as much a conclusion as a foreword.

That's good. The question of representation and of representativeness, of the ordering and shaping of material, of genres and the crossing of genres, of boundary and the breaking of boundary, are precisely some of the questions highlighted in this collection. How does one represent Hong Kong/tell the story of Hong Kong? What represents Hong Kong? What is it to represent Hong Kong? Who is to represent Hong Kong? Is the representation of Hong Kong as simple and straightforward, as innocent and unproblematic, as those representations that we have seen on television, in newspapers and magazines? Is the history of Hong Kong sufficiently embodied in the form of chronicle, a linear presentation of dates and events? What about the ironies of history—painful or otherwise—which abound in the development of Hong Kong? Which version of Hong Kong history is one to take as 'true'—that produced by the British? by the Chinese? by Hong Kong historians? by supposedly apolitical and objective scholars? Are the so-called 'landmarks' of Hong Kong—those listed in tourist handbooks, printed on postcards, projected on to screens in promotional material, or deployed as settings for melodramas—anything more than just tired clichés? Do they really say something about the spirit of the place and the complex character of Hong Kong? Are the people of Hong Kong well and truly represented—represented with any depth—in the existing portraits? The money-obsessed, get-rich-quick men and women on the street; the mahjong players that fill every household; the punters that overflow into the racecourse on horse-racing days; the jewellery-studded tai tais; the empire-building-empire-wrecking taipans; the shadowy and sinister triad bosses (the last three making up the 'three-Ts' observed by commentators as indispensable ingredients of a Hong Kong novel)? Powerful is the avalanche of competing summations of Hong Kong's past, studies about its present, and forecasts about its future, all of which are making their own implicit or explicit claims to being the most representative, the most authoritative, the most definitive. Soon we would be written off by history as having already been written about—exhaustively, definitively, conclusively.

That is why we have to stand back and look at the representations for what they are—not truths, certainly not absolute truths, but just representations, attempts to speak on behalf of something or someone. This point is dramatized by many of the pieces in this collection. With humour or with sizzling anger, with detached irony or with flamboyant self-consciousness, the pieces draw attention to what are central to any act of representation: the politics of re-presentation (what is included and what is left out, what is highlighted and what is suppressed), and of the rhetorics of presentation (*how* to say something rather than *what* to say: the tone, inflections, subtext).

This seems pretty obvious. But when one—a person, a place, a people—is living in an echo chamber reverberating with voices claiming to be speaking on one's behalf, one will either be deafened and muted by the din, or forced to scream above it, or become extraordinarily alert to the politics of re-presentation and the rhetorics of presentation that lie behind those voices.

These reactions are, with varying degrees of intensity and explicitness, articulated in many of the pieces in this collection. In fact, the very collection itself has been brought together with the intention of laying bare the mechanisms of selection and rejection, of personal motives and strategies of presentation that govern any act of representation. Hence the description of this work I gave earlier: 'It is an unashamedly subjective and defiantly idiosyncratic collection—a collage rather than a representational painting.' Taken as a whole, this book registers my own personal response to the many voices that have claimed to represent Hong Kong, or have been proclaimed as representative of Hong Kong over the last decade. It registers my own personal response too, to the many new voices that are now claiming to represent Hong Kong. The collection also marks this individual's attempt to counter the grand narratives, the master images, and the controlling identities—imposed on Hong Kong from the outside—with narratives, images, and identities chosen by the people of Hong Kong for themselves. The aim is not to replace one set of grand whatevers with another. The pieces, though making up a collage, stand in their own right as interesting and absorbing stories and can be read in any order that takes the reader's fancy. For each in its own way illuminates Hong Kong from the inside, throwing light on its culture, its vicissitudes, its inhabitants, its striking features.

Matches struck in the dark. That's what they are. A glimmer here, a flicker there, a flash elsewhere, lighting up, if only for a while, the faces, expressions, gestures, movements, bodies, shapes, contours, areas, and spaces all too seldom seen by the Western eye. Occasionally in the past, when translations of Hong Kong literature—either in the form of anthologies or of individual works—appeared, glimpses could be caught of what exist in the dark. But, by and large, the inhabitants of this city, who mostly express in Chinese their thoughts, their feelings, their hopes and aspirations, worries and anxieties, strengths and weaknesses, values and beliefs, desires, neuroses and hang-ups, have tended to remain in a world inaccessible to those who do not speak the same language. Now that Hong Kong has crossed without stumbling what many in the world considered to be an incredibly high threshold of history, the spotlight of the international media—welcoming to some, sinister to others, irrelevant to most—has been switched off. But there are matches struck in the dark. They will continue to burst into light, illuminating the different facets of this amazing city, and its amazing people, to all who care to cast their glance this way.

PART I

Prologue

The Story of Hong Kong

By **P. K. LEUNG**
Translated by Martha P. Y. Cheung

This is an expanded version of excerpts from P. K. Leung's book, written in Chinese and published in 1995, entitled Hong Kong Culture. *In this essay, the writer gives a broad overview of the cultural context in which the works in this anthology can be read. Expressing views and sentiments much shared by the editor, this essay can be read as a second introduction to the book.*

A story that is hard to tell

The story of Hong Kong has been told by many people. Some tell the story of a fishing port, others tell the story of a Chinese sailing boat, some tell the story of buildings rising high into the sky, others tell the story of the dazzling lights at night. Yet others tell the story of the fog at Lei Yue Mun, or of the bars at Lan Kwai Fong. The story seems to get simpler; the story seems to get more complicated. It leads to other stories, breaks off and begins again, begins and falters. The story of Hong Kong is getting longer, messier; the story of Hong Kong is getting shorter, flatter. Everyone is telling it—the story of Hong Kong. Everyone is telling a different story.

But then, we don't want to see everyone telling exactly the same story. And so, amidst this clamour of voices, we should perhaps listen carefully: who is telling the story? What sort of a story is it? For whom?

Over the years, there has been a steady stream of people from the outside seeking to tell the story of Hong Kong. These stories invariably have an action-packed plot spiced up with sex and adventure, with invariably a touch of the exotic. Suzie Wong in her cheongsam with high slits greeting her clients in a Wan Chai bar; taipans enjoying to the full the advantages of their race and their economic prowess; cut-throat financial competitions and political intrigues unravelling behind the facade of power and wealth of a noble house—fierce battles to make foreign readers gawk. Hong Kong is hit by a typhoon, landslides, a slump in the stock-market, a run on the banks—all in the space of a week in summer. Interwoven with these amazing events are business battles involving incredibly high stakes, political assassinations, and secret agents from different countries in open confrontations or clandestine struggles, with the bosses of foreign hongs always coming out on top, sweeping away the desired lover and soundly beating their opponents in business. It seems that Hong Kong could always be assigned to play the most absurd role. It is as if the most unlikely stories could, logically and inevitably, happen in Hong Kong.

In a recent film, a bookstore in Tsim Sha Tsui is portrayed as a hotbed of crime; the bookstore owner—a bearded Japanese—kills his gay lover, slices off his skin and uses it to make exquisitely beautiful books. In a recent novel, Kowloon Tong is shown to be a district full of vice establishments and hotels for assignations. The residential areas, universities, media and broadcasting stations which characterize this district, as well as its history, have been erased. The question of 1997 has attracted massive international media attention, but what is presented in the dispatches of even the most experienced and renowned journalists is just an 'internationalized' story based on fleeting glimpses and decontextualized quotations. Hong Kong culture is conveniently or gratuitously reduced to a single image: 'Shanghai Tang'—a nostalgic fashion store—or the 'China Club'—a club for the rich and famous, decorated with paintings striking for their political kitsch. The anxieties and worries of the Cantonese—who make up 98 per cent of the population—expressed in the local dialect and in writings in Chinese have been totally ignored; the focus of attention is trained on the riotous profusion that greets the tourist's camera lens. With these images, it is hardly surprising that people will get the impression that Hong Kong is a place without history, without culture, without dissenting views, a place where all residential districts are red-light districts, and where all publications printed in a language other than English are considered mere evidence of barbarity, as if they too were made of human skin.

Of course, this does not mean that those who know Chinese or can speak Cantonese understand Hong Kong better. A director from Guangzhou who has spent some time in Britain shot a film in Hong Kong. The protagonist—an artist with a background like the director's—comes to Hong Kong to meet his wife, and is taken to a seedy hotel in Portland Street by a taxi-driver who doesn't speak Putonghua or English. In the film, Portland Street is turned into a miniature Hong Kong, and it is like a huge brothel, with everyone waiting to be sold at the best price. The Suzie Wong invented by Western prejudices in the 1950s finds a perfect parallel in the shots taken by this Chinese director in the 1990s. In both these versions of the story of Hong Kong, the ordinary Hong Kong citizen, man and woman, has been excluded; the same goes for the details of their ordinary everyday life. In both these versions of the story of Hong Kong, the voices which can tell their own stories of Hong Kong have been suppressed. Like the colonialists from abroad, the artist portrayed by this Chinese director proclaims that he cannot find any culture in Hong Kong; only on Lamma Island, where the expatriates live, is there a so-called 'Environmental Arts Festival'. And so we see our Mainland artist downing cans of beer with his foreign friends, dismissing Hong Kong society as philistine, dismissing, too, his wife who has been lured by that philistine society to go shopping rather than follow him on his pilgrimage to Lamma.

When these Mainland artists—exiled from their homeland—take the sanitized position of high modernism and dismiss the colonial culture of Hong Kong as materialistic and philistine though actually it is equally accommodating to high art and pop culture, they are looking at Hong Kong from an angle not so different from that of Western tourists in their search for novelty and the exotic. Interestingly, such an angle also turns out to be identical to that seen in stories of Hong Kong produced by the state apparatus in China. From the reports released by the official media since 1949, to the recent documentary, *Hong Kong: 100 years*, produced by the Beijing Broadcasting Station especially for the return of Hong Kong to China, there is the same determined attempt to tell the story of Hong Kong as a colony. This colony is the product of the invasion of China by the foreign powers, of treaties that brought shame and humiliation to the nation, and its history must be put right. In the 1990s, when Britain and China were steeped in political squabbles, every time China wanted to warn Chris Patten to behave himself, the 1959 film *Lin Zexu* (also called *The Opium War*) would be shown in the Leftist cinemas in Hong Kong—to remind him, and the people of Hong Kong, of this 'shameful' period in history. Mainland writers who toe the Party line are set to expose the dark sides of capitalism in Hong Kong and to assert the superiority of socialism. Still relying on the realism with which Mao Dun in the 1930s wrote about Shanghai in his novel *Midnight*, they are fervently committed to producing their three-volume definitive novel of Hong Kong.

But the era of *Midnight* is gone. Many Mainland artists and writers have turned their backs on the severe stance of critical social realism. In the process of modernization, they have, to varying degrees, come under the influence of commercialism. Hong Kong and the Mainland have also worked together to produce many extraordinary political soap operas. In these TV series or long novels, aspiring Hong Kong businesswomen are graced with a new political awareness: despite being mistresses of British merchants, they are selfless enough to help righteous Chinese merchants outwit the colonials—all for the greater glory of the country. In current TV pop music concerts, before the sentimental love songs are sung, there are always respectable male singers standing before a sea of red flags, singing heartily and with devotion 'Be a Brave Chinese', or 'Descendants of the Dragon'.

From all sides people are vying with each other to tell the story of Hong Kong. And they declare in unison: Hong Kong has no story of its own; Hong Kong is unclaimed territory, the wrestling ground for different kinds of ideologies; Hong Kong is an empty box waiting to be filled; Hong Kong is a floating signifier, and the authority for decoding the signified rests solely with them, only they can stabilize it. It is as if Hong Kong is the female protagonist in a pulp fiction; people are pointing their fingers at her, gossiping and inventing things about her. Her story has to be told by others, and it does not matter if she feels that the story is not really about her, that it is too vulgar, or too classy. She has been represented, and she has no voice to tell her own story. Everyone from the outside is convinced they are better suited to telling the story of Hong Kong than the local people themselves.

Over the years, the people of Hong Kong seem to have resigned themselves to this fate. We don't protest much even when a foreigner thumbs his nose at us and tells an absolutely ridiculous story about us. Why? Well for all sorts of reasons. Maybe we are too civilized to protest, or maybe we're indifferent; maybe we're ignorant, or maybe we've just given up.

But it is not only the tourists who, in their search for the exotic, would come up with stories weird and absurd. Many of us have got used to these stories, have internalized them. When Hong Kong has a chance to tell her story, what is told may often be the same story. This is especially true of the cultural activities organized by the government or other 'representative' organizations. Hackneyed stories bombard the ear. One moment, it's the story of a rose garden; another moment, it's the story of fifty years of no change. One moment, it's the story of Casablanca of the East; another moment, it's the story of Shanghai. One moment, it's the heart-rending love story of a patriotic revolutionary; another moment, it's the equally heart-rending love story of financial brinkmanship and ruthless betrayals. One moment, it's the story of a capitalist with a conscience for the nation; another moment, it's the my-fair-lady story of an English gentleman educating a flower girl. Mainland critics strong in Party spirit will declare, upon arrival in Hong Kong, that what is lacking in Hong Kong literature are epoch-making works, works with boldness of vision, works that reflect reality. And we have more visitors touring Hong Kong. One after another they roll up their sleeves to collect their material, draw out their secret formulas, and set down to concoct the great Hong Kong story.

Two familiar types of stories about Hong Kong

The story of Hong Kong has been told by many people from the outside. There is, first of all, the story of Hong Kong as an international city. Like the names of the bars run by the foreigners in Lan Kwai Fong, Hong Kong is the spitting image of Brussels, or Paris, or Casablanca; Lan Kwai Fong itself is turned into the Montmartre of Hong Kong, and Tai O into the Venice of the East. There is no difference between Hong Kong and these other cities. Related to this is also the story of Hong Kong as a metropolis run by postmodern transnational corporations. Cultural critics too, label Hong Kong culture as 'postmodern' and brush away all the messy and complicated social phenomena that make up an integral part of Hong Kong culture. They say that changes come so fast in Hong Kong there is no point capturing them in writing, no point talking about the question of representation. But this in effect is asking us to tie our hands behind our backs and not reflect on the special features of our society and our culture. Everything is levelled off, a mere look-alike of some other things. Hong Kong is London, Hong Kong is New York, they are all the same. And the emphasis is just on the glory of Hong Kong's past, the gloom and doom that awaits our future.

Also belonging to this first type of story is the familiar tale of stability and prosperity. One prominent theme of this story is that the economic prosperity of Hong Kong rests upon her lack of democracy. A variant of this theme is that it is because of the need for democracy that the curses of colonialism have to be accepted. English, the colonial language, is promoted at the expense of Chinese, and its importance is stressed at regular intervals. Even Chinese parents have protested against the policy of mother-tongue education. Retired professors of English who come to Hong Kong from abroad emphasize the centrality and indispensability of the English language. Others make the same point, but their argument is based on 'the need to be useful to China'.

Lee Kuan Yew talked about this 'need' when he came to the University of Hong Kong in 1992 to deliver his lecture 'A Tale of Two Cities—Twenty years on'. According to him, both Hong Kong and Singapore play the role of a catalyst in the economic development of their neighbouring countries. To ensure that Hong Kong will not lose her importance to China, Hong Kong does well to maintain her links with other countries in the world. 'For the more Hong Kong has of these international links, the more useful it will be to China.' Retaining the use of English can help Hong Kong meet this objective.

He who tells this story has his own agenda. It can easily be seen that Lee Kuan Yew wanted to portray the people of Hong Kong as hard-working and deprived—of welfare such as medical care—in order to demonstrate Singapore's superiority. Hong Kong and Singapore are equals only in so far as both enjoy great economic leverage and a fairly strong legal system, but when it comes to political identity, Hong Kong had better remember that she is very different from Singapore: 'Singapore has been nation building to develop a separate and distinct identity. Hong Kong has not. Singapore's geographic distance plus its demographic setting has led to a Singaporean identity which is separate from the Chinese in China. Hong Kong did not attempt, indeed was not permitted, to develop one.'

To illustrate his point that the people of Hong Kong willingly identified themselves as Chinese, Lee Kuan Yew even used the reaction of Hong Kong to the June Fourth Incident as an example, and contrasted it with the reaction in Singapore, which saw only about thirty-odd university students in a mild protest. Those who know Singapore well may have a different interpretation of the situation; the identity of Hong Kong can also be discussed in a more complex manner. But what commands our attention urgently is the question of what the story reveals about the story-teller's stance. Lee Kuan Yew has a stance of his own—as can be seen also in the political measures he adopted in the past. The story he told is meant to convey a message: Singapore has a unique identity of her own, the adoption of English as an international language has a purpose, is conditioned by Singapore's historical background, and serves a practical function. In this story, Singapore is the protagonist, Hong Kong just a supporting character.

The other type of story about Hong Kong repeated equally frequently is the nationalistic story. Unlike accounts of Hong Kong as an international city—which stress the *status quo*—the nationalistic stories are critical of the current situation and believe that the territory's ideal future would be return to the embrace of the motherland. These stories have been told often enough by Chinese writers since the May Fourth Movement. In 1925, for example, Wen Yiduo wrote a poem entitled 'Hong Kong' in which the colony is compared with a 'yellow panther' separated from its mother:

I'm like the yellow panther guarding the palace gates,
Mother, my post is strategic, though lowly my state.
Here the savage Sea Lion preys on me,
Devours flesh and bone, warming itself with my blood
I cry, I wail—Mother! But you hear me not.
Let me take shelter in your arms, quick, Mother!
I want to come back, Mother! Oh Mother!*

Since then, stories about Hong Kong have often compared her to a 'helpless girl', 'an orphan', 'an illegitimate child'. Some have gone further and described her as ignorant or vulgar, or even as a victim of rape. Vulgar, too, is the Chinese used by the people of Hong Kong, which has come under attack frequently and vehemently: it is impure, its syntax is convoluted, it shows 'the poverty of a backward colonial culture,' wrote Wang Lixi in 1939. Related to this, of course, is the view that Hong Kong is a 'cultural desert'. Commenting on the inferior palate of the local people, Yang Yanqi remarked in his 1941 essay, 'Six months in Hong Kong', that Hong Kong people 'don't even like pork and eat only barbecued pork'. His standpoint and conclusion only expose the limitations of his vision and his observations. Strangely, while Hong Kong was sneered at for its lack of culture, these writers of the '30s and '40s, who had fled the Mainland and come to live in this cultural desert, often boasted to their friends back in Shanghai about the wonderful films they had seen in Hong Kong. This kind of narrowness and these ambivalent feelings still permeate the travel writings of some of the Mainland writers today. Changing times do not seem to have brought any significant changes.

In 'Love in Sham Shui Po' by Hu Chunbing, written in 1941, Hong Kong takes the form of a young woman filled with admiration for a Mainland visitor. Clasping his hand in hers, she listens to his stories about the motherland, and soon her grip tightens and she would 'leap up or exclaim with an "ah" or an "oh"'.

---

* Wen Yiduo's poem on Hong Kong, and the works of the other Chinese writers mentioned in this section, are all collected in *The Sorrows of Hong Kong*, Lo Wai Luen (ed.), Hong Kong: Wah Fung Publishing Company, 1988.

Here, the exclamations printed in English in the Chinese text ridicule the use of English by the Hong Kong heroine: English is not seen as the instrument of international communication which will ensure that Hong Kong remains 'useful' to China. But there is one similarity between this story and Lee Kuan Yew's account: in each Hong Kong has been reduced to a figure of speech, a useful foil for others, it is granted only a marginal existence, and what is said about it reveals rather the story-tellers' own dubious desires and fantasies.

No stories in this humble city?

While everyone is scrambling to tell the great Hong Kong story, many artists and writers in Hong Kong don't seem to be keen to take part in this race. Perhaps they are suspicious of the crushing grandeur of the grand narrative? Or of the carefully designed 'script' that sets the blueprint for Hong Kong's political, cultural, and economic developments? Some even shove the grand narrative aside to avoid over-determined meanings. Casually or self-effacingly, with caution or with the self-abandonment of a drop out, they prefer to tell their stories from the space they open up for themselves in different borderlands—the borderland between past and present, between their native country and a foreign country, between commercialism and art, between a policy and its implementation, between the grand narrative and the plain, low-key story.

If one looks carefully enough, one finds that these borderlands are actually rich with stories. Wang Tao, a nineteenth-century scholar whose career went disastrously wrong in China, came from Shanghai to Hong Kong and founded a newspaper—the *Chun Wan Daily*. He divided the paper into two sections, the 'serious' and the 'entertaining', and started the tradition of newspaper supplements in Hong Kong. Newspaper supplements did become, and still are, a distinct characteristic of Hong Kong culture. It was also in newspaper supplements that the local writers found a space for their works to be published. In the 1940s, Huang Guliu's novel, *The Story of Shrimp Ball*, was first serialized in a newspaper before it appeared in book form. In the 1950s, San Su, noted for his eccentric political commentaries and his fictional works—written in the Cantonese dialect—about the ordinary

11

folk, also had his works published in newspaper supplements, *Diaries of Middleman La* being a good example. Louis Cha, founder of *Ming Pao*—now one of Hong Kong's leading newspapers—wrote the editorials for his paper and serialized his enormously popular Martial Arts fiction in the supplements section. In the 1960s Liu Yichang made his living by writing popular fiction serialized in newspapers, whilst at the same time he satisfied his literary aspirations by publishing experimental fiction, also in serial form, in the supplements. All these writers, in their different ways, carried on the various traditions of Chinese literature, but they also managed to create and establish new genres. They all belonged to an era which saw constant conflicts between different opposing forces—commercial as well as political. Nevertheless, their works helped to build up an embryonic sense of identity for Hong Kong literature. Furthermore, the achievements of these writers showed how circumstances often forced the intellectuals and writers in Hong Kong to play different roles at one and the same time, to make strategic retreats or ingenious advances at the fringes of the commercial or political playing field.

The post-war generation continued to eke out a living in the borderland between high art and popular culture. They relied upon their parasitic existence on the periphery of the newspapers to develop and enrich the unique characteristics of Hong Kong culture. An increasing number of writers adopted a Hong Kong perspective in their writings, and in the 1970s, as the metropolis culture of Hong Kong began to take shape, they attempted to tell their own stories of Hong Kong. Roaming freely in the space provided by the metropolis, they found all sorts of niches for themselves in mainstream consumerist culture; at the same time, they experimented consciously with new techniques and styles, hoping to develop multiple perspectives in their modes of thinking, attempting to tell, from their own niches, stories which are a little different.

The impact brought about by Margaret Thatcher's visit to China in 1982 and the signing of the Joint Declaration in 1984 have been explored, in fairly great depth, by local writers. The tensions between Hong Kong and China, the complex relationships between people from both sides of the border, the obsessions and neuroses caused by the 1997 issue, the question of emigration, of June Fourth—all these feature prominently in the fictional and non-fictional works of the time. In addition to investigating what happens when two cultures meet, and clash, local writers also carried out a complex, many-sided enquiry into the cultural identity of Hong Kong, or they would reflect on history and on their culture and relate their observations to everyday politics. Even if they made no specific temporal or spatial references to Hong Kong, they would use parables and other imaginary or fictionalized landscapes to reveal the special features of the culture of Hong Kong and her situation, or rely on mood and images to tell their stories of Hong Kong.

For decades, Hong Kong writers have tried to survive in the interstices they discovered on the margins of their society and to make their voices heard. The strategies they have developed are significant and deserve respect. None of these voices should be suppressed. Perhaps it is when these many voices sing in chorus that the texture and complexity of the story of Hong Kong can be felt.

Revised version, June 1997
The Chinese original has not yet been published.

PART II

History

2

Chronicle of a City

By **YU FENG**
Translated by David Pattinson

It is common knowledge that people living under colonial rule have little or no sense of history, or a distorted view of history; their modus operandi is to work for the present and look towards the future. In Hong Kong, the future has been looming large in the consciousness of the people since the mid-1980s. The approach of 1997 has encouraged the Hong Kong people to put their history under increasingly intense scrutiny. The stories in this section reveal how some local writers deal with history. In the case of Yu Feng, he does it with a vengeance, and no apologies are needed.

1

When my father first mentioned my great-grandfather's bitter experience, I was ten years old. That morning there were armed riot police deployed everywhere around the building in which we lived, and the air was filled with the hoots and shrills of police whistles. Helicopters threaded their way through the narrow gaps between the tall buildings. The sunlight which reflected off their fuselages spun with the whirring rotor blades, which in turn cast their inauspicious shadows in all directions. Military police paratroopers, each holding a rattan cane and wearing a gas mask, landed on the roof of the building opposite which housed the Chinese products department store, and took up positions among the huge slogan-bearing banners which had been hung there. From a distance they looked like a few black stains on the white characters and red background of the banners—but just a few stains, which in no way lessened the impact of the impassioned and inspiring messages. At night these slogans were illuminated by lights. As I lay on the upper bunk, through the tiny window facing me I could just see the words '. . . live Mao Tse . . .' written in large characters. Sometimes at night after Mum had chased me into bed, the light from this slogan would shine on me like sunlight, and I would lie there, humming revolutionary marches in my head, tossing and turning until late at night when I finally fell asleep. That was how I passed many nights as a child.

That morning I smelt gunpowder. The chaotic smell of gunpowder came in through the tightly closed window, irritating my eyes so much I began to shed tears. Then I started to choke and cough unceasingly. My little sister was so frightened that she curled into a little ball under the big, round wooden table and cried, but nobody took any notice of her. Ignoring Mother's scolding, my little brother sat on top of a chest of drawers with his face pressed against the window, looking down unperturbed over the performance of the military police laying siege to the department store building. Never once during the whole drama did his stern and haughty face show the slightest flicker of fear. In our room we could often hear the sounds of hurried, whispered arguments coming from the corridor outside. Sometimes there were the rapid footsteps of pursuer and pursued. This ebb and flow of sound was punctured by the loud smash of something being struck to the floor, followed by the metallic crash of a steel security door being forced open then violently pulled shut. I thought our front door was going to be the next to be smashed in, so I quickly dragged all the chairs over in front of it. My young brain stored these chaotic sounds and smells well, as all these years later I still clearly remember the atmosphere of terror which filled our home that day.

That morning when my thirteen-year-old brother got up, he felt thirsty, so he went over to pour himself some hot water. As he did that he accidentally scalded his left hand, and a blister as large as a hen's egg formed on the spot. Mum quickly put his hand in iced water and applied some ointment, but nothing she did had any effect at all. The blister grew and grew, until it covered the entire back of his hand. After breakfast, Mum realized that nothing she could do would make any difference, so she took my brother to see the doctor. As they walked along, they noticed that there were few cars on the road, and the people who passed them

18

had solemn, concentrated expressions on their faces. The owner of the herbal drinks shop on the corner warned Mum that a curfew would be declared at any moment, and so most of the doctors wouldn't be seeing patients. My mother and brother rushed to the nearest general store, bought some canned food and fruit, then quickly made their way back home. Unable to get treatment from a doctor, my brother sat in a corner and groaned. His left hand, as if taking advantage of a riot nearing its peak, became red and swollen, and the pain spread from his left hand, up his left arm and into his chest. We all wondered why he didn't throw a tantrum. Knowing his irascible temper, he should have started throwing things around by this time, but he didn't. Instead, since that day, he became extraordinarily docile, completely unlike the person he was before.

Not long after my mother and big brother came home, a cacophony of police whistles suddenly rang out in the street. Mum stood at the window watching for a while, then rang up a workmate who lived downstairs. She was told that military police were searching some of the buildings nearby, probably trying to round up those behind the riots. Mother turned pale, put down the phone, ran into the other room, and dragged out a big pile of my father's left-wing newspapers. The front-page headlines of these papers were printed in big red characters, and beside them were large photos of Chairman Mao and Lin Biao. The rest of the page was covered in small, crowded text, punctuated here and there with the heavy, formal type of the article headlines. From under the coffee table Mother pulled out some magazines with red flags and colour photos of groups of people on the covers, and threw them all into a huge pile on the floor. Then, shaking with fear, she ordered my father, who was home on strike, to tear them to shreds.

As was his morning habit, my father had just put on a record of majestic revolutionary songs. These songs carried my young mind to a distant and seemingly unreal world where people did nothing but shout slogans, chant the sayings of Chairman Mao read from the 'Little Red Book', sing songs and take part in marches. How I wanted to live in that world, or to change the place in which I lived into that ideal world! Mother turned the record player off and scratched the record with a screwdriver.

When she saw the 'Little Red Book' with its plastic cover in the pocket of my father's white shirt, and the shiny badge on the collar, she grabbed the shirt. Father didn't resist, but just sat gloomily in the rattan chair and let Mother snatch away the little book and remove the badge. At that moment a cold light suddenly flashed past my eyes like a knife, very nearly blinding me, and I almost cried. In that moment the lofty image I had of my father in my child's mind was shattered completely. The father who had stood with the workers confronting the police on the streets and demonstrating, the father who with my uncles and aunties sang songs celebrating the imminent return of Hong Kong to the Motherland, the father who had stood up on the podium arguing the cause so eloquently, ceased to exist on that day. The seeds of our inability to get along were sown then. But on that morning, I didn't know that; I was simply overwhelmed by the feeling that the world of my dreams had begun to fall apart and would never be the same again. I couldn't understand why, but I didn't cry.

From that day on, my father became reticent, hardly saying a word all day. He gradually lost contact with his comrades and after my little brother and my grandmother died, he left the trade union, and started a small business with some friends. He never said another word about the passionate beliefs of his youth, about those ideals which were now completely forgotten. Or perhaps not forgotten, but rather buried by his own hand. A few years later, after the People's Republic began to open its doors to the outside world, he moved into China trade, and actually made a bit of money out of it. By the time he fell ill and had to stay in bed, he even started to wonder when a sister of his who was living overseas would be able to get foreign citizenship, and urged my brother and me to do something soon about emigrating. How long life is—long enough to allow one to completely change the beliefs of one's youth! Or maybe it is too short, so that there isn't time for one to understand why such abrupt changes occur. But those rapid changes took place many years later.

My mother had thrown those badges into the toilet. I can still remember how the sound of the toilet flushing and the reports of guns firing tear-gas canisters in rapid succession rose in a crescendo, then faded away together into silence. Many years later, when I began to write stories about Hong Kong's past and recalled the events of that morning, I realized that the moment my mother flushed the toilet was precisely the time when the riots were crushed. The sporadic strikes, demonstrations, and street bombings that took place after that were just the tail of a comet. Unfortunately, two months later the tail of this comet killed my younger brother—an outcome I would never have dreamed possible on that terrifying morning.

———

My brother was killed on the last day of my tenth year. I saw with my own eyes a young and sensitive life end in an indistinct pool of blood when one of those street bombs marked 'Fellow Chinese Keep Away' accidentally exploded.* At that moment my childhood came to a premature end. I became quiet and brooding. I was strangely curious about death, and began to ponder the meaning of life and death. As I grew up, I sank further into the depths of depression. I grew apart from the playmates of my childhood, and buried myself in the world of books, seeking truth and comfort.

My great-grandfather's bitter experience also occurred on the last day of his tenth year. Likewise, it brought his muddled childhood to a premature end. According to my father and grandfather, my great-grandfather's life was as ordinary as could be. He wasn't born into a wealthy family, and there was no rags-to-riches story to tell. I've never heard of any heroic deeds being attributed to him. Like so many other people in those tumultuous times, he was born, grew up, grew old, and died, and that was it. Not a thing is recorded about him and those of his generation in the history books. And I have no intention of making his life the basis of an epic family saga; I haven't got the talent. When I started writing down some of the things that had happened in my family over the years, I was just the resident manager in a joint-venture factory in a township on the Pearl River delta. In the evenings after work when there was nothing else to do, I would sit by the window looking out at the high, dark yet star-studded sky of the countryside, and scribble a few things to pass the time and forget about the pressures of my job. From my ancestors who fled the

---

* During the 1967 riots these bombs were left in the street and were targeted at non-Chinese, who presumably couldn't read the warning.

fighting associated with the collapse of the Yuan dynasty and came to southern China, * to those who moved from place to place over the centuries till my great-great-grandfather's generation settled on the coast of Guangdong, to my great-grandfather and his children and their children who lived, grew up and multiplied there in the Pearl River delta, there had never been a single person who had done anything of note. So I thought I'd simply make an honest record of some of the ordinary things they had done in this city before it was a city.

My father had never seen my great-grandfather as he died, at the grand old age of ninety-six, three months before my father was born. All the stories my father knew about him were told to him by my grandfather when my father was young, and my father in turn told them to me. In the process, these stories went through war and upheaval, hardship and deteriorating memories, until the details of each of their stories became complementary at times, conflicting at others, and occasionally so absurd as to be almost implausible. So I sat in my dormitory weighing up the different versions, trying to fill in the gaps, including this and omitting that, until I was able to put a few disjointed chapters together. No doubt they are a long way from the truth, but that's the best I can do.

As my grandfather lived in the countryside, I rarely saw him. But a year before he died, I worked at a factory close to where he lived, so there were a few chances for the two of us to be alone together. And I was able to learn quite a bit more about my great-grandfather. My grandfather spoke Cantonese with a strong local accent and, because I could only understand a bit of it, talking to him was hard work. In two to three hours, I might be able to catch twenty to thirty per cent. But whenever my normally taciturn grandfather saw me, he would grow loquacious. Between the morning when my father first mentioned the incident which happened to my great-grandfather all those years ago, and the evening when I heard the same story from my grandfather's mouth, fully twenty-two years had passed, though it seemed like no more than a day. During this time, I had grown into an adult,

---

* Approximately the middle of the fourteenth century. The Ming dynasty was established in 1368.

had experienced much of the joy and pain of life. It is natural, therefore, that many of the strong feelings I had then should now seem quite ordinary. But we will leave them aside for another time.

———

The first time, and indeed the only time, my grandfather talked about what had happened to my great-grandfather on that day many years ago, was on the evening after I had had such an almighty row with my wife Shuk Fan in a long-distance phone call we nearly decided to separate. That was a period when both family affairs and national affairs gave me great cause for anguish. For several weeks on end, I would sit in my dormitory by myself watching television until the small hours of the morning, before finally heading off to bed. One reason why I stayed up so late was to watch the current affairs special reports, but the main reason was to wait for Shuk Fan's phone calls from Hong Kong. At that time, I only got two days off once every fortnight. However, every time I went home, the two of us would argue a lot, neither willing to give in to the other. The feelings we once had for each other had disappeared with time, and we were now distant. Once I had returned to my dormitory, though, I regretted my stubbornness. When I turned on the television, the screen was filled with marching students shouting rousing slogans and delivering impassioned speeches, and fully armed military police. I put away my personal emotional entanglements for a while. Sometimes I even had an irresistible urge to run out on to the streets and join the protesters in marching and shouting slogans, as if in this way I could solve my own trivial vexations and the problems facing the country at the same time. But when the television was turned off, when the commentators' drawn-out analyses, reviews and predictions faded into the silent space, into the past, I was left sitting alone in the room, looking at the high, black sky of early summer outside the window, and a great wave of despair would suddenly sweep over me. Only when it was nearly light could I force myself to go to bed, and even then I slept but lightly, a sleep without roots.

That evening after I had put down the phone, I got on my bicycle and rode to my grandfather's home a few kilometres away.

Riding into the setting sun, I travelled along the asphalt road through many abandoned fields, disorderly industrial areas, groups of grotty apartment blocks for workers, and muddy wastelands. Workers were waiting for public transport in groups of three and four. I turned into a small road which ran between some fields, on one side of which was a pond with a few ducks swimming on it. My grandfather was sitting alone on the steps at the front of his house. Beside him was an old banyan tree with dangling roots, while the deep orange sun hung low in the high, blue-grey sky, so that his face seemed to be framed between the old tree and the sun. A little thin silhouette. The evening wind brought a cold draught, and there was chilliness in the air. In front of the silhouette a tiny flame flared briefly, feeble like my grandfather's tired life. I hesitated, unsure as to whether I should go forward and disturb the stillness of the scene before me.

My grandfather lived alone, with just a yellow dog and a few chickens for company. The house had only been returned to him a few years ago as part of the government's policy of handing back to their original occupants homes that had been taken from them during communization and the Cultural Revolution. What was he thinking as he sat there? The greatest regret in his life was probably the death of my grandmother, and that happened a long time ago. Was he thinking of her? Did he regret not listening to her advice and staying in the countryside, staying in that frenzied land during those years which glowed red with fire, and watching with his own eyes his wife being denounced and tortured to death by the Red Guards? I suddenly recalled what Shuk Fan had said to me: her complaints about me, her fear that she would end up drifting from place to place just like her parents' generation, her misgivings about a future that could not be known. All these became reasons for throwing all to the wind and leaving Hong Kong no matter what, just like her relatives, former school friends and colleagues, who had packed up everything and gone overseas. But I could never make up my mind, and took this job as a factory manager in Guangdong. This move had caused irreparable damage to a relationship that was already strained.

I left my bicycle by the road and stood there for quite some time. When the sun finally set behind the hills, I walked up by the tree not far in front of him and sat down in a broken old rattan chair. My grandfather slowly turned his head around, his dry, wizened eyes seemingly still in some distant time. We began chatting, and gradually came round to talking about his childhood, his brother, and finally the incident that happened to his father on that day long ago. As we talked, his eyes brightened. It became very late, the clouds in the night sky were absolutely still and not a star could be seen. Later, as I rode back to my dormitory, I noticed that lights were on in all the houses, but there was not a sound save the faint drone of televisions and the occasional bark of a dog. Only after I got back to the dormitory and turned on the television did I realize that it was probably just at that time that many people collapsed in pools of blood in a distant city.

However, when my grandfather mentioned the incident that happened to my great-grandfather on that day long ago, the first image that appeared in my mind was that of my mother taking the badge off the collar of my father's shirt on that panic-stricken morning when I was ten years old. That piece of shining metal flashed in front of my eyes like the cold gleam of a sharp knife. My father was tearing up his magazines, while at the same time telling us about the incident that had happened to my great-grandfather. I was helping, and didn't say anything. My mother inspected the torn-up pages, and ripped the bigger pieces into smaller bits, so all the fiery slogans, ideals, -isms and whatever were completely destroyed. The sound of the toilet flushing was the last roar those papers could let out.

2

That year my great-grandfather was ten years old. As he hid among the rocks on that stony beach, he remembered that similarly cold morning some four or five years before when his father had come in and woken him up. He had not seen his father since then, and now he couldn't remember what his father looked like. Many years later, when my great-grandfather returned to the family village, only the family of his aunt—the wife of his father's younger brother—was still there. His uncle had long since gone off to live somewhere else. Still later his aunt told him that after his father had left him that night, he and his younger brother had taken a boat to Canton, the provincial capital, where they were sold off as coolies to work in America. For the first few months he had sent money home, but after that he had been heard of no more.

On that visit back to his family village, as my great-grandfather came around the bend in the yellow dirt track, he saw his aunt standing in the doorway wiping tears away and saying: How tall you are! How tall you are! He noticed that the banyan tree beside the house that they used to climb as little children was now a huge, swirling mass of branches. He couldn't have known that, over a century later, after that house had collapsed and been replaced by a new one, the tree would still be there, and his son and his great-grandson would sit under it and recall what happened to him on that fateful day. In the conversation under the tree, time passed like the fleeting shadow of a tree in the wind: a momentary flutter and was all.

On that similarly cold morning, my great-grandfather's father had picked my great-grandfather up from his bed in his brawny arms. A cold northerly was blowing outside, whistling through the broken window with such force it seemed the window would fall out at any moment. My great-grandfather shouted for his mother, momentarily forgetting that she had died several months ago. Without a word, his father wound his queue around the top of his head, wrapped his son up in an old cotton-padded jacket, then picked up a basket containing his clothes, opened the door, and left this poor, decaying village without so much as a glance over his shoulder. In my imagination, many years later, as my great-great-grandfather lay ill in the cold country to which he had gone and recalled what happened that day in his home back in China, he must have held his head in his hands and wept uncontrollably. Because of this his illness became worse, and when he died and was buried in foreign soil, the story of our family's migration from the north of China to the south was buried with him. For this reason the history of our family can only be a modern one, beginning with my great-grandfather.

The trip my great-grandfather made with his father to Canton that day was the first time in his life that he had travelled so far. It was a long journey. They crossed mountains and rivers, and passed through seemingly endless villages and paddy fields, arriving at their destination only after night had fallen. His father did not say a word for the entire journey, and whenever my great-grandfather cried because he was hungry, his father would give him a piece of biscuit to quieten him down. One biscuit for an entire day. The sweet taste of the biscuit stuck in his memory. Later, during the many times he was hungry at night, it was this taste that would come back to him, and his recollection of it was much more vivid than any memory he had of his father's face.

My great-grandfather was left with some distant relatives there in Canton. That night his father left him forever. He didn't cry, he was so tired he fell asleep on the wooden bench and was snoring when his father finally departed. All he could remember of Canton was a few dark, narrow houses. These distant relatives lived on the upper storey of one such two-storey house. The lower storey was a smoke-filled den which men whose bodies and minds had been wasted by opium frequented like apparitions, floating in and floating out again. My great-grandfather was still young, and because the wooden steps that led downstairs seemed high and steep, and creaked and shifted under one's feet, he did not venture out but stayed in the room all day, looking at the paintings of some gods on the wall and the incense burning on the altar below it. These relatives were poor too. All the men worked as coolies for the hongs, and when they came home at night all they did was drink and shout, and hardly took any notice of this child from the countryside. The two meals a day they gave him were no more than the carrying out of the responsibility which his father had entrusted to them.

A few days later my great-grandfather was again taken away, this time to some friend's home in a poor village on some barren island. A man who worked in a quarry collected him from the provincial capital and together they walked a long way till they reached the Pearl River, where they boarded a fishing boat. It was overcast that day, and the biting north wind rocked the little boat terribly. My great-grandfather vomited all the time, but he was very excited, and could hardly take his eyes off the boatmen rowing and adjusting the sails. After sailing for a relatively short time, the boat pulled over to the bank where they moored for the night. The next day the boat arrived at the mouth of the river, and as they made their way through the area where the river ran into the sea, a misty rain began to spray them, and the wind became even more piercing. Between bouts of dizziness and vomiting, my great-grandfather saw squadron after squadron of large European sailing ships sailing in the direction of the grey river. Some of them had cannon, strange flags flew from their mastheads, and some foreign devils looked out over the sea. Soon the boat great-grandfather was on sailed into an increasingly narrow waterway, flanked on both sides by towering mountains which seemed to converge into a single range in the distance. White-capped waves tossed the tiny boat around, so the boatmen took the sail in and began the arduous task of rowing. Sometimes the boat rocked so hard it looked as if all on board were going to be thrown into the sea; at other times the boat seemed certain to be flung against the rugged shoreline, smashing everyone to death. But then the mountains suddenly gave way to flatter ground, and the waterway along which they had been travelling opened up to reveal a completely different scene. All around them were islands, some big and mountainous, and some no more than rocky outcrops. Even the wind died down somewhat. Nearby was a succession of beaches punctuated by ragged headlands, between which small fishing boats floated in twos and threes. That afternoon the boat my great-grandfather was on was brought up to the shore and moored where a mountain ran down into the sea.

In my great-grandfather's eyes that mountain was an exceptionally ugly one. It was separated from the mainland by a long, narrow channel, and its various peaks seemed to stick out of the sea for no particular reason. There was hardly a tree on it: it was all just pale yellow sand covering the steep mountain slopes and precipices that soared above. The only other things in sight were a few deserted houses. The craggy shoreline rose and fell, occasionally giving way to small bays with stony beaches broken up by rocky outcrops and the occasional dilapidated jetty. It was at one of these jetties that my great-grandfather's boat tied up. When my great-grandfather finally set foot on solid ground after all that excitement on the boat trip down, he remembered his father and his relatives back in Canton, and irrepressible feelings of sadness welled up inside him. He began to cry and refused to go a step further, howling that he wanted to go home. It took the combined strength of all the others, with much shouting and yelling, to carry him up on to the shore. At the time my great-grandfather would never have guessed that he would spend the rest of his life travelling up and down between this island, Canton and his home village. This first voyage was like a dress rehearsal. And he wouldn't have known that for many, many years after that, his children and grandchildren would also flee to this once barren and ugly island.

———

On one cold morning some four or five years after settling on the island, my great-grandfather was beaten up on that stony beach, and was lucky to escape with his life. Of course, such a minor incident has never been recorded in any book of history, but it has been passed down in the family from generation to generation. He lay groaning and shaking between the rocks on the beach from noon till dusk before he could find enough strength to stagger up. When he did finally manage to stand, he discovered that everything around him had changed. The mountain and the whole island now looked completely different from how it had looked when he came down to the beach that morning. On the hill in front of him, a strange flag fluttered alone in the wind, and the red, white, and blue pattern on it had swept away the dull grey in the sky, leaving it extraordinarily clear. A ray from the setting sun broke through the thinning stratus clouds and just happened to fall on the hill where the flagpole stood, and to my great-grandfather looking up from below, the flag appeared sacred and unreachable as it fluttered there in the sunlight. My great-grandfather climbed up on to a large rock to look about. The desolate mountain range on the opposite shore seemed to be rushing westwards, rising and falling, but the momentum was stopped abruptly when the towering mountains reached the sea, a sea which seemed uncrossable. All the boats that had been on the sea were gone, and in the dim twilight he could see that the waves had white caps on them. The sky grew darker and darker. My great-grandfather turned to make his way home, but perhaps because he was tired, or because of the beating he had received, he began to feel dizzy. Suddenly stars appeared before him, dancing in the air, increasing in number and density as if they were flying towards him and landing on the mountains about him like dazzling jewels. My great-grandfather was dumbfounded as he watched all this, and the hubbub of horses, carts, and people rose in his ears, louder and sharper even than the street noise he had heard back in bustling Canton. He put his hands over his ears, and in his confusion he tripped over on a rock. After a time, all the stars and the noises suddenly vanished without trace. The surroundings resumed their tranquillity: a vast sea and a vast wind.

The clothes he was wearing had almost been torn to shreds by his assailants, and he had lost his shoes. The scene of the beating he had received that morning suddenly reappeared in his mind as clearly as if it was happening right at that moment, and he always said that he could recall every detail of it accurately, so much so that as he lay on his deathbed, he could relate the whole story to my grandfather without missing a thing.

———

That morning the weather had been particularly cold, and my great-grandfather had been lazing in bed. His uncle tore his quilt off him and hit him as hard as he could because he wanted my great-grandfather to go out and help mend the farming tools. He remembered how on a similarly cold morning a few years earlier he had been picked up out of his bed by his father's strong hands. As he thought about how he had been dumped on this island so far from the mainland, far away from his relatives back in his home village, he cried. Then he gritted his teeth, got out of bed, threw on his cotton-padded jacket, and ran out of the house.

He left the gully where the village in which he lived stood, and made his way aimlessly along the shoreline which ran along the foot of the mountains. Many years later I, his great-grandson, would try to retrace his steps, but I lost my way at a busy intersection. The shoreline of those days has already been buried under tall buildings and city streets, and looking up through the jumble of shop signs overhanging the street, all I could see was row after row of tower blocks, the mountains having disappeared from view. But on that day my great-grandfather had definitely made his way westwards along the winding shore and across the place where the creek ran into the sea. He walked along the rocky beaches for about half an hour until he reached a place where a hill rose sharply out of the sea, and just beside the hill was a shallow pit. Not far offshore there was a small boat from which an old man and a young girl were catching prawns. My great-grandfather squatted on a rock for a while and watched them idly. Just when he was about to get up and go, he suddenly heard shouting, and looked around to see a group of red-haired devils swarming out of several small boats which had already been pulled up to the shore. My great-grandfather immediately hid in the gap between two rocks. The old man and the girl had disappeared, and several triple-masted ships appeared from the west. Then troops were sent into small boats which transported them to the shore. Great-grandfather covered his head with his arms and wriggled further into the gap between the rocks.

Now the tramping of leather boots could be heard everywhere, filling the world around him. My great-grandfather was terrified, and had no idea how he could slip away without being discovered. Suddenly a pair of boots made their way in his direction, and stopped right above his head. He heard the sound of heavy breathing, followed by the rustle of clothes being loosened. He held his breath. Then came the sound of water, first splashing on the rock beside him and spraying on to him, and then moving over and landing right on his head. The water was warm, and had a somewhat rancid smell. He thought it was rain, but when he looked up, he saw a powerfully built red-haired devil buttoning up his breeches. The soldier saw him and shouted. Some other soldiers rushed over and surrounded this small, skinny boy who was now covered in mud. Shouting wildly, they kicked him and trampled on him. He grabbed a handful of stones and threw them at the soldiers, who then flung themselves at him, seized his queue, and started swinging him around as hard as they could. He had never received such a vicious beating in all his life. He bit the hand of one of his attackers with all his strength, and tasted a salty trickle in his mouth. Then he blacked out.

If it had not been for a series of shots from the cannon on the ships offshore, and the sound of bugles from the shore, those red-haired devils would probably have beaten my great-grandfather to death. So the fact that I, his great-grandson, was able to be born over a hundred years later because of the ceremony by which Britain took possession of Hong Kong must be one of the absurdities of history. The soldiers let him go and raced to the small hill. The cannon fire on the ships became more and more rapid, and echoed so loudly in the surrounding mountains that my

31

uncle and the other villagers, in spite of the distance, put down the farm tools they were mending, looked up at the clouds of gunpowder rising up into the sky, listened carefully, and didn't know what to make of it. My great-grandfather lay on the rocks groaning. The cannon volleys followed one another in rapid succession, and the several dozen soldiers who had come on to the shore were shouting and singing wildly, while some fired their rifles into the air. For a while the ground trembled and the mountains shook. Maybe the founding of a city was no more than that. Just that.

The fumes from the gunpowder enveloped my great-grandfather and he started to choke and cough. With tears in his eyes, he shivered in the cold wind. Much later, the soldiers boarded their boats in a noisy confusion and left, his existence apparently forgotten. So my great-grandfather passed the whole afternoon there, lying between those rocks.

After the stars and horses and carts had suddenly vanished from his mind, my great-grandfather climbed up the hill and found the courage to try shaking the flagpole, which stood about twice the height of a man. He found that the flagpole was not as sturdy as it had looked from a distance, but had just been stuck between a few rocks, and as soon as he shook it a few times, it fell over. He removed the flag and lifted the pole up, then threw it like a spear towards the mountains to the north. Those mountains looked like the body of a dragon which threatened to leap across the sea and grab this outsider who dared challenge it, and to swallow the entire hill. But my great-grandfather wasn't strong enough: all he did was assume the stance of a spear-thrower, the stance of laying down a challenge, and although it looked good, it wasn't much use. The flagpole landed rather lamely just a little way in front of him, and silently broke into two. My great-grandfather took no further notice of it, but wrapped himself up in the flag, and swaggered home along the shore. His clothes were torn to shreds, and if he hadn't had this flag with its blue, red, and white pattern to protect him, there would have been no way he could have made his way home in the strong northerly gale that sprung up at dusk. Later, many years later, as I was trying to retrace the steps of my ancestors in order to write these stories of old Hong Kong, I went to that place which had once been a beach and was now city streets. Amongst the shops, restaurants, and banks, and the dust and fumes from the buses and trucks, I couldn't hear the thunder of cannons marking some great historical occasion. In that city, which had been old Hong Kong, everything had but a fleeting presence and the people were good at forgetting; they were too busy looking to the future. And that stony beach had long lain buried under the city, forgotten.

But my great-grandfather never forgot. He would revisit this spot many times in his life. When it was still a stony beach, he came; when it was no longer a stony beach, he still came. Several decades later when the place had become a district of ill repute, he would hang about there. Whenever he had had a few drinks, he would tell the story of that morning long ago, though naturally he left out the bit about him being beaten to within an inch of his life. His audience would nod their heads, not quite sure whether to believe the story this scrawny old man was telling them or not. Then some of them would put on a look of amazement, humour him a little, and go back to their drinking games.

Chinese original published in *Su Ye Literary Monthly*, No. 9, 1992.

3

The Walled City in Kowloon: a space we all shared

By **P. K. LEUNG**
Translated by Janice Wickeri

*In the early nineteenth century and well before the British came to
Hong Kong, the rulers of the Qing dynasty maintained a fortified
headquarters in Hong Kong. Even after the New Territories had been
ceded to the British in 1898, and after the Chinese officials and
soldiers stationed there had been cast out, the legal status of this
area, surrounded with walls fifteen feet thick, somehow remained
unsettled. The British government never insisted that the Hong Kong
administration should apply to it the municipal regulations in force
in Hong Kong, and yet it was not run by the Mainland authorities.
However, whenever plans to tear it down were proposed by the
British, the Mainland Chinese would object. As a result, the enclave
became a sort of no man's land and was known simply as the Walled
City. It was said that as late as the 1970s the only real administration
there was provided by the triads. In this story the writer takes a look
at the place and its history as plans for its demolition are finally put
into action.*

A huge wrecker's ball shatters the walls: the Walled City in
Kowloon is finally coming down. It is an event which stirs in me
a lot of mixed feelings.

A friend of mine spent her childhood in the Walled City. She once said, 'Outsiders always think that the Walled City is mysterious and frightening; for us, it's the place where we grew up. When I was a kid, I played in its streets. I have a lot of happy memories of the Walled City, there's nothing scary about it.'

She may feel that way, but outsiders most certainly do not. When she was in primary school, she gave her address as the Walled City and this attracted a lot of strange looks from her teachers and classmates. Maybe she was just being sensitive, but she had the feeling they didn't like her very much. Before long she switched schools. At the new school, she gave a different address. When she first started dating, she told her boyfriend to park his car in front of a building some way from the Walled City, pretending that she lived in that building. And she made sure that he was gone before she came out again and ran the long way home.

'It took me a long time to be able to tell people I grew up in the Walled City,' she told me. By then, she had married and divorced, and had been living outside the Walled City for years. In 1987, after the Hong Kong Government announced the clearance plan for the Walled City, some of us wanted to go in and have a look around. She offered to be our guide, even though she had not been back for a long time.

'The boys used to wash themselves at the street taps and play marbles on the street. They were so naughty; they shot sparrows for fun with their catapults.' Though lost in memories of her childhood, she didn't forget to point out how things had changed. 'There used to be two parts to the Walled City; on one side were the tall buildings of Tung Tau Tsuen, on the other the squat wooden huts. My house was over there.'

That was her story. As for the earlier history of the Walled City, it was left to the old people there to tell us. They had been through several earlier 'demolitions': in 1936 they put up a strong protest and the plan was abandoned; in 1948 a demolition team arrived, together with an anti-riot squad, but they quickly left after the residents started throwing stones at them.

All this happened before we were born. While we were growing up, we didn't have any history books telling us about these events. And now a doddering old man was taking us back to the past. There was even a hint of excitement and indignation in his voice:

'Someone went up to Guangzhou to seek support. Guangzhou students demonstrated and pulled down the flag at the British Consulate there, someone set fire to. . . .'

Then in 1962 the Hong Kong administration announced again that the Walled City was to be pulled down. But the Chinese government made a strong protest to the British government, and demanded that all demolition cease.

And so the Walled City was saved, but inside it something was quietly changing. By the time of our visit in 1987, when the Hong Kong Government had once again announced that the Walled City was to be torn down, there was no opposition from the Chinese side. Indeed, the Ministry of Foreign Affairs expressed its 'complete understanding' of the necessity of such a plan. With the approach of 1997, this must have been another of the secret deals struck by the two sides in the negotiations—Britain and China.

What concerned most ordinary folk in the Walled City was the simple matter of survival. The old man asked, 'Who is there to speak up for us? This time they [meaning China] said we should fight it ourselves, take some proper legal action. We're like animals in a cage.'

Would the compensation be adequate for them to rent some similar space outside and continue to make a living? More importantly, should a place which is not ideal be preserved or should changes be introduced, thereby upsetting the *status quo*? Most people who lived there saw the place as home. They wanted to preserve it, and fought the changes being imposed on them as hard as they could.

What kind of a place were we talking about? The old cannons we saw abandoned in one of the alleys seemed a good indication. In the last century there had been a pier for merchant ships nearby, guarded by a small stone fort. Later, the pier was demolished and the ramparts were torn down to be used as rubble for extensions at the airport. The boundary represented by the walls had disappeared, the line of the old sea-wall was no more, and the boundary between old and new wasn't all that clear either. What kind of a place was it?

Well, Old People's Street led to an old people's home, and there really was a well on Great Well Street; just about everything lived up to its name, it couldn't have been clearer. But then how would you explain Bright Street? For many years, its brightly lit shops had been the primary purveyors of 'white powder' (heroin). Prostitution, gambling, and drugs; all had their niches here. Not far away, just around a few corners, was the place where my friend played as a child—a happy and carefree place. Here, prostitutes installed themselves on one side of the street, while on the other a priest preached and handed out powdered milk to the poor; social workers gave counsel, while drug addicts squatted under the stairs puffing away at their pipe dreams; what were children's game centres by day became strip-show venues by night. It was a messy, complicated, intriguing place, difficult to generalize about, a place that seemed frightening but where most people continued to lead normal lives. Just like Hong Kong really.

Never mind that people said it was an area without law and under no jurisdiction. In fact, in recent years, a lot of the crooked businesses had been curtailed, and most people were engaged in making an honest living. Particularly well-known were the small factories that made fishballs and pig's blood. It looked such dirty, unhygienic work, but the resultant products were regarded as the tastiest of snacks in all the highways and byways of Hong Kong. The area also boasted an exceptional number of dentists; those from mainland China who lacked the proper qualifications could practise here with impunity. This shadowy, obscure zone permitted a sort of life in a no man's land, though, of course, the people who lived here were constantly worried that it all might suddenly come to an end.

We went up to the roof of a building during our visit, and my friend led us from one building to another by an unmarked path. We ducked under an electric cable here and clambered over a structure there. In a place where normal rules were suspended, it seemed a matter of course to take irregular short-cuts. We walked just above people's heads, feeling as if we were running on an uninhabited barren mountain. The busybodies among us felt they had discovered a secret cavern from which to spy on the alleys and rooms below—until we looked up into a broken mirror on a wall, saw our own images, and were suddenly shocked to discover that we were part of this place ourselves!

I never went back to the Walled City after that visit. My friend has left Hong Kong and said she wouldn't come back. When I travel abroad, I have frequently come across friendly strangers, people with a certain air about them who seemed to have come from far away places. When they'd begin to speak I'd realize they were from Hong Kong—this mixed-up, beautiful-ugly place—but otherwise they seemed to have disguised their origins very well. Time and again this has reminded me of my friend from the Walled City, has made me miss her.

When abroad, I often try to explain to people that Hong Kong is nothing like the frightening, formidable place they think it is; and yet when I'm back I start criticizing everything, offending people I know or do not know. When I'm abroad, I tell people that Hong Kong has its own culture; but when I'm in Hong Kong I keep asking myself why we're always following outside standards, why we can't set up standards of our own, establish our own cultural space. I go on and on, and always end up isolating myself. Sometimes, I feel like a stranger in my own home.

It's been a few years now, but many of the disputes caused by the demolition of the Walled City and the rehousing of the people are still unsettled, and the protests have not altogether died down. I often think of the streets I walked through and the people I saw there on my last visit. What adjustments do they have to make in order to survive in the outside world? Will they have adequate resources and space enough to carry on with their lives? But then, I cannot help but also think of the dark dank alleys, the rats scuttling across the gaps between the wooden planks, the useless ancient cannons that seemed to have been discarded along the side of the street. . . . I don't want the place to have been preserved for the sake of nostalgia or as a curiosity.

Nostalgia is perhaps a sentiment born of not being able to face up to history. I see now that when we were there, among the homes of the Walled City, we hadn't realized that they were really like our home too—yours and mine. Everywhere, people were chatting about ordinary things: a relative's health, the problems of everyday life. In every street in Hong Kong, under every roof, there must be countless people doing exactly the same thing.

Later, just before the clearance was completed, a few of my friends slipped into the Walled City and brought out a whole lot of junk. They mounted an exhibition called 'Walled City Debts' at the City Contemporary Dance Company's workshop, in an effort to focus attention on the plight of the Walled City's residents. A photographer friend had also gone there and taken many pictures—including some of a nude on a roof—and a theatre friend said he wanted to stage a performance there. Unfortunately, it never worked out. As I strolled among those old things salvaged from the Walled City—sign boards removed from antiquated shops, discarded abacuses, old account books, yellowing photographs—I seemed to have wandered into an old, forsaken city, seemed to be greeted with all kinds of ambiguous signs pointing to all sorts of bizarre meanings. But I knew that those disjointed signs, those scattered artefacts, could never equal the solid, lived-in place from which they came.

The huge wrecker's ball shatters the walls; the Walled City is coming down. If we now think about this soon-to-vanish site, it is not for reasons of nostalgia, but in order to understand better the place in which we live, the space which we all share.

1993
Chinese original published in the local newspaper *Wah Kiu Daily*, 9 January 1994.

4

The Atlas: Archaeology of an Imaginary City

By DUNG KAI CHEUNG

Translated by Dung Kai Cheung

The Atlas *is a fictional work made up of fifty-one short pieces and divided into four sections: 'Theory', 'City', 'Streets', and 'Signs'. The temporal setting for 'City' and 'Streets' is the twenty-first century when the 'City of Victoria' (Hong Kong as we know it) no longer exists and the narrators can only gather, from the maps and atlases of the city drawn at different periods in the past, what the city was like and what changes it went through during Hong Kong's 156 years as a British colony, from 1841 to 1997.*

The excerpts are taken from these two sections. Ostensibly about the historical evolution and vicissitudes of the various streets and districts of Hong Kong, these pieces are yet steeped in the spirit of invention, at times even of the fantastic. Such a treatment of history raises some provocative questions: How true is the 'truth' told by history? How much is the writing of history in fact an act of creative interpretation and of deliberate intervention? The blending of fact and fiction in these stories is particularly effective in highlighting the drama of how different cultures, different ideologies, and different peoples seek, openly or subversively, to read and explain (away) each other, domesticate and contain each other.

Possession Street

Possession Street got its name from a historical event of great significance for Hong Kong. When the British first took possession of Hong Kong, they landed at the north-western part of the island, at a spot which they subsequently called Possession Point. Hence the street there was called Possession Street. However, this street was also the place where a watercourse entered the sea, local people therefore called it Shui Hang Hau, meaning 'mouth of the watercourse'. In fact, not too many locals knew that the street was related to the invasion of the island.

In January 1841, after the first Opium War, when Charles Elliot, the British Plenipotentiary and Superintendent of Trade, and Qi Shan, the Chinese Commissioner representing the Emperor of the Qing Dynasty, were still negotiating the terms of the Convention of Chuanbi, the British man-of-war, *Sulphur*, received the order to occupy Hong Kong Island. Edward Belcher, captain of the boat, recalled in his book, *Narrative of a Voyage round the World in HMS* Sulphur, the moment of landing: 'We landed on Monday, 25th January, 1841, at fifteen minutes past eight a.m., and being the *bona fide* possessors, Her Majesty's health was drunk with three cheers on Possession Mount. On the 26th the squadron arrived; the marines were landed, the Union Jack hoisted on our post, and formal possession taken of the Island by Commodore Sir J. G. Bremer, accompanied by the other officers of the squadron, under a *feu de joie* from the marines and the Royal Salute from the ships of war.'

At first, the British troops were stationed at Possession Point and lived in tents and sheds. For this reason, the district was also called Sai Ying Pun ('West Camping Site'). Owing to poor sanitation and the disagreeable climate, many soldiers died of fever, creating panic among the troops. There were even rumours that an evil spell had been cast on the watercourse's drinking water. After the barracks were moved to an area east of Central District, the rumours gradually subsided, but the curse was not dispelled. As the city developed, the open ground next to Possession Street became the gathering place of entertainers, practitioners of herbal medicine and fortune-tellers. Local people called the place *Dai Dat Dei* ('Large Ground'). Among the fortune-tellers was one called *Sun Suen Dzi* ('Master of Divination'), who professed that the *fung shui* (literally, 'wind and water'—a term connoting the supernatural effect of the environment on people) of Possession Point was unfavourable to the British. On their part, the British also kept away from this potentially dangerous district of suspicious Chinese characters.

The British probably did well to steer clear of this place for the word 'possession', besides meaning ownership and control, also refers to the condition of being under the control of an evil spirit, or to madness. Later on, Possession Street was renamed Shui Hang Hau Street in Chinese. Before the government moved the brothels to Shek Tong Tsui, all the high-class Chinese prostitutes conducted their businesses in Shui Hang Hau. There was one British Health Officer J. A. Davidson who, defying the foreigners' taboo, cultivated a liking for Chinese bawdy-houses at Shui Hang Hau instead of those for Westerners at Lyndhurst Terrace. He fell madly in love with a local courtesan, Dip Yi ('Little Butterfly'). After a night's romance, the giddy Davidson, drunken with passion and alcohol, took a stroll along the waterfront, slipped, and was drowned. Some said that Davidson was drowned because he was 'possessed' by the spirit of Dip Yi's father.

Professor S. Clark, who taught at the History Department of the University of Hong Kong before the Second World War and took an interest in the study of Chinese fortune-telling, described in his book, *The ABCs of Chinese Fortune-telling and its Application to Hong Kong*, the view that the English word 'possession' was too ominous. He suggested changing the English name of the street to 'Exorcism Street' so as to restore the rightful order of things. In Chinese, 'exorcism' translates as *gon gwei* which means 'to chase away ghosts, evil spirits, and foreign devils'.

Scandal Point and the Military Cantonment

In a map drawn in 1880 and showing the military facilities of the City of Victoria, the motives of the military were fully revealed. The map represented the district later called Admiralty. Murray Battery was situated on the slope down Government House on the left of the map. On the lowland to the north-east of the Battery was Murray Parade Ground. To the east of the Parade Ground, separated by an uphill road, was Murray Barracks. Further east, on a knoll, was Head Quarter House, also called Flagstaff House. In the middle of the coastal areas was Naval Yard, with Military Hospital and Wellington Battery to the east. On the slope to the south of Military Hospital were Victoria Barracks and magazines. They occupied the right-hand portion of the map.

Judging from the array of military facilities on the map, one can surmise that the garrison of the City of Victoria was quite sizable. According to historical documents, in the very early phase of the city's development, there had been disagreements between the first Governor Sir Henry Pottinger and the military. Pottinger originally planned to allocate a plot of land in Sai Wan (Western District)—to the west of Possession Point where the British forces first landed—for military purposes. But the army insisted on stationing right at the heart of the city and demanded the hills in Central, where the future Botanical Gardens and Government House were to be situated. The matter was later brought to London, and was finally settled by having the military cantonment located to the east of Central, on a portion of land commanding strategic control of the east-west main thoroughfare on the northern shore of the island.

These are the facts presented by historical records and historical anecdotes. Yet later map researchers, by studying the above mentioned map, arrived at an entirely different conclusion. They argued that the layout of military facilities of the early City of Victoria revolved around Scandal Point (Han Wa Kok) for in the above mentioned map, Scandal Point was situated right in the middle (on a knoll to the south of Naval Yard and in between Head Quarter House and Murray Barracks) and the military facilities of the area surrounded Scandal Point on its east, north and west sides. It was as if Scandal Point was the centre which the fortifications were designed to defend.

The name 'Scandal Point' was invented by the British. It is impossible to trace the actual origin of the name. Strictly speaking, the word 'scandal' implies a measure of public offence, but in its Chinese translation, *han wa*, it became 'gossip', limiting its meaning to 'true or false talk which brings harm, shame, or disrespect to others'. According to Yip Ling Fung's *A Record of the Vicissitudes of Heung Island*, every Sunday, after attending mass at St. John's Cathedral, foreign believers would usually make their way home to the Mid-levels via Scandal Point. On the way, they would, quite naturally, exchange news of the most insidious nature, comment on the social and private lives of personalities, and spread embroidered stories and malicious gossip. Although such an explanation sounds reasonable enough, there is no sound basis to it.

Some teleological map-readers insist that the relationship between Scandal Point and the military cantonment around it was not fortuitous. The purpose of the military garrison was clearly to defend the scandals, and at the same time to imprison and contain them within the invincible walls of guns and cannons, preventing them from leaking out, and also preserving their multiplication.

Aldrich Street

Aldrich Street was situated in Shau Kei Wan in the north-eastern part of Hong Kong Island. It was so named because there used to be a bay here called Aldrich Bay, and one end of the street reached the waterfront. Up on the hill at the other end of the street, there was once an Aldrich Village. The Cantonese transliteration of the name 'Aldrich' was *Oi Dit Dzui*, which means 'love of order'.

Aldrich Bay (Oi Dit Dzui Wan) was named after Major Aldrich. After the signing of the Treaty of Nanking in 1842, Major Aldrich was sent to Hong Kong by the British military to take charge of the plan for the stationing of troops in the newly acquired colony. He proposed a grandiose plan which included a large military cantonment laid out in a beautiful symmetry, as well as a foolproof defence scheme. The location he chose for the cantonment covered areas which later were to become Admiralty Barracks, Central District, Government Hill, and the Botanical Gardens. Aldrich fondly imagined that this invincible giant fortress would become the centre and the symbol of Hong Kong Island in future. But the Governor of the time, Sir Henry Pottinger, was firmly opposed to Aldrich's plan and insisted on retaining Central District for commercial purposes. In the end, Aldrich's dream of the military city was left unrealized.

Major Aldrich's main contribution to Hong Kong was, instead, the straightening out of the army discipline. Since many British soldiers were unaccustomed to the climate or infected by diseases, the army's morale was low. The situation was aggravated by the poor discipline of the soldiers, who took robberies, alcoholism and brawling as the order of the day. Major Aldrich punished the unruly soldiers by having them stationed at the remote A Kung Ngam (Grandpa Rock), where the Lei Yue Mun Battery was later located. He also introduced new rules of conduct and decreed more severe punishments to keep a tight rein on the soldiers. It was probably to commemorate Major Aldrich's contribution that the government named the bay at Shau Kei Wan after him. Certainly, the name Aldrich Bay already figured in an early topographical map of Hong Kong drawn by Lieutenant Collinson in 1845. It was, therefore, most appropriate to translate the Major's name as *Oi Dit Dzui* (love of order).

Major Aldrich was a man of stern self-discipline, down to the most minute detail in his everyday life. For example, even when he was on the battlefield, he would maintain his habit of having afternoon tea at four o'clock. The Major also spoke in a very orderly and well-structured manner, and he never allowed interruptions. In some ways, Major Aldrich could be regarded as an opponent to war because he had a profound dislike of chaos and couldn't tolerate the sight of dead bodies strewing the field in sorry disarray. Nobody knew when and how the apotheosis of Major Aldrich came about. Perhaps it was because local villagers suffered a lot from the looting of the pirates in the early years, and the predilection of the Major for strong fortifications protected the area from being ravaged, so he was venerated as the god of peace by some villagers. As the legend passed from generation to generation, Aldrich the man became enshrouded in mystery. Still later an *Oi Dit Dzui Miu* (Aldrich's Temple) was erected by the seaside, housing a statue of *Oi Dit Dzui Kung* (Lord or Grandpa Aldrich) that looked as dignified as the venerated Kwan Dai (General Kwan), a famous warrior in ancient times. Soon, Oi Dit Dzui Temple became as popular a place of worship as Tam Kung Temple at A Kung Ngam nearby. It was reported that during the riots caused by the fare increases of the Star Ferry in 1966, the spirit of *Oi Dit Dzui Kung* had appeared several times, admonishing people to obey the Royal Hong Kong Police Force.

In the *Hong Kong Streets Directory* of 1997, Aldrich Bay had disappeared due to reclamation works. Oi Dit Dzui Temple and Aldrich Village also no longer existed.

Ice House Street

Ice House Street was a steep road located in Central, its upper end was connected to Lower Albert Road and its lower end intersected with Queen's Road. Originally there had been an ice warehouse there. Established in 1845, Ice House imported ice blocks from America for the consumption of foreigners and for food refrigeration. It also provided ice for free to local hospitals. In those days Queen's Road was by the waterfront, so it was convenient for cargo ships to unload ice blocks and have them transported to the warehouse. It was not until 1866, when an ice-manufacturing factory was set up in Spring Gardens in Wan Chai, that the business of Ice House was threatened. In 1880, Ice House stopped importing natural ice from overseas. In 1918, Ice House and its competitor, Hong Kong Ice Manufacturing Company, were finally taken over by Dairy Products and Ice Manufacturing Company Limited.

Interestingly, the Chinese name of the street, *Suet Chong*, does not correspond to its English equivalent, 'Ice House'. 'Ice' should be translated as *bing*, but local people had the habit of calling 'ice' *suet*, which actually means 'snow'. Furthermore, the translation of 'house' as *chong*, meaning 'factory', is also incompatible with the fact that the 'House' was not a factory but a warehouse (*fu*). The accurate translation, therefore, should be *bing fu*. But there is also a contrary view which maintains that *suet chong* (snow factory) is an accurate description of the company, or at least an accurate description of one of the businesses of the company. According to this view, in the early days of Ice House, besides providing ice for local consumption, it also carried out a research project on snow production. What it did was to recreate the weather of the expatriates' home country by reproducing the virtual experience of snowing. This was supposed to ease the suffering imposed on them by the heat and the humidity, as well as to alleviate their homesickness in a land without a truly freezing winter. *Suet chong*, therefore, is not a mistranslation, but a most appropriate description of the purpose and function of the enterprise. Compared with *bing fu*, *suet chong* in fact comes even closer to revealing the essence of a colonial society. Nobody knew whether the snow production project was eventually successful or not, but one thing was certain—to experience the chilly winter days of the motherland in the ice-storage room at Ice House had once been a popular entertainment, although it was also a closely guarded secret. It was said that a fully furnished English-style living-room had been installed in the factory for the ladies and gentlemen of the time to enjoy in blissful serenity the warmth of a fireplace and the comfort of afternoon tea.

In the early years there was a story that circulated widely among the local Chinese: the British, arriving in Hong Kong for the first time, would head straight to Ice House to have their memories and dreams stored and preserved there, lest they rot in the unbearable heat of the subtropics.

Local people called ice-cream *suet go* (snow cake). Dairy Products and Ice Manufacturing Company Limited, which bought Ice House, was a large ice-cream enterprise. At first, the Dairy Company was located at Ice House Street, just next to Ice House. Later on, the premises of the Company became the home of the Fringe Club, an arts organization which provided venues for artists to act out their dreams, be they sugary or icy.

Sugar Street

Sugar Street (Tong Gai) was a short street lying between Yee Wo Street and Gloucester Road in Causeway Bay, hardly worth mentioning from a cartographic point of view. Its name originated in a sugar factory situated there ages ago. But the street also had another, informal name—Silver Coin Street—for the sugar factory had been preceded by a coinage factory. The two factories, moreover, actually had an interchangeable role and this is of intriguing significance in the development of local history.

In 1866, the government invested $400,000 in the construction of a coinage factory in Causeway Bay, with the objectives of minting silver coins locally rather than in Britain, and of reminting old silver coins for customers. But the business of the factory was unsatisfactory. As a result, the factory was closed down in 1868 and its machinery sold to Japan for $60,000, while Jardines Co. Ltd. bought the site for $60,000 and rebuilt it into a sugar factory. There was, however, another story concerning the closure of the coinage factory. Rumour had it that a strange thing happened when the minting machine first went into operation. The workers had poured in melted silver, but what came out of the machine were white and sparkling sugar grains. The same thing happened time and again in the next two years, and the government, for fear of creating a scandal, compensated the customers with its silver reserve, resulting in a severe drain on its coffers. At first, this huge amount of sugar—an extravagant by-product of the coins to be minted—was allocated only for internal consumption, and high officials and various departments found themselves spectacularly well-provided for with sugar at tea-time. Later, certain portions were allowed to be sold in secret in black markets, or shipped to other British colonies in South-East Asia, or even to Great Britain. It was said, probably with a touch of exaggeration, that Queen Victoria and members of the Royal family were particularly fond of the sugar produced by the Hong Kong coinage factory because of its inestimable value. But although the side-effects brought about by this strange malfunctioning of the mint were not too unacceptable, the Hong Kong government still decided to close it down because of its astronomical costs and for fear that the truth might leak out.

Commentators believed that the sale of the factory to Jardines was only an attempt on the part of the government to cover up the scandal. Some went further and speculated that Jardines had actually invested in the construction of the coinage factory in the first place. After Jardines had formally bought the factory and installed new machinery, its sugar trade business thrived and was probably its major source of profits apart from opium. But this was not the end of the story. In his book, *A Record of Strange Happenings in Heung Gong*, Lo Tung (Old Child) quoted the account given by a worker at the Jardines sugar factory. The worker recalled how every day the machine would be filled with raw material for the extraction of white sugar, and what came out were stacks and stacks of silver coins—glittering, saccharine.

The sugar factory was destroyed in 1874 by a disastrous typhoon, all its machinery and stock devoured by the sea. Some seamen and fishermen bore witness to the fact that the sea water of Victoria Harbour turned sweet after the catastrophe, and the marine products netted in the harbour were all bloated and had a sweet taste. For reasons unknown, the sugar factory was not rebuilt, only the name 'Sugar Street' remained as a testimony to its existence once upon a time.

Lo Tung concluded his narrative enigmatically with a Cantonese colloquialism: 'as the saying goes—a mouthful of sugar, a mouthful of shit'. It remains unclear whether the saying was intended as a general observation on the ruling style of the colonial government in its exercise of political and economic power, or as a comment on the operation of divine justice.

Sycamore Street

Sycamore Street was situated at the edge of Tai Kok Tsui on the Kowloon Peninsula. On the map, it looks like a bow: the arrow passing through the middle of the bow is Maple Street, while the smaller street running parallel to the bow is Willow Street. There are many stories about how this street came to be known as Sycamore Street. The mainstream view is that the English name was the original and the Chinese a translation. According to this view, when the district first began to develop, the government's policy was to name new streets after the names of trees. In the same district there were Pine Street, Oak Street, Beech Street, Elm Street, Ivy Street, Cherry Street, Maple Street, Willow Street, Poplar Street, Cedar Street, etc. All these streets had English names as originals and were then translated into Chinese, so Sycamore Street should not have been an exception. It is obvious, however, that the Chinese name of Sycamore Street, unlike all the others just mentioned, was based on phonetic rather than semantic translation. One quite convincing explanation runs as follows: the semantic translation of sycamore in Chinese is *mo fa guo* (fruit without flower)—a meaning which would almost certainly have been frowned upon by the Chinese, who in those days cared a great deal about *yee tau* (good omens) and would have preferred to see 'flowers blooming and fruits ripening' (*hoi fa kit guo*). Since at that time Tai Kok Tsui was a residential area for local Chinese, the name *mo fa guo* was rejected out of respect for local culture and 'sycamore' was transliterated into the much more elegant *Si Go Mo Gai* (The Street of Poetry, Singing, and Dancing). Certainly it was much more in tune with the residents' wish for peace and prosperity—poetry, singing, and dancing being the sort of activities associated with the good times.

This view, however, is open to challenge. It has been said that there is no knowing what tree the word 'sycamore' actually refers to. In Europe, it is a type of maple tree; in America, it is a type of plane tree; but in lands east of the Mediterranean, it is a type of fig tree. So even if 'sycamore' were to be translated semantically, it would not necessarily have to be translated as *mo fa guo* (fig tree). Perhaps the problem was simply glossed over by a transliteration because local translators of the time were unable to decide on the exact meaning of the word.

There was another widespread story—not so credible but more appealing. It was recorded by Leung Kwun Yat in his book, *A Study of the Oral History of the Kowloon Area*. In the eighteenth century, well before the arrival of the British, the area which was later to become Sycamore Street was adjacent to Mong Kok Village, one of Kowloon's largest villages, and it grew into the centre of cultural activities of the entire district. In those days there was an ancestors' shrine, a school, and an acting troupe in the area, catering for the religious, educational, and leisure needs of the community. Later a *shou choi* (a scholar who has passed the local examinations) from Mong Kok Village named the place *Si Go Mo*, and said that the meanings of these words could be traced to an ancient work of Chinese literature—The Mao Commentary of *The Book of Poetry* (*Mao Shi Xu, Shi Jing*): 'Poetry (*si*) has its root in feelings. When kept in one's heart, it is feeling, and when expressed, it becomes poetry. When something is deeply felt, it takes form in speech; if speaking is not enough to express it, one sighs and exclaims; if sighing and exclaiming is not enough, one sings (*go*); and if singing is not enough, one moves and dances (*mo*).' At the beginning of the twentieth century, with the decline and eventual disappearance of Mong Kok Village, *Si Go Mo* degenerated into a den of libertines and whores; the cultured pursuits of poetry, singing, and dancing gave way to licentious laughter and bawdy songs. When the British developed the Tai Kok Tsui District, they named the street 'Sycamore' because of its similarity in sound to the Cantonese *Si Go Mo*—an act of disrespect for the Chinese tradition and a deliberate undermining of local culture, some would say.

Yet others put forward the view, based on research, that the area was once planted with fig trees, which were uprooted when the street was built. Hence, it was named 'Sycamore', while its Chinese name was chosen for its propitious connotations of peace and prosperity. Later, the government planted the street with bauhinia, the flower of the city, to add colour and verve to the glamour of *Si Go Mo*. In the latter half of the twentieth century, schools sprang up in Sycamore Street, keeping alive the tradition of poetry, singing, and dancing.

Although *mo fa guo* does not have flowers, it bears fruits; the bauhinia has beautiful flowers, but is sterile.

Tsat Tsz Mui Road

Legend has it that Tsat Tsz Mui Road (Seven Sisters Road) got its name from the story of seven girls who took a vow of sisterhood. Ng Ba Ling (pen-name: O Yeung Hak, 'Turtle Sea Visitor') said in 'The Myth of the Seven Sisters'—collected in the first volume of his work *Hong Kong Folktales*—that 'the story is not only sensuous but also fantastic'. In the story, there were seven young girls whose affection for each other grew so strong and whose relationship became so intimate that they decided to take a vow of sisterhood, pledging *dzi suo*, which means literally 'to comb one's own hair'. *Dzi suo* was a custom popular in the villages of Shunde County in Guangdong Province. There it was customary practice for unmarried women to wear pigtails and married women to wear buns, and, when a woman's wedding day arrived, a senior female relative would help her comb her hair into a bun. So *dzi suo* implies choosing to remain single. Later, the third of the seven sisters, on being forced to marry by her parents, took her own life by jumping into the sea. The other six were determined to honour the vow they had made, that even though they were not 'born on the same day in the same month in the same year,' they would 'die on the same day in the same month in the same year.' They followed in their dead sister's footsteps. It was said that when their bodies were recovered from the sea, all seven of them were still holding hands. Some said, however, that their bodies were never found, and that seven rocks emerged on the next day at the spot where the tragic incident occurred, in a formation from the tallest to the shortest, resembling the seven sisters standing side by side, hand in hand. So people called them *Tsat Tsz Mui Shek* (Seven Sisters Rocks). These rocks later came to be buried underground due to reclamation works, and the newly reclaimed land was then named *Tsat Tsz Mui* (Seven Sisters) and became a popular bathing place in the early twentieth century. The bathing place, however, was plagued by the frequent drowning of male bathers and gossips spread the rumour that it was haunted by the ghosts of the seven sisters. But some believed that the sisters had already realized their dream of a separate female world and there was no reason why they should bother to stir up trouble against the detested masculine sex.

There is another version of the legend, diametrical in plot, but not without similarities. In this version, the seven girls also took the vow of sisterhood, but their pledge was 'to get married on the same day in the same month of the same year'. They did fulfil their pledge, and their husbands were seven brothers. On their wedding night, each of the seven sisters was lying in bed with her new husband and performing the same ritual for the occasion when a terrible cry rose from the room of the third brother. The third sister had failed to bleed and her furious husband was threatening to divorce her. In the end, the poor girl, crushed by the suspicion, accusation, and repulsion that continued to torment her, threw herself into the sea. The other six, overcome with grief and anger, also hurled themselves into the sea. It was said that the Seven Sisters Rocks just off the coast were in fact what the seven brothers, including the remorseful one, had petrified into while looking for their wives and hoping against hope for their return. This story is quoted from the feminist scholar Chang Oi Ping's *Rereading Myths of Hong Kong*, published in 1993. Chang argued that the myth of the seven sisters was 'neither sensuous, nor fantastic', but 'a despondent and painful reflection of the social relationship of the two sexes in those days'.

Tsat Tsz Mui Road, lying between North Point and Quarry Bay on the north-eastern part of Hong Kong Island, was built only after the Second World War. It was divided into seven irregular sections, with the last two separated by Model Housing Estate, leaving the seventh section in a forlorn state. Attempts were made by archaeologists to excavate along Tsat Tsz Mui Road the remains of the Seven Sisters Rocks buried underground. Relying on hearsay, they worked out seven possible locations, including one underneath a postbox and one underneath a florist. In the end, they unearthed seven wooden combs, each entwined with locks of hair.

Chinese original published in Dung Kai Cheung: *The Atlas: Archaeology of an Imaginary City*, Taipei: Lian He Wenxue Chubanshe, 1997.

PART III

Landmarks

5

The Man Who Jumped Off the Connaught Centre

By **SONG MU**

Translated by Jane C. C. Lai

In pulp fiction set in Hong Kong, the Connaught Centre (now called Jardine House) is often used as the background for melodramas of all sorts. This story also features melodrama, but it gives a strikingly different feel to the Connaught Centre as a building to which the ordinary people of Hong Kong can relate. Indeed, to many people in Hong Kong, it is a landmark of considerable historical significance. Being one of the first high-rise buildings to appear on the waterfront, the Connaught Centre, completed in the early 1970s, was regarded by many at the time as an eyesore, a monster of a building; and by others as a symbol of modernity, an indicator of how high future buildings would rise, and a symbol of how prosperous Hong Kong would become. In this story it is the setting for a stylistically varied portrayal of the complex feelings existing between Hongkongers and their compatriots from the Mainland.

In the viewfinder, he looked gaunt and shabby, and, for all his attempts to stand straight, his body stooped. I was going to ask him to smile, but I realized that he was already straining himself to do just that.

'Look this way at the camera!' I couldn't see his eyes behind his thick glasses, but his knitted brow showed that he was making an effort. Click! I asked him to move around so I could take a few more photographs of him in the last rays of dusk.

He took a step sideways and stood there, with the Connaught Centre in the background. He said the Connaught Centre was a symbol of modernization, and he wanted a photo of it for a souvenir.

I squatted down and tilted my camera upwards to catch the whole building in the frame. I couldn't fit in the top of the building, so I took some ten paces back and squatted down again.

In the viewfinder, he was leaning on the railing of the pedestrian footbridge, a diminished figure. The massiveness of the Connaught Centre dwarfed his sombre presence. There was no tension in the composition of the picture, only a helpless sense of desolation. It was the same sense of desolation that had struck me that morning when he had taken off his glasses and revealed his deep sunken eyes.

'Hold it!' A shadow flitted across the viewfinder. I moved the camera away and caught a glimpse of a figure in blue. Then I held it up again and took a photograph.

'That's all the film I have. Let's go home!' I put the camera back in its leather case. He stooped to pick up his shoulder-bag, but he could not straighten up again. He tried to thrust his body backwards, but his knees buckled and he fell forward. I caught hold of him before he fell to the ground, and helped him up. He cleared his throat and said something in a thick gruff voice which I heard very distinctly. He said,

'I gave you a hand too, way back. Do you remember?'

Of course I remembered. Thirty years ago, when the Communists rallied overseas Chinese to return to the homeland to serve their country, he—a fresh doctoral graduate—sneaked off without telling his parents, and took a train to China. I was helping him with his bags, and I slipped on the steps of the carriage. He caught hold of me and pulled me up, almost as if he wanted to pull me on to the train with him. I thought of my parents, the woman I was in love with, and my religious faith. I jerked my hand free of his grip. His eyes were bright with passion, his lips set in a confident and resolute smile. I did not wave goodbye as the train pulled away like a long snake and wailed in the distance. I thought of it as a dragon flying to the north. I was left standing at a loss, staring at the Union Jack fluttering over the railway station.

'Back and forth. Why take that trip in the first place?' I came out with the question that had long troubled my mind.

'It was a journey a Chinese had to make!' There was no glitter in his eyes, but there was still composure in his face.

I could understand that, vaguely. He had gone through the Anti-Rightist Struggle and the Cultural Revolution; he had been locked in a cowshed, had had one of his ribs broken, and all his teeth knocked out. He was here now in Hong Kong and was going to America the next day. He had no regrets, and I was silent in my approval of all that he did. Thinking about him, I felt as if I had stayed on the edge of a turbulence and preoccupied myself with trivialities, I felt almost ashamed that I had remained unscathed. He took a deep breath and said, 'I had to come out of there in order to think, to work out what went wrong these thirty years.' He watched the entrance to the General Post Office where hordes of people went in and out.

'We rushed in then. Now young people want to rush out of there.' He bowed his head and sighed. 'That young man just now. . . .'

'Who?'

'The one who crossed in front of the camera. Dressed in blue. Had a blank face. I wanted to call out to him.'

'Why?'

'That was what I asked myself. What could I say? His dreams broken before he even grew up.'

I watched the crowd, looking for the young man. I saw only office workers on their way home. Had they too stayed out of the turbulence?

I held his arm as we walked away, leaving this hubbub of the commercial centre. Thirty years! And now, I was seeing him off on another long march. And I? My wife was waiting dinner for me. A cradle for workers to clean the glass-wall of the building was being lowered down the outside of the Connaught Centre. Could they cleanse me of these clinging thoughts of parting? There it went, down . . . fiftieth floor . . . forty-nine . . . down . . .

Shit! Where were we? Hurry down. Forty! Damn it! Six o'clock already, and not off work. How could I make it to the first race in Happy Valley?

'Ah Sing, be quick about it. Just give it the once-over and move on. Hurry!' Good job Ah Sing did what he was told. Gave me a breather.

Those bums down there had it easy. . . . Eight hours in air-con and then it was bye-de-bye. And those country cousins with nothing better to do than come here and take pictures. What was so great about the Connaught Centre anyway for taking pictures? Real country bumpkins! Not like me! Last weekend I went to Shenzhen, to Lake Xili. I had Ah Chun in my arms, and we went horse riding and took pictures. That's what I call a grand time. Ah Sing gawked at the pictures with such envy and jealousy. Told him to take Ah Kuen with him to Shenzhen and lord it there, but the damned fool just grinned and said, 'Ah Kuen is very proper, not like you and Ah Chun. She wouldn't go for a fling in Shenzhen.' I was stymied.

Sure! I could take Ah Chun in my arms, kiss her and grope her all I liked, but she wouldn't go the whole hog. She always said she would if we got married. Said her mother had told her never to let me take advantage. What eighteenth-century feudal ideas! You could see it all in the movies—what couples nowadays didn't do it? Wait till you'd tied the knot? That was kind of chancy. Would I have to force it?

'Ah Keung, big brother, give us a hand. I can't rush this job by myself!'

'All right. This job is no big deal, but you want help. You're useless.' If I had to do the job, it would be done in no time.

Ah Chun wanted to get married, I knew. So did I. But Mum said we'd have to give a wedding banquet. Where would I get the money? Lots of people just lived together nowadays in Hong Kong, but Mum wouldn't hear of that. Kept saying that my Dad died when I was a kid, that I didn't do well at school, that she worked her fingers to the bone to bring up us monkeys, that she'd never had a grand day in her life, that she had to have on a proper banquet when she took on a daughter-in-law—she wasn't going to lose face. . . . Well, I'd never done a single thing she wanted me to do, and now I couldn't very well let the old woman rant and rave that she'd rather die, can I? But then what about me? My wages

were a pittance, and the boss wouldn't give me a raise. That
arsehole Biu had said that lots of guys from across the border
were queuing up for my job, and the shop would be all too pleased
if I quit, then they could get lots more work done for half the
money.

I got really annoyed at the thought and spat out the chewing-
gum in my mouth. Wow! It flew at least twelve feet, then dropped
all the way down. Ah Sing said, 'You rubbish-lout! A fat lot of
good that's going to do the people down there!'

'The people down there are layabouts. Fat tubs-of-guts! I have
a good mind to pee on them from here and sprinkle them with
waters of benediction.'

'Don't joke about such things. You'll lose your job if you're not
careful!'

I made as if to unzip my fly, and Ah Sing turned green with
fright. I spat. My spit flew about thirteen feet. I felt great.

Ah Sing pulled up his collar and said, 'Hey, someone's looking
at you!'

I was alarmed. Was it someone from the shop checking up on
us? To find an excuse to give us the sack?

I turned around. There, inside the round window facing us, a
man was staring at us.

Rotten luck! It was the sack for sure this time. I looked again.
The man looked odd. Crew cut. Not with it. Dressed in blue.
Every inch a country bumpkin.

'Huh! You idiot! He's a country cousin from the other side. You
think he can fire me? Look at his face. Does he look as though he
would snitch on me?'

The man from the Mainland looked blank. He seemed to see us
and yet he seemed not to see us. It was weird. I made a face, took
a wet towel and wiped the window, as if to wipe away his strange
face. Through the wet glass his face looked as if it was melting. I
felt great. He turned and went away.

'Why did that country cousin come up the Connaught Centre?'
Ah Sing asked.

'What do I care? Hurry up. I'm going to Happy Valley for the
big chance tonight. Win some lolly to get me a wife!' I heaved a
gob of phlegm into my throat, aimed at the imagined face of the
country bumpkin in the air and spat! Great! It flew way ahead and
then down, down, down. . . .

'Look, Mum, something's falling down!' Kong Sang shouted. I glanced at him but didn't bother with what it was. It was almost six, and Heung Sai still hadn't arrived. How annoying! We would be late for sure! I had said I wasn't going, but he'd said people would talk if I didn't turn up. Well, if we turned up late, that would really give people something to talk about! But then people could say what they liked. As far as I was concerned, they had done me an injustice.

'Why isn't Daddy here yet, Mummy? I'm hungry!'

'Daddy is talking business with those people from the Mainland. He may be a bit late. Don't worry. He'll be here soon. Go over to the pier and get me an evening paper, all right?' Just to keep the kid busy.

As I watched Kong Sang thread his way through the rush-hour crowd, I became lost in thought: the boy had just turned ten, but he was nimble on his feet and brilliant at school (no wonder old Mrs Yu next door was always saying what a nice boy he was) and if it hadn't been for that new boy from the Mainland, Kong Sang might well have been the top boy in the class. . . . H'm, those people were such a pain—I'd been with the choir for over ten years, had always sung the lead, and sung at the finale, but in this concert 'Highlights from Opera: East and West', *she* was going to sing the 'Barbarella' from *Carmen* (and she'd only joined the choir six months ago—couldn't even manage Cantonese, let alone French, awful!—and what was worse was the Chinese folk-song style she used—twisting and turning her voice—how could you sing soprano in a Western opera with that?); and I had to sing the wretched selections from *The Hundred Brides*! Heung Sai had said that my not going to the rehearsal was bad form, but if I were to go on stage tonight, I would really lose face. Besides, Heung Sai himself complained too about how difficult it was to deal with this China trade.

I noticed a middle-aged man standing nearby, looking this way and that. Not the smart type; a bewildered expression on his face. He came and said something to me in Putonghua. I couldn't figure out whether he was asking the way to the City Hall, so I said in English, 'I don't know.'

Huh! Was he going to the concert too? Did he know anything about music? When was it that this place came to be full of people from all the provinces, bombarding you with all kinds of dialects and accents? What was the world coming to? We wouldn't be able to stay here in Hong Kong much longer!

I'd long urged Heung Sai to find some way of getting us to the States, but he had kept putting it off. He said that away from Hong Kong the only way he could make a living was to run a restaurant, but he'd find it too difficult to adapt. Well, I found it difficult to adapt now.

'Mum, your paper!' Kong Sang had come back.

I told him to hang on to the paper, I wasn't in the mood to read it. When Heung Sai got here, I'd give him what for: forcing us to come to the concert. He said to meet here at six for dinner first but it was six-thirty already and not a sign of him. Why did he leave me standing here at the door of the Connaught Centre—was I to pose like a model? Or like some miserable exhibit? What would the choir people say if they saw me standing here! How wretched!

'Mum, Daddy's here!'

Yes. Heung Sai was carrying his black briefcase and coming down the footbridge. He was tall, and always walked with a stoop; I'd told him many times not to walk like that but there was no way to change him—he was that stubborn!

He looked tired, looked so much older than this morning—must have had a tough time negotiating his deal, poor thing; but I couldn't be soft: he had kept me waiting the whole time, I couldn't forgive him that. He was looking up. What was it? Why was he looking so stunned? What . . . ?

'Get away! Step back . . . falling. . . .'

I heard Heung Sai shouting. He was waving his hand. I looked up. Something was falling down . . . fast . . . falling down. . . .

The crowd surged towards the Connaught Centre. Someone shouted, 'A country cousin's jumped off the building!'

'Jumped off the Connaught Centre?'

'How could that be?'

'Don't know. He hit that metal ring in the middle of the fountain.'

'The metal sculpture?'

People ran around and spread the word. Some stopped to look, some rushed to the scene, and some looked on and registered nothing.

Now, it was a scene full of action: first, a long shot, then fast-cut into a few close-ups, voice-over some interesting dialogue. Not bad. Could use this scene for the last scene of *End of the Affair* where the male lead abducts the female lead and they go up to the roof. Hordes of policemen arrive. Crowds gather round the building. . . . The Connaught Centre would make a good location, but it wasn't easy to get permission.

And as he moves with the crowd towards the Connaught Centre, still uneasy at heart, the frustrated lover becomes violent, is arrested and taken to the police station. Released on bail, he goes berserk, kills the girl's family. . . . Mixed up in all this would be psychosis, complexes, bruised ego and other things from the dark side of human nature. Plenty of drama and substance. Besides, cases like this had got into the paper more than once. No problems with credibility. But the last box-office flop was still worrying. Could it have been that the ruthless audience had tired of me? What did they really want anyway?

A wall of people closing off the building. Noise and hubbub. A loudspeaker barking orders for the crowd to back away and disperse. Someone squeezing in through a break. The policemen holding back the crowd. A few of them standing in the shallow fountain, as if waiting for the ambulance and some senior officer. In the middle of the fountain, a body dressed in blue lying face down, trickles of blood seeping into the water. The water still clear, the sculpture still intact. A solemn, desolate ending. The cast list rolls up from the bottom of the screen, and the house lights go up, curtains—a classic ending. Very good!

They said the guy was from the Mainland. My male lead would be psychotic. But then psychopaths were no longer in. Nor was Freud. But if the main character was a new immigrant. . . . That was it! A new immigrant. A one-time leader of the Red Guards, wielding power and glory. Now at a dead end, as it were. Nobody to turn to and becomes a villain. Right. A lone gunman. In a brazen armed robbery in a bank in Central. Surrounded by the police. He abducts a hostage and breaks out. Rushes into the Connaught Centre and starts a series of gun-fights in the maze of passages and corridors inside. Blasts into offices, wrecks some executive suite, is riddled with bullets, and falls through the glass window out of the building. Then cut to this scene. Ha! This was going to work. Plenty of entertainment, lots of violence, and a theme too—the Connaught Centre was a symbol of modernization in Hong Kong. A Mainlander enters, destroys the established order, and is himself trapped, and later destroyed in a tragedy. Lots of subtext there. Very good! I would change the script. A Mainlander. The audience would love it.

A middle-aged woman was covering her face, sobbing. Who could that be? A man and a kid beside her comforting her. Was she a relative of the dead man? The man was blocking the sight from her view. That was good. What you don't see doesn't exist. Behind me people were saying all sorts of things. A good time to gather material. Interview some of them perhaps. Lead off with a topic and watch their reaction. Add those to the film. That should add a touch of authenticity. Good for the box-office.

The two old men standing apart were silent, sad. Who were they? The one in thick specs and wide lapels had a mournful face; the other had a deep frown and was saying 'Did you see those thick dark-rimmed glasses? An intellectual perhaps?' Ah! An intellectual turned villain. Good. Lots of conflicts, paradoxes, and therefore good drama!

Thick specs was saying, 'He has big, rough hands. He must have worked in the fields!' Worked in the fields? How could that be?

'Is that so?' said the other.

'I have seen so many.' Thick specs sighed. 'There were so many of them then. And now, even the Hong Kong dream has fallen apart.' He sighed. What was he going on about? Were they a couple of lunatics? And now an ambulance arrived. An inspector parted the crowd, signalling the policemen to keep order. The sergeant went up to meet him, pointed upwards, and the inspector looked up. A cradle such as window cleaners use was rising slowly. If . . . aha! If I put the camera in the cradle, pointing down for a wide shot. . . . That would be a classic scene. Then pull back slowly, in the dusk, slowly, slowly pull back, until you could see the whole of Hong Kong island, in a blur. . . .

July 1984
Chinese original published in *Sing Tao Evening Post: City Hall* (weekly magazine), 25 September 1985.

6

Watching the Sea

By **CHAN PO CHUN**

Translated by Cathy Poon

The harbour and the sea have figured in literary writings about Hong Kong since its earliest days as a British colony.

Huge rectangular blocks line the seaward road like the trooping of the colour, their tinted glass walls of varying shades glittering under the sun. Rising from the middle of the road, the flyover makes a beautiful turn before descending and joining another road. On one side stands a solid row of high-rise commercial blocks and residential buildings, while on the other the great wall of tower blocks is broken by several old, four-storey buildings. The old buildings face the busy main street, proudly displaying their outer walls that have been darkened by time; green paint is peeling from the window sills while the glass windows are bandaged with crosses of adhesive tape, put there as a precaution against storms. This makes the old buildings look like particularly bad dentures in a row of healthy teeth, or sloppily dressed midgets standing beside a group of tall and immaculately attired gentlemen.

The top of a wardrobe slowly emerges from a narrow and dark stairway. Then, with a yell, the man carrying the wardrobe unloads his chestnut-coloured, waist-high load in the middle of a jumble of furniture and household items on the pavement. He pulls a towel from his waist, but accidentally knocks down a yellowing rattan chair by his side. Picking it up with one hand and wiping away his sweat with the other, he yells to his workmate who is lifting on to the truck a tall, marble-topped rosewood side table that looks as if it is going to fall apart. 'Bloody hell! These stairs! If the wardrobe wasn't made of such good timber and might fetch a few bucks, I really would have chopped it up before moving it.'

I

His wife was about to go downstairs for her mahjong game when the door-bell rang.

Slowly, he got out of his easy chair and craned to look into the dark corridor. He saw his wife opening the door for her and heard them murmuring something to each other. Then he saw her slim shape passing through the gloomy corridor, becoming larger and clearer, and finally stopping before him with a smile. He smiled happily back at her.

He *was* truly happy. The days are long when you are waiting for the rare visitor. His wife was either at the back of the house chanting the sutras or downstairs playing mahjong after finishing her chores. When she came for a visit, however, even if she just sat there, somehow the house did not seem so empty. From the happy note in her voice over the phone just then, he could feel she was not as unhappy as he had thought she had been these past months. He felt relieved.

She seemed to be in good spirits. Her newly trimmed hair and pink cotton dress also gave her a fresh look. He motioned her to take the old, yellowing rattan chair beside him, then grabbed the arm of his easy chair and slowly lowered himself into it. She reached out to support him, but he sternly refused her help with a wave of his hand. She could only watch him closely in case he needed a hand. He seated himself and reclined comfortably against the back of the chair. She also took a seat.

'How are you feeling these days?' she asked.

'Fine. I'm all right. It's been several months now, and I haven't had another attack since then,' he said rather proudly, gently patting himself on the chest. As his speech was still slurred, she had to use her imagination to try to work out what he meant from his expression, lip movements, and some intermittent and poorly articulated words. She found that it was not really all that difficult once she got used to it. Besides, she did not even have to guess the meaning of this oft-repeated utterance. Every time he finished saying this he would say with a sigh of relief, 'I've been so fortunate!'

He had indeed been fortunate.

The long corridor seemed endless. She had run in small, quick steps, resenting a little that she was wearing a cheongsam which prevented her from taking bigger strides. Her mind was totally blank.

There he was, lying all curled up under layers of white, his eyes closed.

'Two packs of cigarettes a day? No wonder your lungs end up like this!' The doctor on duty was giving a dressing-down to the skinny old man who was coughing continuously on the next bed. When he finished, he turned to her and said, 'At his age, sudden fainting usually means a stroke. You must be prepared for him to go at any time. He's quite elderly, you know!'

But he had regained consciousness. His eyes had looked slowly around the room and finally rested on her face. With swollen eyes, she smiled and greeted him.

'I've seen the CT scan from St. Paul's. . . . He will be hemiplegic and dysphasic,' said the same doctor matter-of-factly.

Staring at the white wall and the face which seemed to have shrunk and turned yellow against the white sheets, she could hardly fight back tears as she thought about how this energetic old man would have to spend the rest of his life imprisoned in a body that had lost half its mobility. And yet a calm, almost indifferent look slowly appeared on his face. He even extended his still mobile but shaking right hand and lightly patted the back of her hand.

He had had a long, long dream. He felt that he was drifting in a vast sea, all he could hear was the rumbling waves around him. The innumerable tentacles of the huge waves were clutching at him, shoving him towards the shore and then suddenly snatching him back. He felt very, very tired, so tired that he could not move his limbs. For a while, he just wanted to close his eyes and take a deep sleep, letting the waves toss him up and down. He had a feeling that there was an even vaster stretch of ocean, carefree and tranquil, beyond these huge waves. He could hear the call of the ocean. He relaxed his body and, slowly, sleep closed in on him like a fog. His senses were numbed and he was almost asleep. But when the huge waves had tossed him forward and were about to pull him back, he suddenly had a glimpse of a glittering white beach. He saw his second wife—her step-grandmother, that quiet woman who kept everything to herself—walking alone on the sand. He also saw her. She seemed still very small and was happily collecting shells on the beach by herself. Suddenly she raised her head, looked around the desolate beach, and began sobbing and crying out for her grandpapa. In his anxiety, the heavy fog of drowsiness enshrouding him dispersed. With great difficulty, he summoned his last bit of strength and started crawling towards the beach. Why did his limbs feel so leaden? A big wave came crushing down and he was swept to the bottom of the sea before being pushed up with a gush of black sand. . . . Suddenly he had a feeling that he had flown into a dark tunnel. There was a spot of light ahead and he could hear the faint but clear sound of bells. He had no idea how long he had been flying, but at long last he had slowly opened his eyes.

He distinctly heard what the doctor had said. 'That would be more terrible than death itself,' a voice inside him said.

Almost at once, he heard another small voice inside saying, 'That can't be true! Don't you believe him! You've always been in good health.'

But almost at the same time the first voice retorted, 'He's the doctor. If you can't trust him, who can you trust? After all, you're well over eighty now. Didn't that "northerner" you used to bump into when you went for your morning exercise often say that you'd go at the age of seventy-three or eighty-four even if Yama didn't summon you? You've managed to cheat death this time. Do you think you can be the same person as before?'

'You didn't die, that shows you are still quite fit,' the second small voice broke in. 'Take your medicine, and start learning afresh how to stand and how to walk. You have to do what's necessary.'

Even when he was making painstaking efforts to practise standing up and sitting down and dragging his stiff leg forward, teeth clenched, these two voices still often alternated in his ear.

Now, at long last, he was able to throw away the crutches. Although he could only move forward inch by inch, and had to hold on to the door-frame with both hands before he could pull his leg up to cross the threshold, it was still so much better than just lying in bed all day.

'What's that?' he asked, pointing at the box which she had brought and put on the table in front of him.

'Vegetable dumplings. Eat them while they're hot.' She stood up to open the box, but he had already put one hand on it and was pulling the nylon string with his other hand.

'Let's share them,' he said, but after a few fumbling attempts he was still unable to undo the knot. She reached over, trying to give a hand, but again he brushed her aside. He pulled hard a couple more times and the knot came undone. She went to the cupboard to fetch two pairs of chopsticks and two plates, and poured two cups of tea from the thermos on the tall marble-topped rosewood side table. They started eating.

She enjoyed watching him. She never seemed to have noticed before how nice his face looked, with the short silvery hair sitting neatly on the crown, and the deep grooves on his forehead running sideways down his cheeks. Around the eyes, these strong symmetrical lines branched out like two open fans towards the temples. Below these fans, strong lines again, which ran straight down his face to join the deep folds around the neck. His small greyish eyes looked like two small half-moons set between his puffy eyelids and his drooping eye bags. Deep furrows also ran down the sides of his nose and around the mouth. All these lines moved rhythmically as he chewed his food, and when he smiled, they all tilted upwards.

All of a sudden the lines stopped moving, and they settled slowly to reveal a serious and somewhat worried expression. 'Is it settled?' he asked. Her chopsticks, a dumpling suspended between them, stopped in mid-air; but without hesitation and in as bland a voice as possible, she managed to reply candidly that it was.

'Good for you! That son of a bitch!' he said angrily, the last few syllables sounding unexpectedly distinct.

She lowered her head, then looked up at him again and mumbled, 'Don't be angry with him, Grandpa. It's not his fault!' She had really wanted to say that this was not a question of who was right and who was wrong, but it had come out differently.

He quietly put down his chopsticks. The lines on his face stayed motionless, but a strangely complicated expression slowly surfaced in the eyes—a mixture of surprise, disbelief, reproach, and tender affection—as if saying: even now, you're still on his side. Not his fault indeed! Was it your fault then? You silly girl! But he kept the words to himself.

In fact he had disapproved of Ngai from the start. Right after that first meeting with his future grandson-in-law he had said to her parents, 'Teaching's not a bad profession, but his personality and looks leave a lot to be desired: you just can't trust someone with such a protruding jawbone. He's also a bore. Speaks only when spoken to. Doesn't even pour tea for others. What's more, he looks so preoccupied. Doesn't seem to be someone who can take care of others.'

But he didn't dare say anything to her face. He knew she was stubborn like him, and if he didn't handle it well, she might just marry Ngai at once to spite him. They did get married shortly afterwards, and not much later he learnt that Ngai had lost his job. When asked, she said that he hadn't lost his job, but had left it in order to prepare for an exhibition of his works. He was not all convinced, but asked no more, and felt more certain than ever that she had made a bad choice marrying Ngai. The fact that Ngai could leave her behind and go to the States on his own was good enough proof.

She also knew that he didn't approve of Ngai, and she'd even been secretly annoyed with him. Even now she still thought that he didn't understand Ngai.

'Ngai is dedicated to art and almost incapable of looking after himself in trivial everyday matters, while you are such a motherly figure, Deb. Perhaps you two are made for each other. Congratulations!'

Ngai's best friend Yuen had written this on the wedding card she had sent.

What followed then was a long road that stretched from the city to the suburbs, and at the end of it was an old house in a village in Yuen Long. She taught in a local primary school during the day, and went home in the afternoon to do her housework.

What she remembered most clearly about that village house were the bats that invaded in the evening. As a child she had seen these auspicious little creatures on some of the embroidery at home, and when she grew up, she had read poems with lines like 'Dusk is an embroidery of bats' wings', but she had never once imagined that bats in real life could be so frightening. When she first saw one, she was so scared she screamed. But by and by, she was able to do as Ngai did and bash them with a plank. What else could she have done? Bats would come in whether or not Ngai was there, and Ngai didn't spend much time at home. In fact, life in those years was spent waiting.

Waiting for Ngai to come home from town.

Waiting for Ngai to emerge from his studio, with paint all over himself or with hands covered in clay. Then she would at once put down whatever she was doing to heat up some food for him.

After that it was waiting for news from the Consulate, then waiting for Ngai's letter, or waiting in her dark and lonesome bedroom for a long-distance call which might or might not come.

The sun was particularly warm that autumn. Ngai's hands and lips were like sunshine.

'I'll go over first. You must apply to come as soon as you can.'

'Do we have to? Didn't they say that things will remain unchanged for fifty years after 1997?'

But Ngai said, 'How can you believe the communists? Haven't you heard what happened to artists during the Cultural Revolution?'

'But there's not going to be another Cultural Revolution!'

'Whether or not there'll be one or not is another matter. For people like us, it's always a good thing to go out and see what it's like out there.'

After a moment's silence, Ngai continued, 'I'm not as stupid as Lau and the others who can think of nothing else but democracy and returning to the embrace of the motherland. Going home with concepts of democracy as presents? I'd say they've booked a place for themselves in prison, where they'll have a permanent home!'

Ngai had the habit of rolling his eyes skyward when he laughed, as if he couldn't care less what the rest of the world thought, but the shallow dimple on his left cheek gave his smile an innocent and mischievous touch.

Darkness. She had just woken up from a dark dream and that vast and boundless ocean was still churning in her mind when the phone rang.

'Deb? Just got your letter. There's really nothing we can do now that your application has been turned down by the Consulate.

70

Let's be patient. We'll just have to wait until I get my green card, then I'll apply for you to come and join me. . . . Look, just apply for a tourist visa to visit my sister in Canada. I'll meet you there, and we can work out what we're going to do. . . .'

Ngai's voice seemed so unreal coming half way across the world. Still she made the arrangements and went. She didn't dare tell anyone at home about her plans—not even the old man who had pampered her since she was a little girl and had always listened to her. I'll write to them and explain everything when it's all settled, she had thought.

But when she arrived in Canada Ngai was not there. He telephoned: 'Look, I can't come over and meet you because my visa's expired. Besides, I've a lecture to go to, and after that I have to interview the speaker. Why don't you ask my brother-in-law to bring you over to the States? Just flash my sister's papers at the border. I'm sure you'll get by. You and sis look so much alike they won't notice the difference. Ask him to bring you here, have a bath and take a nap. There's food in the fridge. If you're hungry, cook yourself something. Wait for me. I'll see you tonight. . . .'

She suddenly felt so miserable she wanted to cry. When would this waiting end? In Hong Kong she still had her job, her family and friends. . . .

Naturally she was unable to see the expression on his face. She had put the phone down after saying to him: 'I'm not coming. Let's get a divorce.' But she couldn't help imagining his reaction at the other end of the line. He would be a little taken aback and say, 'Hello? Hello?' before realizing that she had already hung up. He would stand motionless for a while, then shrug and go off to his damn lecture. . . .

How was she to explain the reason for the divorce? Just say that she could wait no longer? She had heard, indirectly, that Ngai had apparently said to someone, 'Deb really has had a tough time these past years. I can't let her go on waiting any longer. I'll make it up to her when I finally make it big, but I just can't keep her waiting forever.'

Was that why he had been so brutally indifferent? She had voiced the word 'divorce' in a fit of anger, and he hadn't even bothered to ring her back and discuss it. Many times she had really wanted to call him up and demand an explanation: 'It was really you who wanted a divorce, wasn't it? I said the word, and you jumped at it.'

But on second thoughts, she doubted what good such bickering would do. Besides, she herself had mentioned the word first. Her wrath would turn into tears every time she thought about this. Gratitude she never wanted. What could he have done to make it up to her anyway? In Chinese folklore, Wang Baochuan spent eighteen long years waiting for her man to return to their shabby cave dwelling, naively believing the reward of a bridal gown would be worth all those years of suffering.

Sometimes she really had no idea how she managed to pull herself through those early months after coming home. Worse still, her grandpa had fallen ill not long after her return. But then out of that jumble of memories and reality a new way of life emerged which she had never ever imagined.

Shakily, a pair of chopsticks holding a vegetable dumpling slowly reached towards her, and the dumpling dropped with a flop on to her plate.

She looked at him. The surprise, disbelief and reproach she had seen a few moments ago had vanished from those small grey eyes, and all that remained was infinite love and a trace of remorse. 'She has suffered enough. I really shouldn't make it any harder on her,' he thought. With this in mind, he pointed at the box and said, 'Come, eat a few more, eat a few more. . . .'

II

The furniture in his bedroom had been rearranged many times before, just like his life had been. That chestnut-coloured waist-high wardrobe was only bought two years ago. Now it stood next to the old wardrobe which he had been using for decades.

She helped him sit on the edge of his bed and asked, 'Are you tired? Do you want to take a nap?'

'No, I'm not tired.' He pointed at the folding chair by his side and asked her to sit down.

With clumsy hands, he slowly pulled open the drawers and dug out some old banknotes, jade buttons, letters, and other things to show her—like a child showing off his toys. Although he had been living in retirement for more than twenty years, he still retained the habit of filing things away as he had done with documents at work. Everything was arranged in impeccable order in the drawers, and he knew exactly where each item was placed. A dark-green folder was holding the *Students' Paper* she had edited when she was studying at the teachers' college. She leafed through those yellowing pages and read what she had once written. The life and thoughts of those bygone years seemed distant and unfamiliar. She had almost forgotten that she was once so sensitive and cared so much about things happening around her. The book reviews had all been written after several careful readings, but she could not remember anything of some of the books she had reviewed. Life really seemed to be a narrowing path for her. Teaching primary school required no research, managing that home, however, had taken up all her time and energies. She had learnt cooking from scratch, and she specially prepared Ngai's favourite dishes. Not long after getting married, all their friends said Ngai had put on weight. Ngai had pointed at her and said jokingly, 'Don't you understand? This is Deb's secret for keeping her husband on a leash. She feeds him so well he begins to look like a stout middle-aged man so no other women would look at him!'

She had laughed and hit him then. But had Ngai been discontented because she had never really learnt how to appreciate his creative works? Why had she never thought of that before?

He looked at her as she sat there lost in thought, but said nothing. He put away the *Students' Paper*, patted her hand, and shakily handed her a photo album. In it she saw him and herself from the distant past, as well as this house and the people living in it in those bygone years. The furniture had seemed so much cleaner and brighter and so much more orderly then. Decked out in a Western suit and tie, he was standing smartly in front of the street-side windows, with the vast harbour and all kinds of ships in the background. She remembered how, when she was still small, he used to lift her up to see the 'motor boats', and how, when typhoons came, the waves were swept sky-high. She also saw a picture of him sitting at an oblong dining-table, with his first wife—her grandmother—in a cheongsam by his side. In the foreground was a Western-style tea set, and in the background a rosewood cupboard and two tall marble-topped side tables. There were large vases on top of the side tables. Her mother, also wearing her cheongsam, was sitting on the edge of a Western-style double bed. And she, who had just celebrated her one-month birthday, was sitting in her mother's lap. Next to them was a pillow, with the words 'Good Morning' embroidered in dark threads on the soft-coloured and frilled pillow case.

'See, you looked like a little kitten then,' he laughed.

She smiled and turned the page. A little girl in a short frock was sitting on the bed and holding up a big apple. Looks like an advertisement, she thought. The little girl then jumped off the bed and ran all over the house, picked up a big yellow-and-white cat and grabbed its paws, trying to teach it to write. Hurt by the pencil and her hands, the cat gave out a sharp cry and struggled to free itself. She went after it. In its anxiety, the cat leapt on to the tall side table. 'Crash!' The large vase fell from the side table and was smashed into pieces.

She was so frightened she burst out crying. He woke up with a start from his afternoon nap, and rushed over to pick her up and comfort her: 'Oh, my baby, don't cry, it's all right, it's all right as long as you're not hurt. No need to cry.'

Grandmother grumbled as she swept away the broken pieces, 'Such a lovely pair of vases, and now one of them is broken. The brat! She doesn't behave like a girl at all. She really needs a good spanking. . . .'

He whispered into her ear, 'We won't spank Deb. We'll spank the cat instead, all right?'

Sometimes he would tell his grandchildren stories—tales about Bandit Cheung, about the pirate queen and so on. But his favourite were stories about those 'three years and eight months'.

'The Japs were really nasty. They often pushed people off buildings and rounded them up for beating and water torture. . . . In those days we had to bow to them every time we walked past their sentry posts. When you bowed, they bowed back, but if you didn't, they would slap you so hard it made your head spin. Okay, if we had to bow we had to bow. Every time I walked past them, I'd tell myself: I'll see if my shoes are clean! I just bent my body, but those devils really bowed back. . . .'

Most of his stories were about hair-raising and bitter experiences. The little ones often opened their mouths wide in amazement as they listened, but the stories were really too distant for children born and bred in peace and stability. For them, the only things concrete about the Japanese occupation of Hong Kong were the military banknotes which the adults had given them to play with from some tucked-away corners. Long before she was born, he had wound up the family business and become a legal clerk in the government.

'What's a legal clerk? Is it the same as those personal assistants to mandarins in movies? Does he wear a two-tuft moustache and a box-shaped hat with tassels hanging down from its corners?' she once asked.

He couldn't help laughing out loud, 'Yes, that's what Grandpa wears to work.'

He was always such a kind person—in her memories and in real life. Yet she seemed to recall a time when she had simple-mindedly and impulsively resented him for his lack of 'national sentiments'!

If she had said yes when she received Ngai's call and had let his brother-in-law take her over to meet him, life might have been different, but she also would have lost afternoons like this when she could sit with him and relive together scenes from the past. If he had not suddenly fallen ill, it would never have crossed her mind that he would leave her one day. Neither would she be keeping him company as she did now. She did not know why she had not thought of him when she was making plans about joining Ngai. She felt as ashamed about this as she did when she thought about how simple-minded and impulsive she had been.

Come to think of it, he had already lost a lot. It seemed that the further he moved on, the more he was deprived of what really mattered in life—the family business was lost overnight during the war, and then those near and dear to him also left him one after another. Upon retirement, he lost a career which kept him interested and occupied. And now, he had lost even his health. Why was he still so happy? How could he talk about the past so calmly and so unperturbed?

Did it mean that one day she, too, would be able to talk about everything she had lost, about those years she spent with Ngai, with equal detachment and calmness?

'What's happened to your leg?'

'I've broken it.'

'What? How did it happen?'

'Come on! Can't you manage a smile? See how you overreacted, my dear! If, like you, I only saw my bad leg, I don't think I could live another day.'

That scene from a movie suddenly popped into her mind. Although she clearly remembered that it was a conversation between two girls, she had a sudden vision that the last sentence was uttered by him.

Obviously he had said nothing. When she raised her head to look at him, he was swinging his more nimble leg contentedly, taking a leisurely stroll into the past.

III

After making tea in the kitchen, she went along the long and gloomy corridor and back to the lounge room. He was now seated by the street-front windows. Today, he seemed to have thought of many more things and of a much more distant past. He was a little tired, but he was fortunate to have so many memories to enrich an otherwise monotonous life. One by one, things which occurred when she was a little girl flashed before his eyes. She had always been a fun-loving, inquisitive girl, and she loved to watch the scenes on the street. Every time she heard that kind of music, she would drop what she was doing, pull a chair over and kneel on it to watch. He would rush over to hold her, and watch with her as the long procession approached from afar and then slowly disappeared into the distance.

'Grandpa, who are those people in white with things tied around their heads? Why are they crying?'

'What's that car there for? Why are these people walking and not riding in that car? Who's the person in that picture on the front of the car?'

She would keep asking these questions. Once she even put a white pillow case over her head and played funeral, and got a good whacking from her grandmother. When Grandmother died, the funeral procession was also very, very long, stretching from the Hong Kong Funeral Parlour in North Point all the way to the Catholic Cemetery in Happy Valley. She was about eight then. . . .

'Grandpa, here's your tea.' He took the cup and had a sip before putting it down on the table in front of him and, with a smile, pointed outside the window.

Just as she had done so many times in the past, she leaned over the window sill, the green paint of which was now peeling off. Outside was the harbour, which had moved further away and been reduced in size. Their four-storey building, at one time right on the waterfront, was now shoved way behind tower blocks thirty or forty storeys high. From where they now sat, they could only get a view of the mountains and the sea framed like a television screen between two buildings. A ship had just emerged from behind one building, but no sooner had it shown itself than it disappeared behind the other building.

The street scene was just as ordinary—nothing but buildings, roads and cars. But when you looked at them long enough you would see a colourful picture. Below the brick-red imitation marble façades of the buildings was a motorway with three rows of 'green islands'. On the green islands, oleanders were interspersed with oriental plane trees; fragrant thoroughworts blossoming white stood next to some unfamiliar purplish-red plants; there were even small patches of grass. Cars of all hues were speeding along the grey asphalt road. . . .

She turned to look at him. He seemed tired today, but a while ago he was still full of zest as he asked if she was going out with anyone, and urged her to find a good man and tie the knot again.

'Get married again? Perhaps. But that's not the only road for me,' she said to herself. All the same, she just smiled at him and nodded. He was still swinging his feet and thinking, and from time to time he picked up his cup for a sip. What was he thinking? She had no idea.

Outside, it was the same small greyish patch of mountains and sea. No ship was in sight, but she knew that behind those tower blocks the sea was still rolling and that there were numerous ships out there—ships setting sail or about to berth, yachts joyfully basking, sampans filled with sorrow, huge warships, agile speedboats—each occupying its own corner of the sea, creating a rich and ever-changing picture. . . .

—

The last of the folding chairs is loaded on to the truck. The rear-board of the truck is secured into position, and, within seconds, the truck becomes part of the colourful stream of traffic.

The pavement lies in quiet solitude in the shade of the brown building across the street.

Wind is blowing across the small patches of grass on the road dividers.

The old four-storey building stands silently under the sun.

The window sill with peeling green paint darkened by time and the adhesive tape on the windows have disappeared behind blue nylon sheets and bamboo scaffolding. The pneumatic drills start blasting away, sending the loosened bricks and dirt shooting in all directions.

Chinese original published in *Hong Kong Literature Monthly*, No. 11, 1986.

7

Old Banyan Trees Moving On

By **XIAO SI**
Translated by Jane C. C. Lai

There are no trees in Hong Kong: the city is just a huge concrete jungle. So say many people, tourists as well as writers—from the Mainland as well as from the West. Xiao Si does not share this view. She also deals with a topic that recurs in this collection—emigration.

By the old Sports Road in Happy Valley there are two old banyan trees, well over a hundred years old. They have stood there to witness the fire at the old racecourse grandstand; they have watched generations of punters—who helped pay for the racecourse turf—come and go, and they have watched all that money come and go.

Now they are moving on.

Botanists say that banyan trees have a lot of vitality, their aerial roots sway in the air as gracefully as a flowing beard, and the roots that touch the ground spread out and hold firm to the earth and never let go. Luxuriant: that's the word to describe them.

Because of a road-building plan, these two trees have to give way. Experts from a horticulture consultancy have come up with a plan to move them to a site in Wong Nai Chung Road, about thirty metres away.

In the hundred years of growth, how large an area must their roots have spread in the earth? Who would know? The experts say that each of the trees and their rootballs must weigh a hundred tonnes. To move them, a special way has been devised to shift and pull them along. Pull an old banyan tree along? It strains the imagination!

Before the move, the trees were given a trim. The spreading branches were cut short, making them look a bit oafish. It made one anxious to think what would happen when they were pulled up by the root. Yesterday, they started their journey to their new home: a difficult three-day journey to travel the thirty-odd metres. And whether they will survive in their new homes is still a matter of concern for the horticulture experts.

'To take root where one lands.' These are reassuring words. But ours are special times and here I am still clinging to concepts left over from an agrarian society. To fly, to bounce, to roam—these are words with panache. To be able to pull oneself up by the roots—that's the way to survive.

Perhaps that is why the banyan trees are moving on.

If one moves in order to survive, then it stands to reason that one must survive after the move. My concern is that the trees might not survive the move. The horticulture experts have naturally worked out the odds, but the old banyan trees themselves must stand this test—a test of their vitality.

If I were a photographer, I would film the whole process of this move—this testimony of life and death.

My good wishes go with you both, old banyan trees. May you stand firm in your new homes to watch more of that money come and go.

Chinese original published in Lo Wai Luen: *Hong Kong Stories: Personal Recollections and Literary Reflections*, Hong Kong: Oxford University Press, 1996.

8

The Bronze Lions

By **XIAO SI**

Translated by Jane C. C. Lai

Xiao Si's writings, noted for the fineness of their observations, often make those of us who have lived in this city for a long time feel that we have never really got to know the place. For Hongkongers over the age of thirty, the bronze lions referred to in this piece will almost certainly play a part in our memories of our growing up experience.

But how many of us have looked at the lions the way she does?

One day, during office hours when others were at work, I went to Central, to the entrance of the main office building of the Hongkong Bank.

The entrance? Where was it? There used to be three sets of big bronze doors, I remembered. I didn't know anything about that postmodernism stuff; all I knew was that the new building was like an unfinished factory, its body cold and stiff and exposed. There was no door; one had a clear view from Des Voeux Road right through to Queen's Road Central, except for the escalators rising in the middle of the lobby. Lobby? You couldn't call that the lobby. The proper lobby for business transactions was one flight up the escalators. Flight? A rather strange one. One stood on the escalators to be conveyed upstairs.

All of a sudden, it seemed to me that many of the concepts, the terms that one was used to had become 'incorrect'. An entrance was no longer a door or space through which you went inside; a lobby had become an open space; and a flight. . . . It was all rather confusing. What could one do but smile.

I went to the main building of the Hongkong Bank for a purpose: to look at the pair of bronze lions.

I had lived in Hong Kong for decades but I had never really observed those lions. So I decided to go and have a good look at them, to touch them, and to read the signature of the English sculptor who cast them.

If Wu Guanzhong, the artist, had not mentioned it in an article, I never would have known that those bronze lions were cast by an English professor at the National Academy of Arts in Hangzhou, back in 1935 when Lin Fengmian—now a world-renowned painter—was President of the Academy. Yes. There it was. W. W. Wagstaff's signature, carved into the pedestal.

The more imposing of the pair, the lion with the open mouth, had sustained many injuries: scars and deep cracks. When were these inflicted? For fifty years, he had opened his mouth but said nothing.

I walked round the lions again and again. Someone, probably waiting for somebody, stared at me, wondering what I—who didn't look like a tourist—was looking at. Well, someone born and bred in Hong Kong is looking, for the first time, at the lions which have been here for five decades. Would you understand that, Sir?

He most probably would not.

I touched the lion's claws and its tail. They gleamed golden, where people's touch had polished them.

Ah. I didn't even get the bank's full name right. It was called the Hongkong And Shanghai Banking Corporation.

Chinese original published in Lo Wai Luen: *Hong Kong Stories: Personal Recollections and Literary Reflections*, Hong Kong: Oxford University Press, 1996.

9

A Government House with a View

By DUNG KAI CHEUNG
Translated by Dung Kai Cheung

Also taken from The Atlas: Archaeology of an Imaginary City, *this story brings out, with subtle but powerful irony, what the writer thinks about the governors of Hong Kong and British colonial rule in Hong Kong.*

In the early days of the City of Victoria, the governors did not have a permanent residence and office, not until the erection of Government House on Government Hill in 1855. Yet in a 1856 map of the Central District, Government House was still only marked out in dotted lines, thus casting doubt on the exact date of its construction. As far as its location was concerned, Government House was undoubtedly ideal for commanding the whole city. According to the *Plan of the City of Victoria* in 1889, up on the slopes behind Government House was the Botanical Gardens, or the so-called 'Garden of the Head Soldier', down the hill in front of Government House, there was the Government Office Building and Murray Battery, to the west of which was the commercial district of Central and the waterfront. In the direction north-east of Government House lay St John's Cathedral, Murray Parade Ground, and City Hall. In fact, from the panoramic sketches drawn by Lieutenant Collison in 1845, one can already tell what a vantage point the future Government House was to occupy.

Sir William Des Voeux, the tenth Governor of Victoria (1887–91), described the view from Government House in his memoir as follows: 'Looking out at night from the front gallery of Government House, before the moon had risen, I witnessed an effect which was quite new to me. The sky, though clear of clouds, was somewhat hazy, so that the small-magnitude stars were not visible, though some of the larger ones were plain enough. Beneath, however, the air was quite clear, and consequently, though the vessels in the harbour were invisible in the darkness, their innumerable lights seemed like another hemisphere of stars even more numerous than the others, and differing only as being redder.'

For over fifty years, the view from Government House was probably not very different from Des Voeux's description. Even in maps produced in the 1940s or 1950s, the waterfront to the north of Government House was only extended a little further. But if we study carefully a 1:5000 map of Central in 1990, and supplement it with other relevant information, we will discover that the view of Government House has been blocked, in front, by the postmodern monster of a building—the Hongkong Bank—and, to its right, by the Bank of China Tower, the tallest building in the city. The coastline of the city has also moved significantly north-ward. Consequently, as seen on the map, Government House has become an inland building.

No documents survive which give a record of the view from Government House in its later days. The only description, culled from the grapevine, is what the last Governor (1992–97) Chris Patten allegedly said to his gardener one night before his departure: 'Looking out at night from the front gallery of Government House, before the moon had risen, I witnessed an effect which was quite strange to me. The sky, though clear of clouds, was somewhat hazy, so that the small-magnitude stars were not visible, though some of the larger ones were plain enough. Beneath, however, the air was quite clear, and consequently, though the buildings in the city were invisible in the darkness, their innumerable lights seemed like another hemisphere of stars even more numerous than the others, and differing only as being more dizzying.'

Chinese original published in Dung Kai Cheung: *The Atlas: Archaeology of an Imaginary City*, Taipei: Lian He Wenxue Chubanshe, 1997.

10

The Sorrows of Lan Kwai Fong

By P. K. LEUNG
Translated by Martha P. Y. Cheung and P. K. Leung

The original version of this work—in Chinese as well as English —was written and first published in 1993, in Dislocations (NuNaHeDuo), a photography magazine. Although revised for translation and publication in this collection, the early 1990s remains the temporal setting for this piece, since the mood and feelings belong to that particular period in the history of Hong Kong. Some of the bars and restaurants no longer exist in Lan Kwai Fong.

In recent years I gave two readings of my poems—not at the university, not in the library, but in Lan Kwai Fong. In the bar of the Fringe Club there is a small stage normally used by bands for playing music, but it caters for poetry reading too. In another bar, 'Post 97', there is no such provision, but when poetry reading still featured as part of the entertainment, the menus were printed with the programme of the month; during the reading, no drinks or food would be served, and every poet would get two glasses of wine for their pains.

On those occasions, I read together with poet friends who wrote in English. I recited my poems in English, too. This made me a little sad. In recent years, I have seldom had an opportunity to give readings in my own language—Chinese. The readings took place either abroad, or in 'Westernized' places like Lan Kwai Fong.

Why is it that local poets writing in the local language receive so little support? What has happened to our cultural space in Hong Kong?

———

In early 1991, a local publisher approached me and my photographer friend Lee Ka Sing to produce a book of poems and photographs about Hong Kong. We accepted the assignment with great enthusiasm, and decided on 'home' as our theme. I had written a series of three poems under the title Home—'The Square', 'Broken Home', 'Home-Refurnishing'. They were my response to what had happened in China in 1989. After 1989, some big businesses withdrew their capital from Hong Kong, certain aspects of our quality of life came under threat, and publishers willing to invest in serious and quality publications were getting fewer and fewer. Cultural space being so limited, Ka Sing and I of course treasured this opportunity, and we threw ourselves into the project. Later on I received a grant to do film studies in New York and spent six months there. Ka Sing joined me in New York and we went on a trip to Eastern Europe before coming back to Hong Kong. The experience we had of other cultures was of tremendous help to us in saying what we feel about this place in which we live.

I remember vividly the different homes I visited on that trip: composers' homes, artists' homes. The libraries—so beautiful, so spacious—were the homes of a huge variety of books. The churches—disused and dilapidated—still provided refuge for the vestiges of people's beliefs. In the former residence of Bertolt Brecht, I could imagine how the dramatist situated himself in his community and his culture. I also saw, in the vicinity, the Berliner Ensemble, the market, the bars, and even the cemetery in which Brecht was buried. I was always so envious of other people's homes. They were bright and spacious, filled with books, records, arts and crafts objects brought home from visits abroad, clumsy but charming kitchenware, menus. . . . They provided a space where one could entertain friends, or simply do one's reading and writing in solitude. At the time this feeling of envy was particularly strong since Hong Kong was going through a difficult period of transition. Everyone was overworked and had no peace of mind, the future was uncertain, friends were emigrating, families had to live in separation. Hardly anyone seemed to be able to find a home where they could live and work without feeling unsettled.

In 1992, Ka Sing and I came back to Hong Kong, the manuscript of our poems and photos on 'Home' ready for submission. But we were told by the publisher that because literary works were doing poorly in the market, the plan to publish our work had to be cancelled. I could understand that. The reality in Hong Kong being what it was, we just had to accept it. So the poems and photos, which carried so much of our feelings for Hong Kong, were shoved into drawers or strewn about in the corners of Ka Sing's studio. They had become homeless.

That is a fact of life in Hong Kong. Getting one's poems published has never been easy. Poetry journals come and go, struggling desperately for survival. Take, for example, the poetry journal founded by Ka Sing and his friends—*Autumn Firefly* (*Qiu Ying Shikan*). It started as a mimeograph, then it took the form of a small-size newspaper; for a while, it was published as a poster, and later as a series of eight postcards printed with poems and illustrations. These postcards were sold in bookstores and galleries, in the hope that readers would buy one set for themselves, and others to send to friends. In some ways it could be considered an attempt to promote poetry through contemporary means of communication and the latest design skills.

Publications like this one have the characteristics of a co-op. It isn't a grand residence, but those who contribute to it feel that they are members of a group committed to opening up for themselves and others a crucial space for survival. But when these publications fold, as did *Autumn Firefly*, the poems lose their homes—like street-sleepers they are abandoned to their fate. All around, there are high walls, closed doors; or else, there is the desolate sight of shattered tiles and dilapidated ruins. Political journals have their own agenda on what to publish; cottage presses are often highly exclusive; different patches are manned by different gate-keepers. Admission isn't easy for those who want to make their own views heard. And soon, you would rather prefer to settle for a space that is less pure but more open, and you find your literary works appearing in photography magazines like

Dislocation (*NuNaHeDuo*), or *In*—a woman's magazine with a feminist slant—or *Crossover*, a small magazine on cultural criticism. Sometimes, in order to speak your mind freely, it would be strategically wise to publish works with political concerns in commercial magazines, or experimental works in magazines where politics are strictly ruled out. An evening newspaper that has just cancelled its literary pages invited me to write a column on food. It looks like I stand a better chance to survive as a food critic than as a poet.

One writes in order to express oneself and communicate with others. But in Hong Kong, the environment is deteriorating for those who want to write. Even if you could tactfully avoid political censorship by having your works published in commercial magazines, these magazines would also apply the scissors to your work or dismiss them for commercial reasons or because the editors are looking for something more trendy. Situations like these make you feel even more acutely the pain of living under other people's roofs. I have been doing my writings in Hong Kong for years, I used to feel that writing for the newspapers was as comfortable as stepping into a popular local teashop for a cup of tea. Lately, however, I have found that it is hard to find a seat, the noise is loud and full of sensational outcries, the quality of the tea is worse, and it is not much fun sitting there. Hong Kong is my home; writing is my profession. But my home seems to have turned into alien soil, and it isn't so easy to carry on with my profession.

To make this place a home where we can live happy and content, many of us have tried to take on different roles at the same time—as teachers, writers, critics, and so on. The purpose is to analyse problems and stimulate thinking. And some of us try to do this by holding seminars on culture and running writing courses in the Arts Centre and the Fringe Club, which serve as a kind of alternative space to that provided by the normally conservative government organizations in charge of the arts. The type of guerrilla warfare we conduct in this city has forced us to venture out from our own grounds into space unfamiliar to us.

It was in the early 1990s, in an unfamiliar American bar in Lan Kwai Fong, that the American poet and translator Gordon T.

Osing suggested to me his plans for translating my poems into English. Before that he had read a few English translations of my poems, as well as others in Chinese. Then, for several weeks, we tried, largely for fun, translating a few of my poems together. Little did I think that this would eventually lead to my homeless poems finding a shelter abroad. Forty of them, translated into English, together with an introduction by Ackbar Abbas and a long dialogue between Gordon and me on Hong Kong culture, were brought together in a book entitled *City at the End of Time*, which was published in a book series on cultural studies. Thanks to cultural studies, these poems of mine, which had found no chance for publication in Chinese, were able to move into what looked like a temporary home in the space provided by a foreign language.

This makes one think about the problem of emigration. Some of my friends (poets included) have reluctantly emigrated because they found living in Hong Kong an increasingly unsettling experience. But for them as well as for my poems, setting up a new home thousands of miles away and settling down in a new culture hasn't been easy. Home might have become alien soil, but it doesn't necessarily mean that a strange land could easily turn into a home. Having to adapt to life in a foreign country is like having one's poems translated into another language—both go through a complex and intricate process of cultural translation, and there is always the danger of losing oneself and of being appropriated by the other.

And so in those days I met Gordon regularly in Lan Kwai Fong which until then had been an unfamiliar, 'Westernized' place to me. We moved from one bar to another when we were made to feel unwelcome for taking up the table for too long. But in some smaller bars we finally found the space we needed. And gradually I felt less apprehensive about this project than I had been at first, I also got used to the strange feeling of having to express myself in a language not my own. I remember spending many afternoons with Gordon in 'Seasons', 'Club 64', and the Fringe Club. We went over words and phrases, searching for expressions that neither exaggerate nor distort the meanings of the original. How can the ideas specific to one culture be retained in translation without their becoming incomprehensible to people of another culture? How can one find a foreign voice without making it sound false and pretentious? We racked our brains over these questions. The obstacles were huge, and it often turned out that the translation became a new creation in a new linguistic and cultural context. Would it really be possible to set up a new home in this dubious land of mixed cultures?

—

Lan Kwai Fong seemed a suitable place for the kind of dialogues and negotiations Gordon and I had with each other. It had started off as a residential area in the early decades of the twentieth century. There were merchants selling flowers and fabrics, and at one time it was a famous gathering place for matchmakers— because the place enjoyed good *fung shui*, so they say. In the 1970s it attracted a number of artists because the rents were cheap and because it was close to Central. My photographer friends Lee Ka Sing and Leong Ka Tai had their studios in Lan Kwai Fong; the avant-garde theatre group Zuni Icosahedron also had an office there in the 1980s. I remember going to their office to discuss collaborations, and we had inexpensive meals on the second floor of a Vietnamese restaurant. One old colonial building, which used to be the premises of Dairy Products and Ice Manufacturing Company Limited, now houses the Foreign Correspondents Club where journalists gather. Another old colonial building is now the premises of the Fringe Club. There are studio theatres and galleries inside the building, and it is the venue for the annual Fringe Festival in Hong Kong. In 1978, the first disco opened in Lan Kwai Fong, and since the 1980s, there have been more and more trendy bars and restaurants. Some yuppie journals such as *City Magazine* began to call this district the Montmartre of Hong Kong. In the same magazine I read of the views expressed by the Artistic Director of the Hong Kong Repertory Theatre at a recent theatre forum. According to him, while local dramatists find it hard to receive international attention because their plays are in Cantonese, the audience of Hong Kong enjoy the enviable fortune of being able to see all good Broadway or Western plays performed in translation by local theatre groups. This, to him, is the best thing about Hong Kong. So the best thing about Hong Kong is what is not Hong Kong, and what is 'international' is good enough to replace the 'local'. Many of us, however, do not think that the best theatre comes from Hong Kong Rep's brand of Western imports, and it makes no sense for a district in Central to pretend to be Montmartre.

For us, the merit of a place like Lan Kwai Fong is that it is an open space where all kinds of people can gather—expatriate and local; people from different walks of life. Of course everyone is trying to stake a claim to the place. And of course many are trying to turn it into a non-Hong Kong enclave. Businessmen set up trendy restaurants here with names like 'California', 'Central Park', 'American Pie', 'Casa Blanca', 'Beirut, 'Mozart Stub'n', 'Indochina', 'Thai Silk'—probably to remind themselves of their homes in distant lands. Those distant lands also evoke a sense of time that is always not the present. 'The '50s' is owned by someone who adores the golden hits of the 1950s, and the owner will occasionally make an appearance to sing the songs himself. But time is not necessarily the nostalgic past. 'Club 64' captures a momentous event in history—4 June 1989; while '1997', 'Post 97', and 'Mecca 97' allude to the future—a tongue-in-cheek attempt to domesticate the apocalyptic perhaps, or a genuine invitation to go beyond the present. East and west; past, present, and future; they are all crammed here, freely, haphazardly. This is a district where the local and the international come together in a big kaleidoscope, where wonton noodles and fish-belly congee are sold right next to Western bars, where health fiends will feel at home with the most ravenous diners. In this place that doesn't seem at all like Hong Kong, the reality of Hong Kong nevertheless creeps up in the most unexpected corners, making it hard to say exactly what kind of a place it is. Nearby, there are expensive antique shops and galleries displaying Qin dynasty terracotta warrior figures and Tang dynasty triple-colour glazed pottery to attract the tourists. And tourists will somehow find in this area something that reminds them of home. Young people come here too, to catch a glimpse of the latest trends in the West while students who have returned from their overseas studies gather here to relive their lives abroad.

But Lan Kwai Fong is not simply a place for sentimental nostalgia, decadent hedonism, and indulgence in the foreign and the exotic. Some artists have tried to turn the less expensive premises in the vicinity into a kind of alternative space. '12 Bar', for example, features alternative music, while 'Quart Society' presents exhibitions of works by local artists. Artists meet at 'Club 64' for forum discussions and music performances. Plans for organizing an annual art exhibition in commemoration of June Fourth were also first discussed here. In the last few years, the bar even offered free drinks for those who came back from the June Fourth March.

So Lan Kwai Fong is not the exclusive domain of anyone or any group, local or non-local. It is not monolithic either. Of course I have no intention of romanticizing the place. There have been incidents of triad infiltration, there are drug problems, and although expatriates and locals do get along on the surface, a few years ago on Christmas Eve, street fights broke out between rival racial groups. Many Hongkongers stay away from this area, or dismiss it as being too 'foreign'. Obviously, Lan Kwai Fong is not a self-contained, autonomous space that can be isolated from the political and economic conditions of Hong Kong as a colony.

———

The unfortunate tragedy of the deaths of twenty revellers on New Year's Eve in 1992 had brought unwanted attention to Lan Kwai Fong. To a lot of people, this confirmed their worst suspicions about the place. But we would do well to consider the aftermaths and repercussions of that incident. The tragedy shows that Lan Kwai Fong definitely is not Montmartre; rather, it is part of the political and social fabric of the society of Hong Kong. After the tragedy, the Governor visited the site and the injured in hospital. Representatives from the New China News Agency made similar visits and also sent messages of condolence to the victims' families. Some Legislative Council members, too, visited the site and the injured in hospital and expressed their concern about crowd-control and other related issues. Their actions drew considerable criticism from the public—it was just a show, an attempt on the part of those councillors to promote their own image and gain political capital. And there was public unease over certain proposals on drinks bans and future restrictions on entry to the area. This revealed the delicate situation that Hong Kong was, still is, in: everything is highly politicized, and worries about freedom of the press and freedom of speech have made people extremely neurotic and paranoid.

While the mourning ceremony for the souls of the dead was being held at the corner of D'Aguilar Street, another group became victims in the aftermath of this incident. The Hong Kong Institute of Professional Photographers (HKIPP), in preparation for a public auction of photographs to raise funds to sponsor young photographers to study abroad, had organized an exhibition in Lan Kwai Fong a few weeks prior to the tragedy. Some of these photographs, which had been displayed on the street, now had to be removed, for reasons which could only be described as bizarre. One of the photographs, *Stun* by Osbert Lam, which showed a blow-up of a walnut shell carved with thirty Buddhist monk figures crowded together against a background of bleached blue leaves, was rumoured to be a prophecy of the number of people trampled to death at the tragedy. Even though this was factually incorrect, the rumour was soon picked up by gossip columns and newspaper reports. In no time, the popular magazine *Eastweek* produced a special issue on this, with Osbert's photograph as the cover, and various *fung shui* people commenting on the bad omens that the artwork embodied. In addition to *Stun*, various other photos were also analysed—ingeniously, imaginatively, with great respect for the logic of free association. Caan-Angela and Carsten Schael's *Red Brick-one*—which features a red-brick building—was said to look distinctly similar to a gravestone; Stephen Cheung's *Pond Lily* was considered evocative of a wreath of flowers on a grave; Andrew Chester Ong's *Untitled*, because it has a clock in it (*zong* in Cantonese) was interpreted to mean *sung zong* ('paying one's last respects to the dying'); David Ng's *Yellow Stone Mists*, with its misty scenery, was said to resemble vaguely—vaguely indeed—the head of a girl lying on the ground. Even the old comb shown in Jen Halim's *Hers* was regarded as indicative of one of the objects accompanying the dead to the grave. The *fung shui* experts, moreover, all pontificated on the cause of the tragedy: the bad *fung shui* of the place, unlucky dates . . . you name it. One even advised all who entered Lan Kwai Fong from then on to put their palms together in a Buddhist greeting and murmur three times: May all bad omens be lifted!

There was an outcry against *Eastweek* for its unashamed promotion of superstition. A few days later I read in the *Hong Kong Economic Journal* an interview with Yip, one of the editors of *Eastweek*, who claimed that his publication was not promoting superstition, but merely exposing the absurdity of the rumours and providing some psychological relief to the readers. There was also an interview with Lee, the spokesman for the HKIPP, which had organized the exhibition. He made no comments on what the *fung shui* experts had made of the photographs, but simply announced that the exhibition had come to an end and the auction would be postponed.

While reading the two interviews and thinking about their different stances, I was struck by the fact that both Yip and Lee were my poet friends and all of us had been involved, not so long ago, in editing *Autumn Firefly*. We must still have piles and piles of postcards printed with our poems at home. I remembered, too, many of my other poet friends. We have all moved on to play different roles. Some have gone back to their old jobs as taxi-drivers, some are selling jewellery in jewellery shops, some have joined TV stations, and some are editing entertainment magazines. But even though we all work and write in different media now, everything any one of us says or does, the works any one of us produces will still affect all the rest of us—and many others as well. Words can kill; rhyme and rhythm can be fatal; reading and interpretative strategies can be used for ideological manipulations. Each of us has had his own difficulties, and each has handled them in his own way. But, in the public sphere that we share, we still run into each other. We had once been members of the same family; could we continue to help make this place good for living and creative endeavours?

———

In the open space above the street in Lan Kwai Fong, the photographs were taken down. They had lost their home, just as my poems and Ka Sing's photos about 'Home' had lost theirs in the previous year. In the shared space in which we all live our lives, what one person says, if only in a gossip column, can have an impact on the public. And, whether we like it or not, we are influenced by public opinion and its outcomes. Public opinion is easily sensationalized and manipulated by the media and other parties, and it grows each day, taking up more space, drowning out other voices—voices of the gentle, the idealistic, the tolerant. Public opinion—it is so unreliable, so unpredictable.

—

Lan Kwai Fong always makes me think of Hong Kong. The space we have is a mixed, hybrid space, a crowded and dangerous space, carnival-like even in times of crisis, heavenly and not far from disasters, easily accessible and also easily appropriated—by political, economic and other forces. Is there anything we can do to ensure that this place remains an open space for all? What appears to be prudence can easily turn into self-censorship; what seems to be free speech can easily infringe upon other's freedom. All sorts of pressures and interpersonal relations keep intervening, affecting how we use words and images to express ourselves and communicate with others. This space that is open to us can all too easily be lost to us. And, without a home that is friendly, stable, and tolerant, we can only drift from place to place lugging with us our words and photographs.

Revised version, June 1997
The Chinese original, upon which this revised version is based, is also published under the title 'Homeless poems, homeless photographs' in P. K. Leung: *A Poetry of Floating Signs*, Hong Kong: Oxford University Press, 1995.

PART IV

People

The First Day

By YE SI

Translated by Martha P. Y. Cheung

This story gives us a glimpse of the life of the working class in Hong Kong. There is, however, none of the outcries against the evils of capitalism which for decades characterized the writings of many Leftist writers in Hong Kong. Ye Si is the pen-name P. K. Leung uses for his fictional works.

The morning light streamed in and shone on a tumbler. Ah Fat glanced at it and saw a wisp of a rainbow gleaming on its surface. He blinked, the rainbow was gone. He narrowed one eye and looked again. There it was: red, orange, yellow, green. . . .

'Hey!' Ah Hung came over and said in a low voice, 'The boss is looking at you.'

Ah Fat blinked again and rubbed his eyes. But it was no use. He felt himself blushing, even his earlobes burnt. A pair of eyes seemed to be following him everywhere, even much later, when the people at a nearby table started to leave and he hurried over to clean up.

He stacked up a few plates and took them to the kitchen. As soon as he opened the door, he was greeted with the heat of the kitchen and the smell of fried eggs. He took a deep breath. The smell of fried eggs was really good! He went into the courtyard, and, as instructed, put the plates into a red plastic bucket. The white plates with the yellow streaks of egg yolk on them sank at once into the greyish soapy water.

When he came out again, he saw a cup of tea standing on the counter. The man they called Uncle Ah Kuen was standing there idly. Ah Fat checked the order, and took the cup of tea to table number seven. On his way, he stole a glance at the boss. Ah, he wasn't looking at him anymore. The boss was now standing by the door and concentrating on frying hamburger steaks.

Ah Fat looked at the tumbler again. It was now empty, with a deep brown ring of tea dregs at the bottom. Tea stains marked the spot on the table where the glass had stood. The patron at that table was now reading a newspaper. Others had finished their breakfast and were leaving one after another. The woman in a green dress at the next table also left.

'Seven dollars,' Uncle Ah Kuen called out lazily to the cashier. Ah Hung turned round and said to Ah Fat, 'That woman is mad!'

Ah Fat would not believe him.

'This is your first day at work. There are many more things you have no idea of!' Ah Hung said. 'She comes every morning, and sits there mumbling to herself.'

'She looked all right just now, didn't she?'

'It's just that you didn't notice,' Ah Hung replied.

The man who was reading the newspaper had put it down and was picking his teeth with care. They went past his table. The floor around his chair was strewn with toothpicks. Ah Hung walked straight on, without so much as a look at them. Ah Fat couldn't bear the sight and swept the toothpicks under the chair with his foot. 'What a mess! That man is such a pain!' he grumbled inwardly.

Uncle Ah Kuen was telling Ah Hung about the greyhound racing the previous week, keeping Ah Hung from his work, 'It just wasn't possible! The fourth race. Who'd have thought. . . .'

Miss Wong, the cashier, chipped in, 'Who'd have thought that you, too, would lose!'

Uncle Ah Kuen snorted in annoyance and said, 'Who said I lost? I just didn't win.'

Miss Wong burst out laughing. Ah Hung turned to Ah Fat and asked, 'You like greyhound racing?'

Ah Fat shook his head.

Uncle Ah Kuen cast a sidelong glance at him and said, 'I guess not. A good lad, eh?'

Ah Fat blushed and defended himself, 'No, it's not that. . . .'

But Uncle Ah Kuen ignored him and turned to greet the boss's wife, who had just arrived. This was the first time Ah Fat had met her. She was standing by the door where the boss was frying hamburger steaks. The hamburger steaks were gleaming with oil, and the sausages were slowly turning in the oven. They looked delicious. She was chatting in a soft voice with the boss. It looked like she was laughing too. Ah Fat thought she seemed a kind and warm person.

Miss Wong asked Uncle Ah Kuen, 'Are you going to watch the military tattoo tonight?'

'What military tattoo?'

'It's the programme for the first day of the Hong Kong Festival. It was reported on TV. It's at the Hong Kong Stadium.'

They went on talking about the military tattoo.

'Lunch is ready!' Ah Hung said as he came in from the kitchen. He told Ah Fat, 'Hurry up and eat. You'll have a busy time at noon.'

Ah Hung sat down at the table and said, 'Great! Soup with pig's bones!' He rested his legs on the chair opposite him and let out a deep breath. Ah Fat tried to do the same, but his legs were too short and couldn't reach the chair opposite him. Still, he let out a deep breath.

The place began to get really busy from about half past twelve midday. People arrived in droves. First came groups of women from the factories. Then office workers from nearby buildings. And then mechanics in blue overalls. As soon as one stood up to leave, another took the seat. Ah Fat dashed about, feeling a little overcome by the heat. His hair could have done with a wash, and the smell of his sweat—mixed with the faint odour of his unknown predecessor's white shirt that he was wearing—was making his head spin. There was noise everywhere. He came out of the kitchen carrying a dish of beef curry with rice and a bowl of noodles with roast duck leg, put them down on the tables of those who had ordered them, then went to collect the coffee cups and sandwich dishes. He saw someone going up to the cashier, and so he shouted, 'Three fifty!' Then he showed someone who had just entered to this or that seat, brought the ketchup or salt to a table over at the other side, took the empty dishes into the kitchen and came out again to clear another table, wiping away with a piece of cloth the bones, stains, and crumpled paper napkins. . . .

Ah Fat was melting under the heat. He unbuttoned his shirt, just as Ah Hung had done. And he watched with admiration as Ah Hung picked up a whole stack of plates, with three or four tea cups on top, and teaspoons as well as forks and knives, and strode off. That was neat! Unfortunately, Ah Hung didn't manage to carry this feat through. The smallest plate at the top fell and smashed to the floor. The boss happened to be around and he flew into a temper. Ah Fat saw that the plate was just a small one, and yet the boss got really angry. 'You people do nothing but break the dishes! You people do nothing but eat.' He kept saying, 'You people', 'You people are like this'. Ah Fat felt that he, too, was being scolded even though he hadn't done anything wrong. At this, a wave of grievance surged up in him.

———

In the afternoon, the patch of sunlight before the door slowly faded. Ah Hung, who was leaning against the cashier's counter, yawned; Uncle Ah Kuen yawned too. Ah Fat, like someone infected with the disease, also yawned.

Miss Wong at the cashier's seat burst out giggling. The boss, who was sitting at one side reading the newspaper, looked up and glared at them, then buried his head in the paper again. He picked up a red pen and started marking down his choices for the greyhound racing.

Uncle Ah Kuen asked, 'Any that take your fancy?' The boss thought for a while, then handed over the newspaper. Ah Fat happened to be standing there, so he had to take the paper from the boss and pass it to Uncle Ah Kuen. Later, Ah Fat saw that his hand was stained with red ink and the dark print of the paper. He was about to rub off the marks with another hand when Ah Hung nudged him and said, 'Here comes the lorry with the soft-drinks!'

Ah Fat didn't know what he should do, so he just followed Ah Hung's example. Ah Hung went to the back of the restaurant, so he followed. Ah Hung lifted up a crate of soft-drinks bottles, so he too, lifted one up. He saw a few dozen soft-drinks bottles on the floor. They were of different shapes; some clean, some dirty. He liked those that were clean and rounded in the middle. He picked them out and put them all into the same crate. But Ah Hung snapped at him, 'Don't dilly dally! There's no time!' Then Ah Hung snatched up a handful of bottles and stuck them all into a crate. No more fussing around sorting them out.

Ah Fat lifted up a crate, carried it out, loaded it onto the lorry, then took down another crate of soft drinks from the lorry and carried it inside. This new crate was much heavier. Ah Fat was huffing and puffing by the time he set it down where the old crate had been. When the job was finally done, Ah Hung sat down to recover his breath, hanging his head. Ah Fat noticed that he looked quite pale, and was rubbing his eyes with his fingers. Ah Fat asked, 'Are you all right?' Ah Hung shook his head, annoyed, and did not reply.

Ah Fat felt a little tired too. He went back into the shop. Someone came in and the boss glanced at Ah Fat. He had to go at once to take the order.

'Tea with milk. Buttered toast.'

Ah Fat went to place the order. All this time, Uncle Ah Kuen was standing beside the customer, absorbed in studying the tips in the newspaper.

Uncle Ah Kuen now sighed and said, 'It's going to be tricky this week!'

Someone else came in. Uncle Ah Kuen still did not move. Again, Ah Fat had to go and take the order.

After a while, someone called him from behind. It was Ah Hung. He went over; Ah Hung indicated with his finger a plate of toast behind a pillar. Ah Fat was quite hungry, and helped himself to a piece. He had taken a few bites when a thought occurred to him, so he leant his head out from behind the pillar—the boss was still buried deep in the newspaper and didn't see them. But Ah Fat remembered what had happened that morning and what the boss had said—'You people are all the same!'

The boss was right. He felt as if something had got stuck in his throat, and he couldn't swallow anything. He was still chewing, but only mechanically, and the taste was gone. Ah Hung nudged him again, and pointed at the remaining piece of toast on the plate. He shook his head, and said he was full.

Ah Fat leant against the pillar, and straightened out his white shirt. It belonged to someone else and was too loose, it didn't fit him. Over on the other side, someone came in. Ah Fat was about to go over when he stopped. He had made a mistake, it was the boss's wife returning. She sat down opposite to the boss and they began talking in low voices, as if discussing something important. Ah Fat looked at them, then turned to study the red and yellow menus pasted on the wall. A fly circled slowly over a table, he followed it with his eyes. It flew inside a glass cabinet full of tumblers through a narrow opening between the glass doors; it dashed about inside the cabinet, banging against the stained surfaces of the glasses, swooping and swishing about in the narrow space looking for a way out, but was hopelessly trapped.

A shrill voice broke the silence. 'You think I don't know? You think I don't know?' It was the voice of the boss's wife. Everyone turned and looked at her.

She went on, 'You make me work my fingers to the bones for you. And you use the money to buy her a watch!' Her face was red, her thick lips opening and closing, spitting out the words. The boss kept his voice low. He seemed to be pacifying her.

'Why shouldn't I talk about it?' She went on in a loud voice, 'I tell you. I know how to use eyeliner too, and I can put on a mini-skirt and a pair of platform shoes!' Her voice, a little hoarse now, sounded as if it was choked with tears. Ah Fat never imagined they would be like this.

Ah Fat didn't know what to do and just stared blankly at those around him. Miss Wong was looking down and adding up the bills, pretending to be unaware of everything. Uncle Ah Kuen was hiding behind his newspaper, but Ah Fat could see from one side the look of derision on his face. Ah Hung was leaning against the pillar behind him, his head lowered; he seemed exhausted, completely oblivious to what was happening.

A customer stood up to leave. Ah Fat hurried over and gave him his bill. Then he took the dishes to the kitchen. He nearly stumbled over a broom. Only then did he realize that the ground along the edge of the ditch was littered with leftover food, bits of fishbones and waste paper, empty lunch boxes, ice-cream paper cups, and a few iron wires. Before he had not noticed these things.

When he came out again, the boss's wife had gone. The boss looked a bit gloomy. Uncle Ah Kuen had put down his newspaper and was setting the tables for the evening.

Ah Fat was nursing his elbows. It had been a very busy evening and his hands were quite sore. Perhaps that was because it was his first day at work, he thought.

All things considered, he hadn't done too badly. Just now when Ah Hung was taking some dishes into the kitchen, he nearly dropped another glass on to the floor again, Ah Fat didn't know whether it was because Ah Hung's hands were shaking or what. Ah Fat began to feel a little worried about Ah Hung; he wondered why there was always this tired look on Ah Hung's face. Right now, Ah Hung was leaning against the seat behind him.

But soon, Ah Fat's mind drifted to other things. He looked up at the clock and thought—just another half an hour and he could get off work! He could step out of the door and go home! Home!

The boss had left, Ah Fat had no idea when. Miss Wong was sitting at the cashier's seat chatting with Uncle Ah Kuen about how exciting the military tattoo this evening was going to be, how spectacular. When she finished, Uncle Ah Kuen began to brag about how good he was at gambling! He even urged Miss Wong to bet a few dollars and try her luck. Once they started, the two really went on and on, non-stop.

The people at a table behind him had left. Ah Hung was not there, so Ah Fat went and cleaned up. When he pushed open the door to go into the kitchen, he saw that it was dark in the courtyard. He put the plates and cups into the bucket, and stood watching as the white plates and cups sank into the greyish black soap water. There was a gust of wind and he could feel a chill in the air.

He went into the lavatory, and pushed open the door of a cubicle. Somebody was there—he hadn't locked the door. The man inside pushed the door shut. But Ah Fat caught a glimpse of the man. It was Ah Hung. He was inside, as if puffing on something! Ah Fat caught a whiff of a sharp, strange odour.

Ah Fat staggered out, and went back into the shop. Uncle Ah Kuen and Miss Wong were still chattering about gambling. Ah Fat found his heart pounding, about to jump out of his mouth. He had stumbled upon a secret, had caught sight of something he had no business knowing. He felt confused, he wasn't sure whether it was what he thought it was. He remembered that pallid face of Ah

Hung, remembered the way Ah Hung seemed to be puffing at something, and that sharp, strange odour! These images were firmly imprinted on his mind, indelible!

He went all the way to the front door before he stopped, as if trying to get as far away as possible from those ugly, haunting images. His heart was still racing. Beside the door, he saw only a few pieces of unsold hamburger steaks on the black iron plate; they looked dry and shrivelled now. Miss Wong and Uncle Ah Kuen were still chattering. Ah Fat didn't hear a single word they were saying.

Not until Uncle Ah Kuen tapped him on the shoulder did Ah Fat realize that they were asking him something.

'What?' He looked up.

'I was asking you,' Miss Wong said, 'how do you feel about your first day at work?'

'Nothing special.' Ah Fat shook his head and forced a smile. He stood there against the gradually darkening sky, smiling as if in a trance, as if in fear.

1974
Chinese original published in Ye Si: *Island and Mainland*, Hong Kong: Wah Hon Publishing Company, 1987.

The Ghost Festival

By **XIN QISHI**

Translated by Cathy Poon

This story, again about the common, poorer people, has an interesting twist at the end. Like The Atlas: Archaeology of an Imaginary City, *legend, rumour, and gossip are woven into the narrative, but in a different way. And, like 'Chronicle of a City', this story registers the writer's preoccupation with the past: how can one know about the past? what can one know about the past? in what ways and forms will the past survive? how reliable will these vestiges be?*

Uncle Shek was stripped to the waist, his back arching like a bow, the deep tan of his flabby muscles an obvious sign of prolonged exposure to the sun, and there were deep folds across his abdomen and stomach. He was wearing an old and mildewed pair of grey shorts which showed his skinny legs and knee caps creased like grinning faces. His short stubby hair, which used to remind you of a hedgehog, was now thinning and grey. There were freckles all over his face. They could have been the black moles which marked the faces of the elderly, but it was hard to tell. His mouth was constantly moving, but all that could be heard was the occasional meaningless sound.

His job was to collect the garbage from four seven-storey blocks. Every day he had to sort out the mountains of rubbish in the garbage rooms and dispose of it in the large containers provided by the Urban Council. Sometimes, when there were pieces of abandoned furniture in the corridors, he had to drag and carry them downstairs. Of course, if he was lucky, he might just find a wardrobe or bed that was still in good condition and could fetch a few dollars at a second-hand goods store. Uncle Shek had been doing cleaning work in the neighbourhood for at least ten years. The locals were so used to his being around that they saw him as part of the garbage too. Normally they did not notice his presence, but whenever he fell ill or when garbage piled up around New Year or on other festive occasions, they would automatically think of him.

Sweat was slowly dripping down Uncle Shek's forehead. The soft glow of the setting sun was shining on the street and on the dozen or so huge garbage containers along the roadside. Uncle Shek was again muttering something as he made his rounds between the garbage room and the garbage containers. He had started work unusually early today. As he wheeled his cart along the corridors on each floor shouting, 'Garbage time!' people noisily pushed open their doors and iron grilles, dragging red and blue and yellow plastic bins into the passages. Some said hello to him, or asked him, 'Aren't you a bit early today?' but he just went on muttering to himself. Occasionally he would say a word or two in reply, and when he did, his exceptionally loud and husky voice seemed incongruous with his physical form.

Over the last two days, Uncle Shek had started work about half an hour earlier than usual, and today even earlier, so early that some housewives complained: you must have gone nuts, garbage man, coming so early one day and so late the next, we haven't even finished preparing dinner! Uncle Shek never showed much displeasure or pleasure towards these complaints, just as he was unmoved by the gifts given him on festive days. All he wanted was to finish collecting the garbage in those four seven-storey blocks as quickly as possible so that he could hurry over to the football ground on the other side of the street, where a lot of work was waiting to be done.

The street was lined with small shops of all descriptions. Some people were having their dinner on the pavement and big plates of meat and vegetables were laid out on the tables. The greyish dust hurled up by passing vehicles danced about in the golden rays of the evening glow before landing on people's feet and faces or on the white rice or meat soup. Some people were standing in front of the shops, their backs leaning against the display windows, looking aimlessly into the street while picking their teeth. The owner of the Yee Loong rice shop was bragging about the 'Numerous Offspring' lantern which he had bought at the football ground the night before with the highest bid. Now the lantern was hanging in front of the shop. It was no different from those trotting-horse lanterns one saw at the Mid-Autumn Festival, except that a piece of pink paper hung down from the lower end of this lantern. Decorated with the characters 'A hundred sons and a thousand grandsons', the paper was fluttering wildly in the wind. Like the rice store, the medicine shop also had a lantern at its entrance. This one had a huge light bulb inside, and on the outside, the characters 'Ghost Festival Festivities' and 'Senior Director' were written in red ink on either side. In fact, eight or nine out of every ten shops on this street had similar lanterns bearing characters such as 'Senior Director', 'Junior Director', 'Financial Administrator', 'General Affairs Manager', 'Vice Chairman', or 'Chairman', depending on how much money the owner had donated the previous year.

Each year, for three nights following the fourteenth day of the seventh lunar month, the local people would come to the football ground to burn incense, watch operas, bid for lanterns, or simply take a stroll. Some mothers would not allow their children to go downstairs for fear they would encounter bad luck. Some mothers, however, could not wait to see their little ones go out so they could start their mahjong game. A month or so before the Festival, some Chaozhou-speaking organizers in kungfu suits would go from door to door, donation books in hand, asking for contributions. People could offer as much or as little as they liked and few would refuse to give anything at all. Was there ever a family who had not lost a relative or two? It might be fine to offend the living, but offending a ghost is something else.

Naturally, businesspeople were major targets for donations, and they could not pledge too small an amount for fear of losing face when the sums donated were made public. A well-respected and public-minded businessman would be chosen by Buddha himself as chairman each year, and the man was expected to contribute both money and services. True, organizing the festivities involved a lot of tedious work and arguments were common, but it was, after all, a favour bestowed by Buddha. For this reason, very few people, if chosen to be chairman, would turn down the offer. But it took more than just handsome donations to be offered the job. Who in the world of business does not have some money?

To begin with, on the second day of the Ghost Festival, pieces of red paper bearing the names of the candidates were placed before the altar, then one was drawn from the lot to see whom Buddha had picked to be chairman for the following year. It was a great honour. Just the chairman's lantern alone hanging in front of your door would lend lustre to any humble home. Then there were the title-bearing coloured ribbons. Worn pinned to the chest, they were status symbols that allowed the organizers to move about the arena as they pleased, smugly telling people to do this or that.

The rice shop owner had been chairman the previous year. He had donated 500 catties of rice, but other than getting his share when the mountains of buns and the three small wooden pots of rice placed on the main altar in the football ground were distributed among all involved parties at the end of the festivities, his family had not benefited much.

According to custom, the wooden pots containing the rice were wrapped with red paper and put on the altar as offerings for three days. Those who got a small pinch of this rice would take it home with deep reverence in the hope that it would bring their family peace and prosperity when cooked and served. The previous year the rice shop owner had treated it as an auspicious star that was worth much much more than the rice in his own warehouse. He had hoped and prayed that, after eating the rice, his wife would quickly produce a chubby and healthy son. For that he would have happily donated much more than a mere 500 catties. But a year had passed and, although his wife had gained weight, there was still no hint of a son on the way. This year, since he had not been favoured by Buddha and had not been chosen chairman, he had only donated 100 catties of rice, securing the title of 'Senior Director' for the occasion. But he had successfully bid a high price for the 'Numerous Offspring' lantern to give himself renewed hope for the year ahead. However, people were whispering behind his back: the miser, he didn't want to part with his 500 catties of rice last year—not even for Buddha—no wonder he couldn't get the son he wanted so badly even after years of prayers.

Most of the inhabitants in the neighbourhood were Chaozhou people, and because of the proximity of the place to the market, most of them were engaged in the rice and grocery business. Following redevelopment, many of the shops had moved to the new market to continue their business. The Yee Loong rice shop with its 'Numerous Offspring' lantern, two medicine shops, four provisions stores, one watch shop, one coffee shop, and one restaurant were the only shops that continued to operate there. Locals of the older generation could still vaguely remember what this street was like thirty years ago. They could tell you who was indebted to whom, who bore a grudge against whom, where houses had been torn down, where new buildings had been built, and when the well which supplied their drinking water was sealed. Of course, the hardest to forget was the fire that changed everything. It had burnt for one day and one night, the racing flames painting the sky red. It was only the howling north wind which blew people's tears dry. Having moved from the Mainland to this small, faraway enclave, and after going through so many hardships, they had thought they could finally settle down in peace. They little expected to see everything go up in smoke, their homes destroyed, and themselves injured. Eventually they moved into housing units built by the government for the fire victims. These seven-storey blocks with no kitchens or toilets were frowned upon by people now, but in those days, they were sanctuaries for those who had escaped with nothing but their lives. Had it not been for that big fire in Western District, the old folks on this street would never have come together and shared a life for so many years. Some had made it big and some ended up down and out; some had moved away and some had emigrated; some had departed blissfully for the other world while others remained to live out their lives of ill health. Stories about the street never ran out, but since the old were getting older and the young didn't care for things that had happened several lifetimes ago, the tales were slowly falling into oblivion with the passage of time.

The government had recently launched a massive programme to redevelop the area, and all but Blocks 11 to 14 had been demolished. These were the four blocks Uncle Shek had to look after, and the Yee Loong rice shop was also in one of these blocks. Uncle Shek was an old-timer. He had seen it all, seen the rapid spin of the wheel of fortune, but all his memories were locked away inside him. He was probably not even aware that he had been living in the same place for over thirty years. Sometimes he seemed to know what was going on around him, but often he was confused. Only the garbage had his undivided attention. After leaving the mental hospital more than ten years earlier, he had had a relapse and created a scene which drew a crowd of curious onlookers into the street. On that occasion, he was crying and yelling, pulling his hair and tearing his clothes in front of the Yee Loong rice shop, and had to be forcibly taken back to hospital by several robust men. The old proprietor of the rice shop kept saying to the crowd, 'He gambled and lost, it's as simple as that. I didn't steal from him. The son of the owner of the Yau Lee store can be my witness. He's a grown man. He has no business crying like that.'

When Uncle Shek returned to Western District and, with the assistance of social workers, found work as a garbage cleaner, he was a much quieter man and remained calm when he walked past the Yee Loong rice shop. The only thing that could divert his attention from his miserable home and rubbish heaps were the annual Ghost Festival activities. In the beginning, he had just strolled about, watching people burn incense and chant the sutras. Later, as chores mounted and help was needed, the organizers asked Uncle Shek to give a hand with the manual work, and they gave him some rice, flour, and foodstuffs in return.

At that time there had been a lot of gossip about Uncle Shek. Some were saying, 'Pity the poor man! He must have done something evil in his previous life! See how he gambled away his shop and lost his wife who ran away with his kids. And now he has to slave around here after serving as chairman for several years.'

Others said, 'The old proprietor of the Yee Loong rice shop had something up his sleeve for a long time. He was jealous of Uncle Shek because Uncle Shek's shop was on the main street. He somehow ganged up with some swindlers and conned Uncle Shek out of his shop, breaking up his family and driving him mad. The ruthless rascal! See if he doesn't get punished. He is going to die without a grandson.'

The old scholar who made a living in the street writing letters for others also pontificated, rocking his head from side to side, 'Alas, great is the harm of gambling!'

With the passage of time and the death of the old proprietor of the Yee Loong rice shop years ago, all such gossip and rumours died down. Occasionally though, silver-haired people who walked past the shop and saw the 'Numerous Offspring' lantern would whisper to their children and sons- or daughters-in-law: it's all because the old proprietor didn't do any good deeds for his descendants.

Ever since the big fire thirty years before, Western District had been holding Ghost Festival activities. That fire killed many people. Some of the victims had lived alone and their bodies went unclaimed, probably because their families were still on the Mainland. Out of kindness, local people started to observe the Ghost Festival for these victims. Every year at the Festival, sacrifices were offered to provide temporary food and lodging to wandering souls, while rice and foodstuffs were handed out to all, rich and poor. It was said that after eating the buns and cakes offered to the spirits, adults would live long and prosperous lives and children would grow up quickly. It was all some kind of blessing.

This year, as in past years, at the corner of the street a ceremonial archway had been built, on which were inscribed the characters 'Ghost Festival Festivities, Western District Neighbourhood Association'. Near the crossroads was mounted a flagstaff with a long flowing streamer and two lanterns at the top to light the way for wandering souls to reach the site where the offerings were made. The festivities had been going on for two days already, and would reach a climax that evening. In addition to distributing the food and handing out the rice, there would be the 'burning of sacrificial objects'. During this ceremony, paper gold and silver ingots, paperwork bridges and mansions, as well as sacrificial banknotes and clothing would all be put into the offerings furnace and set alight, as if suggesting that all sorrows and griefs would vanish with the smoke.

In the past when government controls were less stringent, paper offerings would have been piled up here and there on the pavement like little mountains, and a dozen or so fires would be burning at the same time every evening. The fires tinted red the faces of people in the upper storeys who had not yet gone to bed, and small flames flared up in the eyes of the onlookers. Dark corners of staircases would be intermittently lit up by the flames, as if there were ghosts and goblins hiding there who were afraid to come out in the open and could only quietly accept the offerings from a distance. The spectacular sight of the raging flames during the burning of paper offerings, and the hair-raising scenes of children nearly falling into the fires as they scrambled for the buns which had been offered to the spirits, had all but disappeared in recent years, probably because scenes like those led to traffic congestion and could easily result in another fire. Now the burning of paper offerings was restricted to the small tin-house-like furnace at one corner of the venue. The splendour had gone. However gloriously it burned, the fire had to be splashed with water to prevent its tongues from licking the nearby bamboo scaffoldings, paper screens, and tree branches.

Pushing his wooden cart, Uncle Shek hurried over from around the corner. He could see from a distance a crowd gathering in front of the school, opposite the football ground, and knew that he was late. How could he help it when there was so much garbage to collect? Outside the school, he waved at a man wearing a straw hat and shorts. The man signalled him to go in and carry to the truck the gunny bags bearing the characters 'Chinese Rice'. After working for a while, Uncle Shek stopped and started mumbling to himself. The man with the straw hat patted him on the shoulder in an understanding way and said, 'Don't worry! You'll get your share.'

The playground on the street-side of the school was surrounded by a tall wire-fence. Outside, kids were climbing all over it while a crowd of busy on-lookers gathered. When people spilt on to the road, the police who were there to keep order tried to disperse them. A man's voice came over the loudspeaker, saying again and again that all the rice had been handed out and that those who had got their share should leave at once and not gather around the gate. Slowly, some started moving away, but they still kept looking back, ready to turn around at any time. Many did not understand why so many bags were being carried back to the truck when they had been told that it was all over. Meanwhile, in the playground, people with coloured ribbons pinned to their chests were busy moving the iron railings, borrowed from the Urban Council to maintain order, so that they could clean up the rice and litter when the playground was finally vacated. They had borrowed the playground from the school and now it had turned into a real mess. In just over an hour, hundreds of people had packed into the place, even the iron railings were crushed. People who had already received their rice thought they had too little and returned to the end of the queue or even elbowed their way back to the front, pushing and yelling so hard that the police had to intervene.

The rice was distributed in little bags, each one holding about a catty. As he worked, Uncle Shek saw people cradling these bags in their hands, softly as if they were little kittens. He saw another man in a straw hat pass one of these 'kittens' over the fence to a boy outside. But when the truck carrying the rice finally drove off, the man in the straw hat handed Uncle Shek not a soft 'kitten' but just a long loaf of white bread as his reward for cleaning up the playground.

This was the main alms-giving event and it took place on the third evening of the Ghost Festival every year. Rice and provisions donated by shops in the neighbourhood were divided into small portions, and, while the stock lasted, everyone, rich and poor, could claim a share. People came in droves for the hand-outs. It was said that the whole family would enjoy peace and good luck and children would be obedient after eating these offerings to Buddha. And so Uncle Shek was, for the moment, satisfied with his loaf of bread. He put it carefully into his wooden cart, strapping it tightly with a piece of rope for fear it would be snatched away. Some people asked him, 'Uncle Shek, can you finish that loaf all by yourself?' His expressionless eyes suddenly seemed to spark and he broke his usual silence and answered in a loud, clear voice, 'I'll take it home and share it with the kids.'

The main festival site was just opposite the school. The air was heavy with the smoke and smell of candles and joss sticks. A horizontal banner bearing the characters 'Ghost Festival Festivities. Peace throughout the Land' was hanging above the main table, in front of which was an offering table about two feet wide and twenty feet long. On this table, there were tin incense burners, candle-stands, and all sorts of offerings—small mountains of buns and cakes, 'prosperity' sponge cakes sprinkled with incense ashes, fruits and peanuts, wine cups and flowers, as well as the three buckets wrapped in red paper containing the rice to be divided amongst the chairman, directors, and helpers when the festivities were over. In front of the offering table and before an ancient sacrificial vessel, devout men and women knelt on cushions, praying and kowtowing.

Presents donated by local residents were displayed on the main table. They included gold, silver, and jade ornaments, antiques and vases, table and wall lamps, radios and televisions, clothing, socks and shoes. These were auctioned each evening, with the proceeds funding the alms-giving. To the left of the main table was a makeshift conference room and to the right was a reception room. The conference room was always full of people with coloured ribbons pinned to their chests, although nobody knew exactly what it was they were discussing. Behind the conference room was the warehouse where the donated rice and provisions were stored.

Next to the main table was a tall, glittering altar. A huge silk umbrella hung above it while yellow curtains, richly embroidered with lotus blossoms and seedpods, hung in layers from the front to the back of the altar. On it stood a sacrificial vessel, and statue of Buddha flanked on both sides with pictures of arhats. On one side of the altar was a long narrow table, on which the sutras were placed. It was still early. Around eight o'clock, the monks would start to chant the sutras, although naturally people coming to hear the prayers would be fewer in number than those watching the opera, and the deafening gongs and drums would drown out the quiet chanting. But noisy or quiet, it did not really matter, for the Ghost Festival was not meant for the living. Western District used to present two types of operas during the festival: Cantonese opera on one evening and Chaozhou opera on the other two. In recent years, only the Chaozhou opera had been presented because it cost too much to have both. The show started at eight each evening, and people in the neigbourhood, starved of their native opera in Hong Kong, would bring along their own chairs, ready to sit through the whole evening even though the artists were unknown.

At the other end of the football ground, there was posted the list of donors with their names, their companies, and the amounts they had donated written in black on red paper. In the middle of the site were three gigantic joss sticks. Every time the wind swept past, ashes fell on the heads of those walking beneath them. Stalls

selling snacks, congee, and noodles were confined to the right of
the area behind the opera stage, where many stools and wooden
boxes were placed. The site was brightly lit. In sharp contrast to
all this was a shed bearing the three characters 'Home-watching
Terrace'. It stood shrouded in a cold bluish light, with a pair of
couplets hanging, one on each side. Inside the shed were paper
'people' in blue and white. On the long table facing the front of
the shed were offerings of steamed rice and vegetarian dishes
brought by people in the neighbourhood, and a rectangular incense
burner packed with slender joss sticks. The shed exuded an eerie
feeling and the children all kept away from it. Since this was the
last night of the Ghost Festival, the offerings in the 'Home-
watching Terrace' shed would be handed out long before the night
was over. Those who had not yet received any rice or who had
only got a little in the school playground knew that there was
more food to be handed out here, and that the exact time depended
on the orders of those in charge. The patient ones, therefore, hung
around the shed and waited, or kept asking those sitting and
chatting in the makeshift conference room, 'Sir, when are you
going to hand out the food?'

At long last, someone wearing a straw hat and carrying a white
towel slung over one shoulder started heading towards the 'Home-
watching Terrace', and those waiting began to drift in, ghost-like,
from all directions. Women and children jostled one another at
the front. Beggars in rags who had been wandering around in a
trance with their bowls also stretched out their filthy hands to
grab at the dust-covered steamed rice in plastic baskets. Grannies,
who had already managed to snatch their share, were eyeing what
others had got. Several boys were fighting each other for the food.
The boy who won immediately dashed to the rear and handed his
spoils to a woman with a face wrinkled by a lifetime of suffering.
She was carrying a baby on her back, and beside her there were
already a few small baskets of rice offerings, closely guarded by
her other children. Some of the rice had a few pieces of fried fish
on top; some was mixed with bean sprouts. The man handing out
the rice shouted, 'Don't come snatching if you've already got your
share. The rice cannot be thrown away. Those who do so will be
cursed.' A dozen or so hands grabbed at each basket, almost
tipping it over before he had time to pass it to anyone. It was
common for people to beat up and abuse one another on such

occasions, and they would not stop until the men in the straw hats chased them off.

Uncle Shek could not hide his disappointment when he saw the long table with nothing left on it. The twisting of his mouth became more frequent, but no one understood what he was muttering about. He was staring at the baskets in other people's hands, even following closely on their heels. A fat greasy-faced woman, who was carefully putting several baskets of steamed rice into her canvas bag, was completely taken aback by Uncle Shek as she turned around. All at once, she let loose her wild tongue, hitting Uncle Shek with insults like rocks tumbling down high mountains, her language so foul women blushed and men grimaced. But Uncle Shek only took two small steps backwards and stood there shuffling, as though it was too hot under his feet and he could not keep still. A small group of people swiftly gathered around them.

Someone said to the fat woman, 'Give him some, you've got so much.'

This drew another attack from the woman: 'Give him some? No way! I've had to fight for it. We all have to fend for ourselves. He should have come earlier. Why the hell should I care just because he comes late and doesn't get anything?'

It really had been a day of bad luck for Uncle Shek. Earlier on he had missed out on the rice and had only been given a loaf of bread. He had thought he could wait for the steamed rice to be handed out in the evening, but he had been called over by one of the men in straw hats to carry bags of rice from the warehouse to a unit on the ground floor of Block 14. When he had returned, he saw grains of rice strewn all over the ground, but nothing was left on the long table in front of the 'Home-watching Terrace'. He grumbled to himself, 'What lousy luck this year. Didn't get anything.'

As if his luck was not bad enough, he had bumped into this sharp-tongued vixen. The woman was still yapping away, repeating her words over and over again until someone in the crowd shouted, 'Shut up while you're ahead! Why argue with him? He's not right in the head!'

The person was the owner of the Yee Loong rice shop. Others expressed agreement and tried as gently as they could to push her out of the football ground, leaving Uncle Shek standing there like an idiot. When the crowd had dispersed, the rice shop owner again joined the other organizers in front of the conference room, chatting and laughing, cigarette in hand, greeting familiar faces that went past. The chairman of the current Ghost Festival—the proprietor of the Wo Hing Restaurant—carried three heavy paper bags over to a police patrol car and bowed and smiled to the sergeant, thanking him and his men for keeping order. When the police van had driven off, he returned to his chair and started puffing on his water-pipe. It was already dark. Drums and gongs had started again at the opera stage, the chanting of the sutras had begun at the altar, and more and more people were coming over after dinner to pray, have fun or watch the opera. Over at the 'Home-watching Terrace', fires were burning high in the offerings furnace and ashes were flying all over the place. Local residents were bidding for the donated items displayed on the main table. The organizer in charge was shouting the bidding prices over the loudspeaker and saying all sorts of propitious things.

Uncle Shek went on with his unfinished business—carrying bags of rice from the warehouse behind the conference room back to a unit on the ground floor of Block 14 not far away. The owner of the rice shop squinted while watching the movements of the actors and actresses on the stage from afar. And now, a doddering woman with three little children began to pester one of the straw-hatted helpers, begging him to give her some rice. But there was no more. No one paid her any further attention, except those who couldn't disguise their great disgust at her. The old woman ignored them: 'Please have mercy. I didn't know the way. I went round and round and got here only just now. Please give us some rice. The three children have no parents and don't always have rice to eat. Give us some rice, please. May Buddha bless you with a long life and a house full of gold and silver.'

'Stop pestering us. We've told you already we've finished handing out the rice,' said the man in the straw hat.

'But isn't that rice inside those bags?' asked the old woman innocently, pointing at an odd-job man like Uncle Shek who was pushing a cartful of rice.

The rice shop owner could no longer concentrate on the opera. He stood up impatiently and yelled at the old woman, 'That rice is to be distributed to those who have donated money. The rice for alms-giving has long gone. You only have yourself to blame for coming late.'

'I couldn't find my way and it was dark. It's only once a year. Please, have mercy! Have mercy on us!'

'That's right. It's only once a year. All the more reason why you shouldn't have come late. It only shows you're not sincere. Even Buddha does not watch over you,' the rice shop owner snorted. He then waved his hand and said, 'Off you go. Stop bothering us.'

The old woman reluctantly moved away with the three children. But they lingered under the horizontal banner with the characters 'Peace throughout the Land', still hungrily eyeing the big bags of rice being carried away.

When Uncle Shek came out with the last bag of rice, the old woman left the three children behind and walked quickly up to his cart, closely following it and saying, 'Please give me some rice, Sir. Please give me some rice.'

Uncle Shek walked faster and faster, the four wheels of the cart spinning so fast it looked as though they were ready to fly off. He pushed the cart to the corner of a building and stopped.

'Quick, quick,' he said in a muffled voice. Before she had time to show her surprise, the old woman had already opened her bag and Uncle Shek quickly scooped some rice inside, leaving a lot scattered around the cart. He then urged the old woman to leave at once, and, so hurried was her departure, that she could only show her gratitude through her eyes.

This episode soon became known all over Western District. The organizers scolded Uncle Shek soundly, but he only looked at his feet without saying a word. It was only when the rice shop owner patted his own forehead and said repeatedly, 'He's crazy, it's a waste of time questioning him,' that Uncle Shek suddenly raised his head and looked straight at the rice shop owner, a fierce intensity in his glowering eyes. Everyone was stunned speechless by the burning hatred in that look.

Pointing at the shiny nose of the rice shop owner, Uncle Shek retorted clearly and loudly, 'It's you who's crazy.' Then he turned and walked off, pushing the crowd aside as he swaggered away. That night, Uncle Shek did not return to claim his share of the buns and sponge cakes which had been offered to Buddha, and his wooden cart and loaf of bread were left lying forlornly in one quiet corner of the football ground.

In the small hours of the morning, after the burning of paper offerings and money for the nether world, that year's Ghost Festival officially came to an end and people began to disperse. By the time things were cleared away and the lights switched off, most were tired and ready to go home. At that moment, someone was heard yelling for help from the men's toilet in Block 12, then a man dashed out and rushed over to a food stall to call the police. Only then did people realize that someone had been killed. It was the owner of the Yee Loong rice shop.

Before daybreak, news of the murder had spread all over Western District, and in the days that followed, all kinds of rumours and gossip swept the place, making the people's lives that much fuller. Elderly people repeated what they had said before: 'The old proprietor brought disaster upon his descendants because he did no good deeds in his lifetime.' And the people in the neighbourhood did not tone down their criticism of the rice shop owner just because he was dead. They talked about his conduct, about how dishonest he had been doing business, how he had cheated customers by giving them too little or by mixing his rice with impurities, how he charged exorbitant interest on his loans, and so on, as if he had deserved to die. Meanwhile, the garbage had remained uncollected for three days, and the whole place was stinking. Uncle Shek was nowhere to be found. The neighbourhood folk had even more things to say about this, mostly superstitious and idle remarks about retribution and paying for one's wrongful deeds.

December 1981
Chinese original published in Xin Qishi: *The Blue Crescent Moon*, Taipei: Hung Fan Book Store, 1986.

Uncle Che

By **LOK SIU PING**

Translated by Janice Wickeri

The efforts of Hong Kong people to relate to immigrants from the Mainland is a recurrent theme in local literature. This story depicts such an attempt with fine insight into the complex feelings the local people undergo in the course of such a relationship.

Looking back at my relationship with Uncle Che, I can see that I always treated him as my elder, with the respect we confer on an elder. When I was young, my head filled with ideals, I saw him as greater than he actually was, and there was a time when I set him up as my life's model. When I think back on those youthful impulses now, I have to laugh at myself. It seems obvious that as I came to understand him better, I began to feel resentful and annoyed with him. This drastic change in my feelings towards him astounded me. I was forced to reflect on how my own thinking had changed, what sort of psychological process I had gone through, that I ended up hating him like that.

I think I rejected him mainly because of the stubborn way he clung, for decades on end, to his own pipe dreams. I believed those dreams were dangerous, all the more so if they were actually to come true. I did feel sorry for him because all his dreams were so unattainable. Yet if I could have pulled them up by their decades-long roots, I would truly have done so.

It has always been my belief that as you grow up, you gain some understanding, more or less, of your own strengths and weaknesses. Along with that, comes a bit of self-knowledge to help you assess the inordinate ambitions you once had, so that in the end you can rid yourself one by one of those you realize to be absurd. I too had many youthful, unattainable dreams. Actually they were very simple ones: the tiniest bit of achievement to provide a modicum of ego satisfaction, a bit of affection, work I like—that would be enough. Yet humble as these aspirations were, trying to fulfil them was a real strain for me, and I could only manage it with intermittent success. Compared with the hidden ambitions of Uncle Che, mine were hardly worth mentioning.

Right then Uncle Che was sitting fairly close to me, facing my friend who had just dropped by, and pressing his impertinent question once more, 'Which newspaper does your family read: *Ta Kung Pao* or the *Sing Tao Daily*?'

I saw my friend frown. The question mystified him and I felt more or less responsible. I was going to have to explain to him the real meaning of Uncle Che's query, so I said, 'What Uncle Che means is, he'd like to know what sort of political background you live with on a daily basis.' I saw my friend's eyes open wide at that, and the look he gave me said he was at a loss. I knew I'd have to be a bit more explicit. It would be best if he first understood something of Uncle Che's background.

'Which national day does your family celebrate: October 1st or October 10th?' Uncle Che came out with another tricky question.

This time I didn't have to explain. My friend understood the nuances of the question right away. He finally saw what the question was really getting at. He let out a sigh of relief, and, slightly abashed, confessed, *The Economic Daily*!

The answer was a challenge for Uncle Che. Assuming a stern face he said with righteous indignation, 'Never heard of it!'

———

When I first met Uncle Che, I was still a young girl of fifteen or sixteen. I remember that the electrical goods shop my parents ran was still in business then. Uncle Che appeared one evening at dusk. He wore a blue-grey work overall with a blue neckerchief and blue cap. His voice was full and coarse and he spoke Cantonese with a pronounced accent, the speech rhythms all jumbled up. There was hardly a pause between one syllable and the next, as if his mouth was a cryptograph, emitting signals rapid-fire, like disaster coverage broadcast live. It was my father who finally understood what he was saying. It seemed Uncle Che worked at a nearby dockyard and by the time he got off work the news-stands were all shut. He asked if we would subscribe to an evening paper for him, so he could stop by the shop for it after work. My father reluctantly agreed. And so every evening he would come to the shop to get his paper. He loved to talk and would always stay a while to chat. The moment he opened his mouth, he attracted the attention of passersby who would always turn as one to stare at him, because when he spoke extreme anxiety, joy, and indignation passed one after the other across his features. He stamped and gesticulated with short, explosive movements. What's more, he was a big burly man, strong as a horse, who exuded such an air of discontent with things as they were that our neighbours concluded he came every night to pick a quarrel with us. And then, newspaper under his arm, he would leave.

He struck people as a new arrival from the Mainland, non-Cantonese, filled with homesickness, or as a wildly patriotic soldier. But he called himself a sojourner in a strange land. . . . My parents showed him every courtesy and enjoyed shooting the breeze with him. We sisters all deferred to him as our elder, and gave him his due respect. His age differed from father's by only two or three years, so when he spoke to us girls, it was always as an elder. His voice was somewhat grating and he spoke in an authoritarian manner, which struck us as not altogether civilized. But having been raised in a patriarchy, we girls were always pretty compliant. We all liked to gather round him and hear what he had to say. For his part, he would perk right up, his fatigue forgotten, his voice would grow louder and he would wave his arms around like a performer. He was always repeating himself, but he had a strong streak of gumption and a tenacious fighting spirit. His was a personality seldom found in his generation and that was one of the reasons he attracted my youthful curiosity.

'You girls need physical exercise. Karate would be best. First, it'll make you strong; second, it's good self-defence; and third, third is that one day when your country needs you, you'll be ready.' His tone drew the customers who had come into the shop and they wandered over to hear what he had to say.

I was at that rebellious age, and I welcomed such stirring talk, all this about involving oneself in society, bringing glory to the nation, giving your life for justice—it was all meat to me. And what's more, I was studying modern Chinese history in school then—the Opium War, the territorial concessions, the Treaty of Peking, the May Fourth Movement—and I'd recently begun to collect new big-character posters from the Mainland. All this gave his manner and words a heightened sense of immediacy for me. When he spoke of the Japanese army attacking China, he looked so impassioned, it was almost as if he was the sole victim of the whole disaster, the sole witness. Finally he said, 'Japanese ambition is great, you have to be on your guard, keep your vigilance up.' It sounded like a military command, not like casual chat with an elder. We nodded as we listened, and thought that he'd had some extraordinary experiences for sure. It suddenly came to me that he'd always been on his own. He never mentioned a family. I wanted very much to know his story, but I was shy by nature and did not dare to ask.

'You have to have a sound foundation in maths, be good at science—then you can contribute to the nation's future development,' he would go on. I was exceptionally bad at maths, I hadn't achieved a pass grade since Primary Four. In fact, all my life I had been looking for ways to avoid maths.

Uncle Che's talk was repetitious and, as time wore on, we weren't as attentive as we had been, and his talk fell off as well. If, however, there happened to be a new face present, he would perk up right away, trot out his principles and discourse on them at length. Our shop had become a frequent haunt of his. My father was actually a little resentful of the fact, but he couldn't bring himself to say anything and so he too spoke to Uncle Che less and less. One time, though, my father and Uncle Che spent several hours with their heads together. There was none of the former liveliness about their talk and they kept their voices low and very calm. I didn't know what they were saying and when Uncle Che left, his expression was terrible to see.

Uncle Che had decided to go to sea with his ship. As he got ready for his departure from Hong Kong, there was a period of some days when he did not turn up and the shop seemed to grow very quiet all at once. And then one evening, he brought over some gifts for us to remember him by. Opening them, we found a pair of thirty-pound barbells, a dozen darts and a dartboard, a sled, a bicycle, and a six-volume set of *Karate: The Art of Self-Defence for Girls*. We didn't know whether to laugh or cry, but we accepted the gifts without fuss, on our best behaviour.

It was only after Uncle Che's departure from Hong Kong that we found out what his tête-à-tête with father had been all about. He had wanted to store several pieces of baggage with us. Our parents, naturally cautious, declined and, although I put forward some arguments on Uncle Che's behalf, hoping father might accommodate him, permission was not forthcoming, and I had to drop it. Later, I overheard my parents talking privately and it was clear they were talking about Uncle Che's ambitions. Finally I heard my mother sigh and say, 'If his hopes were realized, then we would really have something to worry about!'

From that time on, we never saw Uncle Che again, though occasionally we would receive postcards he'd sent from Japan, Korea, England, or wherever. He'd write a bit about himself, but mostly they were about technological developments, the standard of living and so on in those places. And once he sent a dozen or so photographs, all of a Japanese cargo vessel, taken from various angles. He seemed to be especially impressed with it. I thought that was possibly due to the connection with his profession, but his letters expressed disgust with life on board ship—the only reason he'd decided to go to sea was for the money. The letter was signed: A sojourner in a strange land.

Later, father wound up his business in the shop because the landlord wanted to demolish the building, we sisters all went our separate ways as we left Hong Kong, and Uncle Che continued to ply distant seas on board ship. We all lost touch with him. Over a decade passed before we saw his face again.

One afternoon, a year after my parents had passed away and we had all returned to Hong Kong, my sister happened to spot an old man in cap and work overalls near her place of work. She recognized him at once. 'Uncle Che!'

I opened the door, and there stood Uncle Che, obviously aged, but still in his work overall and cap—a different colour though, changed from blue-grey to black. He'd stayed in shape. I quickly invited him in, only then noticing that he carried a cane. 'Do you have trouble walking?' I asked.

'No, I just use it for extra strength sometimes,' he said, radiating vigour.

During the ten-odd years in which we had not seen each other, I had changed from a girl into a woman. I married early and my child was now twelve. My personality had undergone a big change too, I was no longer strong-willed and excitable as in the past. I was a mother now and took proper care of my child. This assumption of responsibility had given me confidence in my own abilities. I was proud of my maturity and my ability to bear up. I was fonder of things as they were than I had been in my impressionable youth, things meant more to me. I was better at facing up to my own problems and no longer tried to justify my ineptitude. I just wanted to be an ordinary person, just that and nothing more. I didn't know what Uncle Che would think of this change in me.

The first thing Uncle Che said when he had sat down was, 'Which newspaper do you read: *Ta Kung Pao* or *Sing Tao*?' His voice was as robust as ever, his Cantonese as heavily accented. We chatted a while, catching up on each other's news. He was still a good talker, fond of saying things to get a reaction from people.

I had arranged with my family to come over to see Uncle Che, and one after another they came, all happy to see him again. Everyone talked about how they were doing and very naturally the subject of my deceased parents came up. Once again, Uncle Che was the centre of attention, and seeing the expression on his face as he talked, it was as if the intervening years had never been, and he had been talking to us all along.

'I'm telling you, maths and science are the most important. The reason the big cities I've visited are prospering, is because their governments stress technological development. . . .' Uncle Che was once again gesticulating wildly; his voice rose; he was in his element.

I raised the questions I hadn't raised years ago out of shyness, 'Why did you come to Hong Kong in the first place?'

When he heard that, I don't know why, but his face fell, for all the world as if it was a presumptuous question. His high, strong voice became suddenly weak, 'I . . . I . . . I just came; it's been so many years, if there was a reason, I've forgotten it. Why do you want to know?'

His answer seemed extraordinary to me. He'd always seemed so full of self-confidence, but now he seemed to be evading an answer. So I continued with my questions, 'What about your family, Uncle Che?'

It was as if he was under hostile interrogation, his voice fell even lower, 'I . . . I don't have any family . . . they're all gone . . . in China.'

Just then, my younger sister and her husband arrived and I offered them my seat. Then Uncle Che's spirits seemed to rise again and he was confident as he asked my brother-in-law, whom he was seeing for the first time, 'Which newspaper do you read at home: *Ta Kung Pao* or *Sing Tao*? Which national day does your family celebrate: October 1st or Double Ten?'

I remembered the early days with Uncle Che, when he always greeted a new acquaintance with this question he was now asking my brother-in-law. But now I found the question passé. More than ten years had passed, the world and the people in it had changed; these days the views expressed in newspapers in general were a lot more objective. So I made an effort to tell him that in the course of these ten-odd years Hong Kong had actually changed a lot, but he wasn't the least bit interested in my opinion. He screwed up his face. There was no way he could accept any of it. Looking at me in alarm he said, 'Let me tell you, as Chinese you should all temper yourselves. The best thing would be to learn karate. First, it's good exercise, second. . . .'

My sisters' children had all gathered round Uncle Che listening curiously, heads up, to this novel message. His voice grew louder and more stirring, as if we had an orator in our midst, a leader.

'You must have a good foundation in maths and you must study science. Then, in future, you can make some contribution to the development of the nation,' Uncle Che continued.

I looked at his face, radiant, as if he had become ten years younger and I suddenly felt an inexplicable unease. Then my mother's image came into my mind and I remembered her assessment of Uncle Che, and it was as if I had understood something all at once. I sat in a corner of the room, silently observing him. It was only then I realized that he was not really that strong. He was wearing several layers of clothes under his coat, padding his whole body into plumpness. I began to become aware that he looked like a vagrant, with all his important possessions on him. I looked at the cane in his hand. At first I thought he carried it due to old age, but now I realized it was meant for self-defence. He really had aged and what's more, he was afraid and insecure.

It was while we were having dinner together that I first discovered that his teeth had all fallen out. He carried a small pocket knife with which he diced his food, something that showed conclusively that he was in the grip of old age. He said softly, 'My teeth are all bad and I haven't had false ones fitted.'

Uncle Che was working temporarily in a school, doing some miscellaneous janitorial work and living on the school premises. One day, my relatives and I went to pay him a visit. His room was not large, but it was quite neat and tidy. In one corner there was an untidy heap of books: mathematics, science, politics, etc. His work at the school was very light. We congratulated him on being settled at last and not having to wander around any more. Little did we know that in his heart, he had other plans. He made a request of my brother-in-law, hoping that he could spare a little time to help him solve some maths problems. 'The first thing I need to do is get the basic diploma,' said Uncle Che.

I suddenly thought of how he was always talking about maths and science, so I asked him, 'What will you do with this diploma?'

'I've always worked on ships, but I lost my job four years ago because I had no diploma. But they promised to rehire me if I got one,' he told us.

'You're not a young man, you should take care of your health and look for light work; work on the ships isn't suitable for you anymore,' my younger sister said earnestly.

'I want to work on ships so that in future when the country is in need, I can volunteer for the navy. I have experience in working on ships, the only thing I don't have is a diploma,' he said.

It suddenly occurred to me that Uncle Che was extremely confused in his thinking. There was no way we could know what was in his mind, all we knew was that it must be filled with an overwhelming sense of crisis—he was dressed like a worker-peasant-soldier, he acted like a soldier, his past was a bottomless pool no one could fathom. It was quite obvious many dangerous ideas lurked in this mind. He was seventy years old. The aspirations he had clung to so long and so tenaciously might, in what he knew all too well to be the limited days of his life, drive him into irreversible madness. So I told him, 'The nation is safe now, there won't be another war, you—' I hadn't finished.

'I can get up an army. I'm good at that. What I need is money. With money there's a lot I can do.' Uncle Che spoke from the heart.

I kept calm and told him times had changed. There was nowhere in the Chinese world one could raise an army. If things were really as he said, the world would be a very frightening place.

'I don't agree. Japan's ambition is vast. I want to organize a band of volunteers to serve the nation. The weakest part of the Chinese military is the navy. In the future when China is in trouble, I will go to her aid! I will!' He was worked up and his tone reflected it, but it was also hoarse and low.

Looking at him, I thought again of my mother's assessment of the man.

As we left his room, our hearts were all unusually heavy. The thought came to me that the reason he had come to Hong Kong in the first place might have been to raise an army. Had that really been it?

'You don't have to worry,' my brother-in-law suddenly said. 'To tell you the truth, if he's studied the elementary diploma course for three years and hasn't mastered even the most basic maths, it doesn't look as if there's much hope of his getting the diploma. Even then he'd have to take the mid-level test, then the higher level. That could well take whatever time he has left.'

We all sighed heavily, surprised that in fact we didn't really know him at all. We thought of our innocence, of the simplicity of youth, of Uncle Che's stories that had drawn us in, and we all shivered, but not from cold. However, in the end we all came to the same happy conclusion. We were all glad that in the course of Uncle Che's life, fate had not given him the chance to join the navy, nor the wherewithal to raise a volunteer force. True, we all agreed that when a decades-old dream was finally dashed, the hurt must be tremendous. But among the dreams we knew would never come true, this was one that would not be in the least regretted by anyone, though it be the kindest and most reasonable of dreams. What was more, our encounter with Uncle Che had not led to any sympathy for him. Did that make us insensitive to his plight? Maybe, but for our part, such a response was all too human.

Chinese original published in *Bo Yi Monthly*, June, 1989.

Wood

By NG HUI BUN

Translated by Martha P. Y. Cheung and Chan Nga Ting

Though distinctly different in style, this story can be read as a companion piece to 'Uncle Che'. The writer's portrayal of the myriad feelings that the Hong Kong poet experiences as he seeks to befriend and to understand the Mainland poet captures beautifully the feelings of many Hong Kong intellectuals during the 1960s, 1970s, and early 1980s.

The rain was pattering. The mountains looked even more blurred.

I began to feel a little annoyed. Had she got it wrong? Perhaps he was just an ordinary poet. I should have learnt more about him before I came. As soon as I stepped into the woodland, I began to feel somewhat uneasy. The trees there were of all kinds, their hard sprawling branches blocked the way almost completely, and his house was at the very end of the path. I really wondered whether I should push on. It was early winter. In this deep valley where the sun could hardly penetrate the dense trees, my light coat offered me little protection against the chill of the misty November wind. Then, the path came to an end.

His house looked shoddily built, the walls and roof were some medium-sized timbers put together. The timbers were still overgrown with mosses and mistletoe. In front of the house was a clearing with weeds and logs; the soil was a sort of pale yellow. As I came near the house, I discovered that there was no door, just a very narrow entrance. Some hoarse and creaking sound came faintly from the inside, and it travelled gently, yet unmistakably, in the wind. I dared not enter rashly, so I stopped for a while by the door. The house didn't seem to be fitted with windows, it looked quite dark inside, quite deep, too. I called his name and knocked lightly on the wooden walls, but there was no response. I hesitated, then went in.

The house was empty. In the feeble light, I saw him standing in the middle of the room, his back towards me, sawing a section of a trunk. His long coat, in sober colour, reached almost to his heels. I called his name again. He did not answer and just went on sawing, backwards and forwards, backwards and forwards. His movements, slow and relaxed, were more like those of someone posing rather than someone at work. Then he laid down the saw, picked up a plank, and used it to carefully push open the big skylight above him. The wind gushed in at once, sending the dust on the floor swirling. In the white sawdust dancing in the wind, I saw him turning around slowly. Light from the skylight enshrouded him like a drape, then spread around him. And yet, what an old and desolate face it was! I had thought that he was only about sixty and would still be full of life—the life of poetry— but what I saw now was an old man, gaunt and withered.

'I am a reporter from a magazine house. Can I talk to you?'

He picked up the saw, put his hand on a log lying horizontally on two sections of trunks, and sawed lightly on the log. He was bald; his hair, almost the colour of wood, fell to his shoulders from below his earlobes and the back of his head. In the harsh sawing sound, his dry, wiry, and slightly wavy hair quivered. He was wearing a long, loose, old-fashioned coat, the sturdy, bulky shoulders of the coat standing in sharp contrast to his shrivelled neck. It reminded me of the kind of coat I had seen in old movies.

I went up to him and said, 'Can I talk to you?'

As he sawed, his eyes were not set on the wood, but at a distance about two feet beyond. His pupils were a strange colour, like a tea stain, and they also spread like tea stain, making it hard to tell the pupils from the white of the eye. His mouth could hardly be seen, as he had lost all his teeth and there was nothing to support the muscle around it. Deep furrows ran along the sunken muscle and curved right into the mouth. They looked like the sun's rays etched on copperplate. The sun was a void at the centre, a black sun.

'I've heard people reciting your poems and I really like them.'

I had come across his poems by chance and they had stuck in my mind. It was the Mid-Autumn Festival, my colleagues were having a gathering at a friend's house. I was a little apprehensive of this kind of gathering. I was used to being alone. My interests were different from theirs, or perhaps I was too gauche and tongue-tied to join in their conversation. But I did listen to the young woman when she recited a poem.

They were teasing a colleague about her romance. Amidst the noise and excitement, I saw a huge dragonfly flying into the room through the gap of the half-opened blinds. It was a beautiful dragonfly, with an elongated body almost completely lemon yellow in colour, and transparent wings criss-crossed with dark brown veins. It circled low and rested on the coaster beside me. After a while, it flew off, flitting about over people's heads. Where had it come from? Why did it bother to fly to this city through the dust and the cold?

They were still laughing. No one seemed to have noticed it. Then, I saw the young woman sitting slumped in the rocking chair next to me raise her head slightly in the direction of the dragonfly. She had soft shoulder-length hair and one of her hands was resting on the arm of the chair. My heart started to pound, faintly. I had seen her before—she had written many charming and sad stories for the magazine. Sometimes I ran into her, but she just bowed her head and walked past me softly.

Soon, she noticed me too. She bit her lower lip and smiled quietly, brushed back the hair draping over her forehead, and settled back into the chair. I took a step forward. They were still chattering behind me. The light seemed too glaring.

'You saw it?' I asked.

'Yes,' she replied softly, glancing at me, and lowered her eyes again.

'Beautiful, isn't it? Few of them are dark brown in colour.'

'Yes, it's beautiful.' She leant an elbow on the arm of the chair, then rested her chin on the back of her hand. Under the white lamp, the colour of her scarf looked soft and mellow. 'Do you know this poem about a dragonfly? "Between dream and silence you skim, stirring the hesitation in the water".'

'What?'

' "Stirring the hesitation in the water"—that might be used to describe it,' she said lightly.

'I don't know it. How does the whole poem go?'

She recited it softly. Her head tipped to one side, she fiddled with the end of the scarf on her knees and rocked slowly in the chair, coming in and out of the light, in and out of the light. The glimmering light and her soft voice made everything appear unreal. Then, she looked up and smiled shyly.

'You like it?'

'Oh, yes. I've never come across people writing in that way.'

'I'm surprised you like it. Your poems are very different.' A tuft of her hair was dangling down and she tucked it back behind her ears. Then, she stared at the bits of paper on the floor.

I felt a little hot.

'Whose poem is that?'

'It's the work of a very strange man. He came to Hong Kong a few years ago. My aunt knew him in the past, and likes his poems very much. She said he had published two volumes of great poems, but she hasn't seen him for years.'

'Where does he live now?'

'On one of the outlying islands, I can get his address from my aunt. If you like, I can give it to you in a day or two. It's difficult to find him, though. Some of my friends went there once but failed to meet him. Maybe you can have a go. You write poems; he may be willing to talk to you. I do want to know how he's getting on, it's just that I don't feel like venturing out on my own.' She rolled the scarf in her hands and bowed her head slightly.

My heart was pounding madly, probably because of the heat. Feeling a little thirsty, I stretched out my hand to reach for the cold water on the table. But I was so nervous I dropped the coaster, which fell by her heels. I put down the glass at once, but she was already bending down slowly for the coaster, her scarf brushing the floor.

'Your scarf is soiled.'

'Oh!' Then she broke into a smile again.

———

'Can I read your poems?'

But there were no books in this house. It was almost empty, not even a bed could be found. All that could be seen were boards of different sizes, piled high along the walls, some long, some short, some thin as a sheet and half transparent, others cracked, looking like the face of a clock, or hollowed out in the middle, like a wheel. Many were covered with moss, patches of grey clustered together in the corners of the walls. They were soggy, and smelt of damp. Many were rotten and useless, but still had grains. What did he want them for? Did he sleep on them?

'I've heard that you've been here quite a few years. Do you still write poems?'

She had told me that he had stopped writing poems at least a decade before he came to Hong Kong. In all that time, he had published just a few articles. Nothing else was known of him; there was no way of finding out more information. And now his silence made it hard for me to continue asking him questions. Was he the right man? Could it be that he and the poet just happened to have the same name? Watching his expressionless face as he went on sawing, I began to feel a little uneasy. He didn't seem to be concentrating on his work, and he didn't seem to be deep in thought. He must have noticed me, but why didn't he pay me any attention? I had asked him a very simple question. Why this silence? Once in a while, he'd raise his head and look at the sawdust quivering in the white sunlight, but he didn't stop sawing. The rust-coloured saw continued to slice through the frosty air, backwards and forwards.

Then I left.

What kind of person was he? He puzzled me. Did he really write poems? Had she perhaps made a mistake? When I came back from the visit, I could not help phoning her and asking her to come out and meet me. Well, just to ask her about him.

Standing by the lamppost opposite her house, I felt a little nervous as I waited for her, my coat fluttering against the occasional car that swished past me. I was the sort of man who could not be sure of a lot of things, who was afraid of loneliness and yet could not get along well with others. Nothing decisive would happen to me.

'Have you been waiting for long?' She walked towards me gracefully.

'Not really.'

It had rained earlier on and the road was filled with big puddles dark with the reflections of trees in clumps. She was wearing a chequered dress, white on beige, and a long scarf with alternating bands of beige and brown. In this gloomy weather, it greeted me like a cool, bright smile.

'I wanted to meet you because I want to know something about him.'

'Haven't we just discussed him on the phone?' she smiled and said gently.

I had no reply.

'You really went to see him?'

'Yes.'

Then I told her about the meeting in detail.

When I came to an end, she frowned, as if in disbelief. 'I can't believe it,' she said.

'What did you think he'd be like?'

'I never imagined he'd be so old and gaunt. I learnt his poems from my aunt. When my aunt came to Hong Kong, she stayed with us. Whenever she couldn't sleep, she'd recite his poems. I slept in the bed beside her, and gradually I remembered the poems by heart. But lately my aunt has changed. Doesn't say much, and every so often, she raps on the desk with her knuckles. I'm afraid of her.'

She stretched out her hands to receive the falling leaves.

'You know many of his poems?'

'A dozen or so. There's one I like very much, "Bottle". Let me recite it to you.'

Then she began. Her hair streamed in the wind behind her back, revealing the gentle lines on her forehead. Her soft voice wafted rhythmically through the chilly air.

When she had finished, she looked up and asked, 'Do you like it? Don't you think his poems are gentle and charming? They are full of love and hope. My aunt told me she used to have a big album bound between white boards. It contained all his works which had not been included in his poetry collections and were precious. But, someone took it away when they began criticizing him. She couldn't get it back no matter how hard she tried.'

'What did they criticize him for?'

'I don't know. My aunt didn't say. She's not the chatty type. She only told me that he had never written any love poems and had always been alone.' She kicked a stone before her carelessly, slowly unravelling the scarf she had rolled up in her hands. Then, letting her hair drape over her face, she asked softly, 'You haven't written any love poems either, have you?'

A motorcycle was fast approaching us from behind. It sped past us, but the loud roar of its engine vibrated in the air for a long time before it died out, like a quenched flame. I felt a little flustered.

'Look at that motorcycle!'

'I can't understand some of his poems though. I just think they're so unaffected, so charming. Anyway, I like them. . . . Well, I don't understand many of your poems either, but I like them too.'

She broke off at the stem a leaf which was leaning towards her, and rubbed it gently on her face. She tilted her head to one side, looked at me, and grinned. She was not the kind of girl who was always happy, but in the sunlight, her face glowed and she looked quite radiant. I caught a whiff of the fresh scent of leaves on her, I could hear the gentle rustle of her clothes as she walked beside me. But I was aware that a lot of things were just fleeting shadows, shadows of what I hoped would really happen. A tuft of my hair was tickling my face, and I flicked my head to toss it back. I took a deep breath, then a step forward. I'd better not go off into wild flights of fancy. I wanted to say something, but I couldn't find the words. She also grew quiet and we walked in silence. I didn't take the chance, so nothing happened.

'This is where I live,' she said at last.

For many days after our meeting, I could not calm myself down, and kept wondering why she was so fond of his poems. She was a sensitive girl. When I had seen her in the past, she had always looked down and walked on softly. It was hard to believe she could discuss his poems with such childlike tenderness. It had been a long time since I had last met a girl like her. However, I was no good at taking my chances, I worried for no reason. I could feel faintly that I was going to spoil something. But why did I keep thinking about her? Weren't the poems enough to think about?

What kind of person was he really? Was he as wonderful a poet as she had made him out to be? What had come over him? How had he got through those few decades? I couldn't find out anything more about him. The friends I knew well—none of them had heard of him. And there was just no way of finding his poetry collections. How could a person just vanish into thin air? What had he gone through? Where could his poems be?

In the reference room of our magazine house, I went over the bound volumes of *Humanities Literature* published over the last twenty odd years. I didn't find anything.

In the end, I learnt about an institution specializing in providing information on Chinese literature and history for foreign scholars. I went there on the pretext that I was helping a French reporter, who had recently arrived in Hong Kong, to find some material on modern Chinese Literature, and borrowed several rolls of micro-film of a few literary journals. Then I borrowed a micro-film reader from a professor friend and studied the micro-films carefully.

But still, details about him were scanty. None of his poems could be found, and there were just a few articles denouncing his works. His poems were accused of being glutted with images and lacking in clarity. One critic said he was like a goldsmith, interested only in refining words in his own laboratory, and he used excessively accurate words to 'create a philosophical maze'. In an age when there was a general trend towards clarity, he sought to lead the masses to an 'open grave of obscurity'. Strangely, however, another critic attacked him for writing in too 'objective' a manner and for being too 'frosty' in his attitude. His descriptive passages, this critic said, were too plain; there was no implied meaning, no love, no concern for the people in society, and no social consciousness. Yet, another critic dismissed his poems for being too materialistic. His poems, according to this critic, 'have a tendency to fetishize objects and reveal an infatuation with the industrial civilization. While they are good at describing cities, there is no glorification of progress to lift the spirit, no far-sighted vision about the future, and they show a lack of confidence in humanity.'

These comments confused me even further. How could a man be charming as well as frosty, full of love and yet lacking in concern for others, have hope in things and yet no confidence in humanity? Why were these critics' views the polar opposites of hers? Were they talking about the same man?

Night had fallen. The moon looked a little clumsy and grimy.

It couldn't possibly be she who was mistaken? Her face—so soft, so still—rose up in my mind. And that pair of fair hands shading her eyes as she looked at the sunlight that crept through her fingers! I felt a gentle surge of something in me, but when I was about to reach out for it, it was gone. Oh, why was I thinking about these things?

I decided to visit him again. If I could get him to talk to me, then everything would be clear. Surely, she'd be interested to know too.

When I arrived at his house, I could not help but hesitate. The sun was blazing, the soil a dazzling yellow. The material I had brought with me felt even heavier.

Inside, everything looked the same as when I last visited him, except that the place seemed even dimmer. The skylight was closed. There was no light except what could seep in through the narrow slits around the window pane. I could just faintly make out the window pane, blurred at the edges: it looked like a wound that might heal well. By the door lay a newly felled trunk; its branches, still uncut, stretched clumsily to the corner of the wall.

'It's me again.'

I had not expected any replies from him, still I could not help but feel a little sad. What had I come here for? I had no way of knowing if he would speak to me or not. I looked at him, at a loss what to do. He had no shoes on; his feet, covered with sawdust, seemed to have turned the colour of wood. His movements were light, it was as if he was working on a delicate job, and there was no salvaging it if he went wrong. He pulled the saw as far backwards as possible, waited a while, then pushed it gently forwards. Between these two movements, he drew a luxurious arc in the air with his elbow. Sometimes, when the saw got stuck in the wood, he would stop, sweep away the little twigs sticking out from the teeth of the saw, then pull it backwards again. Suddenly, I thought of his eyes. They were not the colour of tea stains, they were the colour of wood—the brown sawdust scattering in the air.

'Can I talk to you again? I came once before . . . also at this hour. . . . I am from a magazine house. . . .' He still did not look at me.

'I just want to ask you a few simple questions. . . . I've heard your poems . . . and I like them. Why don't you write poems now? . . . Or is it just that you don't publish them? . . . Your poems are charming, why did some critics say you're frosty and obscure? . . . When did you last publish your poems before you came here . . . ? Are you living alone . . . ? Why have you sawn off so many logs? Do you mind stopping for a moment? . . . Oh well, it doesn't matter, it's all right if you don't stop. . . .'

The whole house rang with my voice. Outside, the wind was rustling the trees. My throat was seized with a pricking pain like that brought on by a coughing fit. I grasped a twig beside me and rolled it on my palm, the bark hurt my skin.

'Could you please answer my questions? I write poems too. . . . I just want to know your views on poetry. I really like your "Dragonfly" poem—really like it. Say something, please. I will understand. I write poems too. . . . Not great poems, but I keep on writing. Please say something. I can understand. I really write poems myself—no kidding. I can understand everything. . . . Say something, please! I'm not making this up—do believe me. I really write poems—really. . . . Shall I recite my poems to you?'

I was sweating all over, my mouth seemed to be watering with acid. I felt suffocated.

Then I heard a voice reciting a poem. Bitter, trembling, that voice floated into the chilly, murky shadows. I panicked, was that my own voice?

The wind began to rise from some remote mountain area. The distant sound of wind sweeping past the branches, rocks, and brown soil could be faintly heard. The room was filled with swirling sawdust and dust. The pale sunlight penetrated through the clouds and crept in through the slits between the planks on the roof, enwrapping him in a tangle of dusty, quivering lines. He looked even less like a living man. Suddenly I was filled with rage. I scratched hard a section of a trunk beside me, leaving deep white lines on the surface, which looked bloated, swollen and ugly. How could he be a poet? He was just a madman working on a ridiculous job at the wrong time and in the wrong place. His past setbacks had worn him out, there was nothing left in him except some habitual movements. Why did I bother to come here? What had he got to do with me? I wanted to move him with my poems, but he just went on marking time with the rhythm of his saw. He was living in another world, where there was no memory, no feeling, no shadow, no people, and no self. Why did I bother to recite my poems to him?

For days after I left him, I didn't feel like talking to anyone. It could be because I had never tried to reach out to people, never given anything to anyone, and had never even been aware of this. I had been wasting my life and I could no longer afford to do so. But perhaps there wasn't much I could give now. When we were young, we were so foolish, so wasteful, we could hardly imagine that anything would come to an end. But now, even before the end was in sight, we just grasped anything that came our way and wouldn't let go. But why did I keep thinking about such things?

I stayed at home for days. Outside all was quiet. Only snatches of conversation from some television programme and the occasional barking of a dog drifted in. The sounds rose slowly and steadily into a perfect arc, and then was no more, in sorrow gone. Sometimes, I thought I heard an aeroplane passing by, then everything returned to silence.

I never again touched the films I had borrowed; the micro-film reader was littered with old newspapers, many of which were stained. He simply wasn't a poet, why should I bother?

And yet, a letter from a far-away friend changed all that again.

———

I had wanted to write a novel about palace dance in the Tang dynasty, and had asked this friend to help me find a few old dissertations in his local library, as the material there was more abundant and complete. One morning as I left my house, I received a small parcel in the mail. The sun was shining brightly on my desk before the window. I sat down and tore off the wrapping paper. Inside were photocopies in different shades— extracts from various journals and books. Under the sunlight, I looked over them. Then, in a blank space on the last page of an article, 'Blue Sorrows, Ensemble Dance', I found a poem written by him.

It was a poem about trees. Different kinds of trees. Trees dead or dying—rotten and disfigured by the wind, sunk deep into the ground, or struck dead by lightning, cleft apart, their branches stretching out like scorched fingers. Trees washed away by waves, shapeless or misshapen; trees ravaged by weather; trees, sulphur yellow, fallen to the ground, their bearing lost. But behind all these, behind the lime, grit, scars, and salt, there was 'the firmness and the scent of wood, the scent of growing trees weaving its way through the delight of night and the colours of seasons.' It came into his room, and his fingers caressed the rough texture of the trunk, the pricking sensation of the bark. And still the rings continued to grow, round and round, 'rising above the abyss of destruction, decline, decay, and death to join the songs of rivers'.

My face was now in full sunlight. There was a touch of winter scent in the air. On this December morning, the distant mountains were shrouded in mist—a light veil of yellow. I could feel faintly a warmth spreading through my body. It was a feeling at once familiar and remote. There had been a time when this feeling was lost, I couldn't tell why. But now it came back to me again in the hazy winter mist. Was that why he continued to work? I remembered how he had stood there, his back arched, sawing the logs slowly and tenderly, letting the planks crack in his hands and filling the narrow space of his room with the fragrance of wood. It was like a hint, a sign of perseverance, like what he said in his poem. But what had he been through to make him end up as he now was?

I wrote at once to ask my friend to help me find out more information about him. I also continued to work on the micro-films. There was, however, nothing about him in the journals for many years after.

I began to feel a little apprehensive. Had he vanished? Just like that? Then, in the March issue of the 1958 volume, I found a notice carrying his apologies to the public, in which he admitted to a few mistakes he had made in an article he'd written on poetry. The notice was short, the mistakes were not explained. And in a 1967 article published under the name of Jiu Feng, I found this sentence, 'He could have spent these few years on a careful self re-examination; unfortunately, he made no attempt to consolidate his progress; instead, he took the road of retrogression and strayed farther and farther. . . .' What had happened to him in those few years? And for what reason?

I spent three whole days and nights on the micro-films, not giving myself a break until I finished reading everything. But his name never appeared again. Was that when he had stopped writing poems for good?

I told her at once all the things I had learnt, hoping that her aunt could help. But her aunt could no longer speak. His poems, though charming, could no longer soothe away her haunting memories of the past. She remembered only her life in those days, endless days when she stayed shut up in a house, listening to the dull, repetitive sounds droning in the cold street outside. Thud. Thud. Thud. It was the sound of death. A vehicle drove away with a carload of dead bodies.

Was he thinking of the past too? He was old: how much longer could he last? I was a little frustrated. Why was it that one could only get to know another person within such narrow confines? Why was the link between people so fragile?

I already felt a little uneasy when I was talking to her on the phone. I had been going on and on about my discoveries, then I noticed the iciness coming from the other end. When I arrived at the coffee shop, she was already there. She had on a greyish-blue woollen sweater, and was leaning against the brown plaster wall. She stirred her drink slowly. Her hair draped over her face again. It was still a soft and peaceful face, but the sun was shut out. I told her the story again from the very beginning. She listened quietly. Sometimes she raised her head, and then continued to stir the coffee, which had long gone cold. When she talked about her aunt, she rested her chin on her hands, and her voice became cold and distant, as if that was already consigned to the past. The air extractor above me rumbled, I gathered my spirit.

'His poems are really great!'

I quickly drew out from my pocket that poem of his which I had copied down and handed it to her. She read it for a long time, put it on the table, and said lightly, 'It's great, but there are parts I can't quite understand.'

I wanted to tell her my views, but her indifferent expression choked my words. She was gazing at a poster on the pillar.

'You want to go and see the German puppet show?'

'No, not really. It's so cold.'

It started to rain when we left.

I felt defeated. Two people had failed to meet due to some time lag, and could not be together. This could well be all my fault. I had messed up everything and now she had withdrawn into her own web. There was nothing I could do to save the situation. I was a man who didn't know what to do with love. I supposed I could only look for a safe haven somewhere else. But what could the poet give me? Throw me into even greater confusion probably.

Why was it that everything always came to a deadlock at a certain stage?

Time passed; nothing happened. I kept waiting. For a long time, there was no news about either of them. Perhaps everything had simply vanished. I spent my days waiting.

After several months, I got hold of a diary.

The diary was quite thick. It belonged originally to my friend's uncle, a book-seller of pirated editions. He passed away not so long ago, and his family gave my friend all his books and manuscripts. My friend sold most of the books, keeping just a few for reprint, and the manuscripts were laid aside. I was in his house and happened to be leafing through the diary when suddenly I saw his poems. Without thinking twice, I asked my friend to let me have it.

The whole diary was filled with poems. Beside his poems, there were the works of many other poets—good ones, bad ones. About twenty pages were scribbled with his poems. Not many, but good enough for me.

Having got hold of the diary, I read and re-read his poems at one sitting, not stopping until dawn arrived. It was early summer now, and a few stars were glittering in the clear sky. I caught a whiff of something, like someone cooking wheat. In the car-park behind the house, the sparse shadows of trees swayed visibly. It was very tranquil. Occasionally, some wandering cats ran by and rattled the gate, then all was quiet again. I felt a wave of uneasiness rising in me. Was that because of her? But still, I felt happy.

I read his poems again, and once again. Then, I closed the diary and sank into deep thoughts. His poems could be divided into three main categories. Poems in the first group were about simple feelings and ordinary things—the rising sun, the rain, the rocks, some plums, autumn tinted with the colour of palm trees. Poems in the second group dealt with streets, cities, houses, and buildings. The last group was purely about objects. There was some truth in what the critics said about him, but they had all taken the part for the whole—they had simply seized one aspect of his attitude towards life, imposed on it their own attitudes or beliefs, and then claimed that this picture of him was a full portrait. My understanding of him was no more complete than theirs, having read so few of his poems. Still, I had the feeling that he was more interested in the simple things of everyday life than in abstract concepts. He loved the seasons; he loved salt, bread with a sweet taste, coffee, sleep, fresh air, friendship, and trees; he loved what you could see and touch. If some of his poems were charming, that was not because of his choice of subject matter but because the way he presented to us this ordinary world was extraordinary and charming. He let us see that our monotonous everyday life could also be charming, let us feel that there is poetry in even the most mundane things.

He rarely wrote about himself. He always wrote about objects and events in the outside world, as well as the relationship between the two. That was why some described his poems as 'objective'. He seldom wrote about sad things either, or chanted slogans. He planned everything he wrote with meticulous care. Yet, beneath the apparent detachment and behind the objects and events he described, one could feel the turbulent flow of his emotions, his warmth and concern for people. In his poem 'Window', he wrote about a man sitting alone in a house and then hearing a blind fortune-teller walking past his window, the tap of the fortune-teller's walking stick resounding in the desolate darkness of the night. The poem was written in a plain style, but its impact was strong. We could feel the darkness outside the paper window, the blind man groping and shivering in the cold. We could hear, in the clang of the fortune-teller's gong, an ominous note presaging the fate of man.

His poems about streets and objects were also not purely descriptive. The various shapes, colours, and arrangements were all richly suggestive in meaning. One was about a big red oil tanker parked right at the edge of a flight of stone stairs. It was a very powerful poem, heavy with a sense of impending thunderstorm, of danger and disaster. It was amazingly close to a prophecy. His most recent poems were mostly descriptions of things broken or discarded—cracks in the walls, plaster flaking off the ceiling, crushed earthen jars, abandoned wooden carts, cement floors, cold glints on broken copper knots, wood fragments wrinkled or gnarled, and worn-out bamboo baskets—as well as hanging objects like strings, hangers, timber articles, coat-hangers, deer carcasses. The threat of death was palpable, but there was also an unyielding spirit, a stubborn refusal to give in.

And that explained all.

When I finished reading, it was already about six in the morning. I rang her at once. She was probably still in bed, but it didn't matter. Surely she would be glad to hear this news, and then everything would be different.

The phone rang for a long time before I heard her sleepy voice. I had really woken her up. I told her my discoveries at once, then hurried out to wait for her in the park opposite her house.

The park was still in cool shadows. An old newspaper was swept by the wind to the middle of the lawn, then swept away again. Under the yellow lamp light, I saw dewdrops glistening faintly on blades of grass.

Then, she came up to me slowly, a figure drifting through the mist. In the dim morning light, she looked even more like an illusion. I waited for her to sit down on a bench, then gave her the diary. She took it without a word, the expression on her face like a kind of sorrow at dawn. She put the diary on her knees, glanced at the cover, then turned to the pages I had marked with narrow strips of paper, and read each page carefully. Sometimes, she turned back the pages and read again. Her head lowered, her hair clinging to her face, I could only see the silhouette of her forehead and nose. In the gentle breeze, under the yellow light, I could feel a drowsy tenderness. Then, she closed the diary and raised her head.

'What do you think?' I asked.

She looked a little confused, her head tilted to one side. The lights in the park began to go out, the sun had not yet risen. The hair on her forehead was streaming back in the wind. How pale she looked!

'I like several of them, like "Plaster on the Wall" and "Rock", I think they are great. But many of the rest I don't much care for. Why did he write so many poems about things shattered and damaged? Decay and disintegration terrify me. Once started, there seems no stopping the process, the sinking will continue, on and on.' Her head bowed even lower. I saw her feet gently rubbing the sand on the ground.

'It won't be like that,' I said in a low voice.

Then, silence fell on us, heavily, steadily, like a grey net over our heads. The sun rose gradually, but I was overcome with despair. She had withdrawn completely into her self now. When she had reached out to me earlier on, I did not have the courage to take the chance, I had hesitated. And now, the only remaining link between us was gone. She was no longer interested in him. She would feel we had nothing in common anymore, and there was nothing much we could talk about. I, too, was a sinking person: what could I give her anyway? She was left with her own silence.

Then she stood up.

It was still quite dark. I offered to take her home. She didn't turn back and just waved her hand perfunctorily. In silence, she slowly disappeared into the gloomy mist. Occasionally, the headlight of a passing car would mark her out in clear relief. And then, the shadows returned.

I felt icily cold. Would everything vanish just like that? I was the sort of man who didn't know how to handle my feelings, didn't know how to manage things.

Back home, I locked myself in my room for days. Full of frustration, I read his poems again and again. Now I had nothing but him. But could I, like him, rise from loneliness, above all that had been lost or destroyed, and continue to grow? Light was streaming in through the windows, the glass top of my desk basking in the warmth of the sun. I could smell in the wind the fragrance of trees from afar. Anything was possible, I thought. I decided to visit him again, he was now my only comfort.

When I reached his house, it was past ten. The trees in the sun were glittering white and silver. The lingering morning mist made his house seem much more pleasant, and his back less crooked. I called him, then sat on a pile of planks by the wall. The fresh scent of newly felled logs filled the air inside the house. Why had I never noticed it before? Next to the entrance, there lay some long twigs overgrown with green leaves—they were not there last time. The skylight was still closed, I went and opened it. The strong summer sunlight poured down in a cascade, waking the dust in the house and dispersing them hastily in the air.

Then, I began to recite my poems. In the sawdust and sunlight, I felt much more tranquil. I had no more reservations, no more fear, no more sorrow, and no more expectations. I recited slowly and smoothly, beginning from my first short poems. I was not a great poet, and had written many shoddy pieces. But I wanted him to know me, everything about me—all my uncertainties, fears, stupid mistakes, happiness, as well as my recent sufferings. I, too, was a simple and taciturn person, so I could only rely on my poems. He would understand me. I was not looking for any response, but I knew he was listening. Was he really? It didn't matter. I heard the hoarse and creaking sound that came from his saw. The aroma of the newly felled logs caressed my face, I felt the dazzling sunlight and the beating of my heart. Wisps of summer mist rose in gentle twirls into the sky, drifting past his loose coat and rippling over his face. The wind stirred the new leaves on the ground; the crickets chirped. We, too, seemed part of the summer days.

Then darkness fell slowly.

Thereafter, I spent many Sundays there. I recited all my favourite poems to him, and told him why I liked them. Snatches of my memories; something from my imagination; some possible meanings. I had never talked so much and probably never would again. But I had never felt more at ease.

Now and then, we would fall silent, and listen to the wind sweeping through the trees and heading straight to the flood-land stretching for miles behind the house. In the calm autumn days, there was sometimes just the continuous sound of sawing and our own breathing. Sometimes as the crimson evening light of late autumn streamed in through the skylight, we would watch the sawdust dancing in the air. Sometimes, we just watched the cloudless sky, or the twittering birds in the distance. And in these peaceful, tranquil afternoons, I felt as if I had been fully compensated—for everything that I had lost through fear and hesitation, and everything that I had failed to obtain because of my own inadequacies.

And in all these days, he still remained silent. The wind and rain came in and out through the narrow entrance. He kept his head lowered and went on working, the creaking of his saw echoing in the room. But, for all his habitual movements and silence, I could detect some slight changes.

On fine days, when the sun no longer dazzled the eyes, he would raise his head, look at the skylight and sway weakly for a good while before stopping. When the wind smoothed out his hair over his shoulders, and the cold sunlight fell on him, I could see a face glowing with a light tan.

Many a time when I recited to him my poem about shabby streets, he would bend down, pick up the saw, rest it in the slit of a log half-sawed, and brush the handle of the saw lightly. Then watching it quiver, he would sigh as if he was humming a harmony. And when I finished, he would carry on with his work quietly.

I noticed too that he no longer just ate the leaves on the trees, and he spent more time outdoors felling trees. When the wind and rain leaked from the skylight, he began to take shelter in the corner of the walls.

All these signs—so consistent and yet so ambiguous, perhaps even meaningless—could not but shook me. I wrote a long poem.

It was a poem about him, about his loss, his obsession with wood, his perseverance, the pose he struck with his movements, his silence, his despair in decrepitude, and also his gradual opening up.

I spent hours on this poem, all at one sitting. I was exhausted when I took it to read to him. I sat on the floor leaning against a big log lying horizontally on the ground and recited the poem quietly. The sun rose. I felt a warm current flowing gently in my body. To my surprise, he was listening carefully, a newly sawn piece of wood clasped under his arm, his head tilted slightly to one side, so rapt he let the wind drape his long brownish hair over his face. Outside the faint sound of branches dropping to the ground could now and then be heard, and the air was rich with the scent of bamboo flowers. I was breathing lightly. Then, I saw him raising his head slowly and looking fully at me. His eyes were the boundless colour of wood. I felt a little stunned. This was the first time he had looked at me in all those days. The sunlight was trickling through his hair and over his clothes, highlighting the edges of his hair and clothes in gold. Amidst the dim surroundings, he looked even less real. I bit my lower lip lightly, and watched him sitting down slowly, weightlessly. The sun had risen even higher, its rays pouring in through the skylight and splashing all around us, engulfing us in the white light of the rising dust.

Then, I saw him handing his saw slowly to me.

The air was still full of the shadows of dust. All of a sudden, I felt a strong gust of wind sweeping in from outside. I shivered, I caught in the wind the strong stinking smell of wood and the damp gathered in the shade. The swirling sawdust choked me, I wanted to roll up my collar. I felt a chill running through my limbs. The sun was still shining, I heard the sound of my body condensing into ice. I froze.

1975
Chinese original published in Ng Hui Bun: *A Collection of Short Stories by Ng Hui Bun*, Taiwan: Dong Dai Publishing Company Ltd., 1987.

15

A Bitter Experience

By **XIAO SI**

Translated by Jane C. C. Lai

Xiao Si is one of the first Hong Kong writers to explore the question of identity in their works.

The day of the Final between the Chinese and the American volleyball team brought much excitement to the people of Hong Kong. The sentiments had nothing to do with politics, but naturally, and without our realizing it, they became linked with nation and race. With a contest like this, the Chinese would naturally take the side of the Chinese team. Yes, naturally. No need to think twice. A happy position to be in.

But I remember a very bitter experience. Even after eight years, whenever I think about it, the bitter taste grows stronger.

On the evening of 30 July 1977, the International Youth Football Championship Final was played in the Workers' Stadium in Beijing: a match between the Hong Kong team and the China Youth team.

The tour that I had joined happened to be passing through Beijing, and the tour guide had very kindly taken the trouble to arrange for admission tickets for our group of Hong Kong tourists to watch the match. As that was an extra item on the itinerary, a chance to see the massive Workers' Stadium and to watch the match, we were quite thrilled.

The Hong Kong team came on the field, and we applauded and cheered. The Chinese team came on the field, and we applauded and cheered. The match began. It was a very even match.

Suddenly we realized that something strange was happening to our tour group: whenever the Hong Kong team went on the attack or got near the goal, we applauded and cheered. In a vast stadium with tens of thousands of spectators, our small group of twenty or so people stood out oddly. Before the match began, I had thought that since both the Hong Kong and the Chinese teams were 'us', it did not matter who won and who lost, and I would watch the game dispassionately and with equanimity.

But as soon as the match started, feelings got out of control and were nowhere as calm as I had thought. Objectivity, detachment, and equanimity just vanished. There was no thinking, only spontaneous response. Caught up in the fierce contest, I became totally involved, I *wanted* the Hong Kong team to win, and their every move in attack and defence gripped me in suspense.

Hong Kong lost two to one. I am sure many people have forgotten about this match, but I cannot.

It was not just the Hong Kong team that lost that day. I lost too. A fact was revealed all too clearly: without my realizing it, I had become a Hongkonger through and through.

30 August 1984
Chinese original published in Xiao Si: *Leaving is not an Option*, Hong Kong: Wah Hon Publishing Company, 1985.

Summer Without Words

By **YAN CHUNGOU**
Translated by Janice Wickeri

*A subdued portrayal of how the June Fourth Incident of 1989 affected
the lives of several people in Hong Kong.*

1

Everyone applauded as the plane took off.

Xinyu settled himself in gingerly. Beside him two girls sat
shoulder to shoulder, crying. A moment ago, Public Security had
taken three people from the cabin. The atmosphere was so tense
it seemed about to explode; expressions were frozen on faces, no
one knew what would happen next.

Outside the aircraft it was pitch dark. The vast expanse of
ground swept by beneath the wings, with scattered lights like
stars unreconciled to concealing themselves at morning's light.

The girl from the Export Bureau who'd been assigned to
accompany him had a deep dimple. She held a glass of red wine,
fingers slightly curved, and the moment she took a sip, she closed
her eyes as if she was drunk. Charming.

2

There was nobody at home. In the middle of the night, an empty
house is like a shrivelled silkworm cocoon. Xinyu turned on all
the lights, inside and outside. From the sitting-room to the
bedroom and then from the bedroom to the sitting-room—the

whole 800 square feet—he walked back and forth without stopping.

It was neat, clean, almost elegant. The slightly dusty air, the muted colours, the unnerving silence. It could have been a scene from a novel by Matsumoto Seicho.

Menglan had left a note by the pillow: '. . . I've told you before, if you go up there on business at a time like this, I won't be here when you get back.'

She'd said this before, she'd said it and now she'd done it. The woman had style. Man and wife, they were birds in the same forest. Well, when the shot rang out, they took flight in opposite directions.

3

Xinyu spent two days calling around looking for Menglan. But it was just as he'd suspected, Menglan was nowhere to be found. He sat in his office. People passed below like a tide. Slogans and singing floated up from the depths. In a place like Hong Kong, Xinyu found the sounds weird, unreal, like a dream.

There'd never been a summer as noisy as this.

Yet the contract reposed securely in the safe.

All the difficulties had been overcome in a single night. Sourcing, packaging, shipping, export licence, everything went without a hitch.

Deputy Section Head Duan had been all smiles at the banquet he hosted for Xinyu's entertainment in a small restaurant well away from Tiananmen. The red wine, the delicate Yangzhou food, the tender fingers like orchid petals, the quivering dimple.

'We don't care about politics, business is business.' Deputy Section Head Duan's smile was more sincere than ever.

The deal had become stalled while Hongming was handling it. That he should have been able to pull it off so easily was really just a matter of luck, of everything falling into place at the right time.

And yet, in less than six months, he'd lost his best friend, he'd lost his wife. The times were really out of joint. Loneliness is: when you're surrounded by peace and quiet, but your heart has gone missing.

4

Thinking of Hongming, some corner of his heart began, faintly, to ache.

He'd seen him last year, in that house of his that was like a garbage dump—a piece of bread growing green fur on the table, the TV smashed and sporting a big hole like an open wound.

He wondered where the man peed, the whole place smelled of urine.

A half-bowl of ashes had been dumped over the sofa.

He talked until he was blue in the face; the only thing he hadn't done was get down on his hands and knees to beg, but Hongming stuck his ground and wouldn't come home with him.

'You're you and I'm me. What I like you don't like; what you like makes me sick!' Hongming was adamant.

'But before, didn't you want to do business too, didn't you want to make money?'

'That was then and this is now.'

5

The TV stations covered the demonstrations. Xinyu made a cup of coffee, put his feet up on the coffee table, and watched it by himself. A young girl, her face tear-streaked. Pure white folded-paper flowers. Horizontal banners of black cloth. Old folks shouting slogans. Fathers carrying children on their shoulders. A stream of people like an endless black dragon.

With the sound of the television turned down low, it looked like odd people doing inexplicable things in a far-off place.

Menglan would be there among the ranks. Xinyu suddenly felt at a loss. All these years, and he'd never really understood his wife.

What was wrong with being in business? Where there was business, the doors were open. If the doors were not closed, there was a ray of light.

Who liked having to bribe officials? Who didn't want a world of peace and tranquillity? But there were ulcers growing on the nation's back, if you excised them all at once, it would die. It was better not to kill the patient with the cure, safer to release the pus gradually.

The camera suddenly focused on a man holding up a sign. He was standing by the railing at the roadside, his long hair fluttering against the sky, his shirt was open over his chest, revealing the thin ridges of his ribs.

Xinyu recognized him—it was Hongming, though he had shaved and washed.

6

Menglan asked him once, 'When you go up there on business, do you have to suck up to the officials?'

'Of course! How can you ask such a naive question?'

Menglan, coldly: 'You people are like poisonous fungus. Wherever business reaches, the government is corrupted!'

Xinyu answered sarcastically, 'Your food, your housing, everything you use is earned by the sweat and tears of this poisonous fungus!'

The next day Menglan went out to look for a job and from then on, she kept to her own space: she slept on the sofa, ate fast food, and even took her laundry out. One month, two months: she didn't call him to come to her, putting him in a terrible fix. All he could do was throw up his hands in surrender.

When he said that from then on all his business would be straight, she was the only one he was fooling.

She didn't have many talents, but she dared to act.

7

The day Hongming handed Xinyu his resignation, Menglan was there.

The harbour was obscured by spring fog, the horns sounded like the bellowing of old cows.

Hongming set up his own company and took nearly half the customers with him. His gaze wavered—after all they'd been good friends for years. After all, it was Xinyu who brought him into the company.

Arms crossed over her chest, Menglan walked back and forth beside them.

Xinyu leant over the back of the chair and gave a tired, bitter smile. He should have seen it coming. Here, being the boss was the biggest temptation.

'Let's hope things'll work out for you; if not, come back and give me a hand,' he'd said politely to Hongming.

Menglan walked over to them and smiled, 'From now on the two of you are business rivals. No point playing polite. Let's go and get some dim sum.'

Hongming got slowly to his feet as though he'd put down a big burden. His face was pale.

8

Xinyu was still looking everywhere for his wife. A man who goes all over enquiring as to the whereabouts of his wife certainly cuts a sorry figure.

She hadn't had a breakdown, hadn't run off with anyone else. No, his wife had left home because of June Fourth. Put baldly like that, no one would believe it.

At the beginning of that year, they had forced Hongming to come home to live. A single man on his own like that, his business failed, his spirit crushed, all that was left was to let himself go to ruin. Xinyu couldn't bear to let that happen.

Menglan said if Hongming had found a suitable woman to marry sooner, things would have been all right. A man who does battle outside all day needs a home to come back to. There at least he'll have a place to lick his wounds and rest.

Hongming meant to put up a fight. He flicked his cigarette ash on the sofa, peed with the bathroom door open, picked his nose and rubbed his feet in front of guests, got up in the middle of the night to sing loudly in the sitting room.

Menglan put up with him without batting an eye. And although she complained behind his back, when she spoke of his former intelligence and capability, his good looks and dash, she could only sigh.

Later, Hongming left, and there was no further word of him.

Later still, Menglan too disappeared.

9

While he was in Beijing, he had only been to the Square once.

It was at dusk. A cavalcade of motorcycles roared past honking. The western sky was a mass of dark red cloud that resembled a slowly coagulating sea of iron.

It was such a mournful red one felt a presentiment that the movement would come to grief. On the Square there was singing and dancing, cries rose and fell from hawkers' stalls. People were lost in their revelry and knew nothing of the nearness of death.

He was suddenly reminded of 1966 in Beijing, of being reviewed by Mao Zedong in Tiananmen. With the enveloping night, the rostrum on Tiananmen had been a swath of white light, east to west and back again; there was no way to tell which one was Mao Zedong.

Now Mao was revered by the peasants as Mao the great god and his image hung up to exorcise evil and ward off calamity.

He almost couldn't get through the passageway because the ground was covered with people lying every which way. It was an exhausted, benumbed, apathetic crowd, like wounded soldiers hanging on, waiting.

Life, death, and fortune struggled there, the great gamble of the whole people. You couldn't tell whether it was the people playing with politics or the politicians playing with the people. A smell like rotting corpses in the passageway nearly choked him.

10

Xinyu waited for Menglan to come home.

He simply waited, not so worried that he forgot to eat or drink.

The Chinese people had suffered a disaster, and there was trouble in his family too.

In the lonely nights he missed this obstinate woman who had, in her own inimitable way, given expression to the summer's sudden fervour.

In the beginning she had been an almost too easy catch, there had been almost no setbacks—suddenly they were husband and wife. Things that are easy to come by are also easy to lose. It's the same in business: if things are too easy, you get a funny feeling about it.

In three days, the goods would arrive in Shenzhen. With the profit from this deal, he would be secure for six months. If he hadn't seized the chance others had abandoned, if not for the fact that all the business people had gone—how could everything have been so simple?

Women's hearts are like needles in a haystack. Menglan too was gentle as a kitten one minute and fierce as a tiger the next. He couldn't figure her out.

He thought of that girl in the Export Bureau in Beijing, and her deep eyes that seemed to harbour endless words. The tiny quivering dimple so pretty it made your heart turn over.

All the trouble in the world began with men, and men's troubles began with women.

11

It was at the memorial set up for the public to pay their last respects to the dead that he finally saw Hongming.

It was meltingly hot. The road was filled with crowds dressed in mourning; faces set, people walked towards the altar. Hongming was taking charge of things. People entered in groups of three to five and formed a line, after which they would make a respectful bow under his direction. His voice was hoarse.

Hongming was unsurprised to see him. 'You've come too.'

Xinyu nodded, 'I've come to have a look.'

'A look?' Hongming smiled sorrowfully, 'Look then.'

'All this time you haven't seen Menglan?'

'No. Isn't she at home?'

'She left long ago, she's in the democracy movement too.'

Hongming understood then and smiled broadly, 'A million people in the city are involved, it won't be easy to find her.'

It was too hot, Hongming's long locks stuck damply to his face, when he turned, a strand stuck in the corner of his mouth. He looked like the hero in a play, determined to fight on to the end.

12

Xinyu looked up as he stood beside the containers. The sun struck his eyes like a lance and raked his skull like a jolt of electricity.

Three full containers of goods, none of which tallied with the specifications—carton upon carton, like stacks of coffins filled with corpses.

He made three long-distance phone calls, but couldn't locate Deputy Section Head Duan. His urgent faxes sank like stones.

There were still five days to go on his contract with the overseas firm. The containers couldn't stay parked on this track forever, but warehousing them meant a big outlay in rent. The contract with Songxiang had to be signed tomorrow and Tuesday they had to negotiate the transaction on galvanized iron sheeting. Menglan was nowhere to be found; Hongming was immersed in the democracy movement; people were being arrested all over Beijing; Hong Kong was in a state of constant anxiety.

Loneliness is: when you look up without seeing a familiar face, your heart a speck of floating dust.

Deputy Section Head Duan had got away with a considerable commission, while he, Xinyu, might have to forfeit his wife and sustain heavy losses over the failure of the deal.

13

It was raining in Beijing. As the car travelled down Chang'an Avenue the atmosphere was desolate, ominous. Along the road were armed soldiers in rain gear, standing rigid in the foggy drizzle like pillars of stone. The distant Square was a vista of disorder.

The muscles in the driver's face were set. When he turned to glance at the Square, the corners of his mouth twitched.

Suddenly in his ear, a tide of voices came rushing toward him. Shouts, laughter, cries of anger, of pain, broke over him in waves.

All at once he was seized with fear—he was passing through history here—bloody, unbearable, history—irrevocable.

History was all at once very near. He was walking in a crevice of history, and history flowed over his heart.

14

Deputy Section Head Duan was at home. He lived in a compound, with a row of flower pots in front of the steps. The rain had let up and Deputy Section Head Duan was busy with a pot of orchids.

He straightened up, clapped his hands to get the dirt off, and brought over a chair without a word, gesturing to Xinyu to sit down.

He handed Xinyu a cigarette, then sighed softly as he slowly made tea.

'I've done all I can.' He shook his head. 'Everything's all screwed up now, nobody knows what will happen tomorrow. I don't have much, a fridge, a 14-inch colour TV, my eighty-seven-year-old mother. . . .'

A young girl came silently towards them, leant against Duan and put her arms gently round his neck, then she turned her head and looked Xinyu up and down with her deep eyes.

Xinyu asked, 'Is this your daughter?'

Deputy Section Head Duan laughed, his expression a mixture of emotions. 'No, my granddaughter.'

Xinyu stood up. 'I heard a lot of people died in the Square?'

Deputy Section Head Duan shook his head. 'I didn't see it. One can't make rash statements about things one hasn't seen.'

Xinyu smiled and left in silence.

'It's raining; I'll give you an umbrella.' Duan came after him.

But Xinyu was already far off.

The rain increased. A young man ran past him, panic on his face.

15

They'd run into Hongming again last winter.

That day a cold front was moving south. Xinyu and Menglan were passing by an MTR station, when not far from the entrance, they saw Hongming huddled by the front door of a bank, wrapped in a blanket.

The weather was dark and chill, and the cold bored into the soles of their feet. At the mouth of the alley, puffs of steam rose under the lights of the open-air food stall. They pulled themselves together and rushed towards Hongming.

All of a sudden a girl burst across their path. She had something in her hand and she ran towards Hongming.

They stopped where they were and watched the girl hold out a styrofoam lunch box to Hongming. The two of them began to eat, taking mouthfuls in turn.

Standing in the shadow of the tree, Xinyu gently held Menglan back. As they watched Hongming from a distance, something tugged at his heart. Here was a bum, without a thing to his name, yet he had a woman to love and care for him, to live with him on a bowl of noodles a day.

He remembered the past—Hongming coming into the office in his well-pressed suit, the girls, radiant as spring, casting loving glances at him from eyes brimful of tender feelings.

As long as your life is one you've chosen, it's a good one.

16

That evening Xinyu was in a hotel. Outside the window a driving silent rain. Lightning flashed in the distance. The city was laden with grief and anxiety.

'Tears pour down like torrential rain'—a line of poetry from Mao Zedong.

Xinyu's heart had never felt so heavy.

Where would Menglan be on a night like this?

The doorbell rang and Xinyu went to answer it. A girl stood outside, the hint of a dimple on her cheek.

Her entwined fingers twisted uneasily, she eyed him nervously, several times she was on the verge of speaking, then stopped.

Her younger brother had been killed on Chang'an Avenue, her father had fled, she despaired of China.

'I can't stay here any longer, can you help me? I'll go anywhere. . . . Lend me some money, I'll go to Australia, or to Argentina, I'll definitely pay you back. I'm a woman of my word. . . . I'll do anything for you, what do you want me to do? Do you . . . do you want me to . . . stay here?'

She did her utmost to be enticing, giving a very forced smile, drawing herself up and slowly undoing the buttons of her blouse.

Xinyu opened the door and saw her out. He couldn't promise her anything. There were tears in her eyes as she said in a low voice, 'Do you despise me?'

He was taken aback and muttered, 'It's . . . it's me I despise.'

17

He was back in Hong Kong, but there was still no one at home. A failure returning to his failed home.

The year they got married, Hongming was one of the party. When the group photos were taken, he hid in a corner of the garden smoking. When asked why he was in a bad mood, he said: 'I envy you'.

163

The two men had always been close friends; who could say they hadn't always been enemies as well?

Even if they were enemies, they respected each other.

Business had suffered a lot, Xinyu ran around night and day. Making money isn't everything, but if that's the path you've chosen, then you have to follow where it leads.

One day on the street Xinyu came across a group of demonstrators. He began following along behind them. They were mostly young people. They walked along with solemn expressions. They didn't shout slogans, they didn't have any placards, they just walked silently along. Suddenly it dawned on Xinyu that you can't always do things perfunctorily, even if it's just walking along.

And so he walked behind them for a long, long time, until they entered Victoria Park. There was a gathering in the Park, a month had already gone by since June Fourth.

It was nice and sunny. In the pavilion, there were people making fervent and rousing speeches. Along the paths was an exhibition of photographs and other materials. There were people handing out flyers; there were people donating money. He sat on a small rise, not really listening and not feeling particularly touched or anything. He just sat there and felt that he was taking part in something.

A woman passed by in the distance walking towards the meeting. The shadows of the leaves on the trees slid slowly over her back. All of a sudden Xinyu had the feeling that this woman had a very familiar back. He took a good look, it almost looked like Menglan.

He jumped up and headed down the hill, his heart overflowing with a wild joy. He pursued her into the meeting ground, searching everywhere, but found no trace of her. Anxiety was rising in him when he suddenly saw a woman going up on to the platform. He looked more closely. It was indeed Menglan.

She'd cut her hair and looked radiant and heroic. He didn't take in whatever it was she was saying, he just kept thinking how attractive she was.

He waited for her beside the platform and they exchanged a few words standing there. She was happy to see him taking part, but she wouldn't come home for the time being. She said she was living at a friend's and working in a mass organization. She had a salary, she was doing all right.

Xinyu didn't want to press her, he just urged her to take care of herself, and then they parted.

That evening Menglan phoned and they talked for a long time and he felt it was like it used to be when they were dating, he knew that at the other end of the phone was a woman who was a kindred spirit, that they cared for each other. He would think of her as he fell asleep.

18

The summer passed very slowly. When he came home from work, Xinyu would turn on the air-con and slump on the sofa watching TV. That was when something called nonsense patter started to become popular. Xinyu laughed along, laughed till he felt quite lonely. Democracy, after all, was just a burst of bright colour in a far-off painting.

Often Menglan would phone. She was slowly growing depressed. She said she was tired and what's more she didn't know where things were leading even if she did carry on. Sometimes as she was talking there would be tears on that end of the line; after hanging up Xinyu would be sunk in melancholy for a long time.

Xinyu got in touch with the girl from the Export Bureau and agreed to help her apply for study overseas.

He came to an understanding within himself beforehand that he would never expect any sort of compensation from her. It wasn't because she had such a charming dimple, but because her little brother had died on Chang'an Avenue.

Business gradually settled down. This summer had been a difficult one, both for the Chinese people and for himself.

One day on TV he saw Hongming again. His hair was as long as ever, a beard covered his face. He and his companions were in the act of storming the police barricade to get into some cocktail party or other. He was knocked down in the scuffle and his mouth bled.

Xinyu shook his head in disapproval, thinking to himself that Hongming had never been the type to get all worked up—everyone had changed over the course of this summer.

Though everyone had the same deep feelings for the nation and the people, in the end individuals had their own ways of dealing with things.

One night—it was already quite late—Xinyu suddenly heard the doorbell. When he opened the door, it was Menglan.

She sat on the sofa for a long time without speaking. Xinyu poured her a glass of water. As she drank, she started to cry. She said people had forgotten everything. The association was on the verge of disbanding. They had been handing out flyers on the street corner, but a lot of people were unwilling even to take one.

Xinyu took her gently into his arms, he didn't know what to say to her.

Menglan said to herself, 'Is this how it ends then? Is this all there is to it?'

He patted her shoulder softly: 'It's all right. Look, I've bought the Hami melons you like.'

19

China returned to normal. The earth had quaked, a lot of energy had been released, and then the land settled down and was quiet again.

On the evening of the anniversary of June Fourth, they attended the candlelit vigil. The flames were like a red wave. People had not forgotten.

They ran into Hongming outside the vigil. They didn't talk very much. He gave them a candle and a paper cup and showed them the way in.

It began to rain hard. Xinyu started to open his umbrella, but Menglan stopped him.

Looking at the people all standing in the rain that fell about them like tears, Xinyu no longer felt lonely.

When they got home that night, they saw scenes of the vigil on TV. The brilliant sea of red candlelight dazzled the eye. Menglan sighed: 'How beautiful!'

The world is a foul place, there is no place for true beauty. Maybe that's just the way things are.

Xinyu was holding the hairdryer, helping Menglan blow-dry her rain-wet hair. His wife's shiny hair was as soft as silk to his touch.

Chinese original published in Yan Chungou: *Divine Retribution*, Hong Kong: Cosmos Books Ltd., 1992.

Time

By LIU YICHANG
Translated by Kwok Hong Lok

'At the back of Western minds is some idea of welfare, benevolent states, and equality. At the back of Hong Kong people's minds are ideas like famine, exploitation, and vicious competition,' one Western writer has observed. This story, which vividly captures the pace of life in Hong Kong, offers a different portrayal of what lies at the back of at least some Hongkongers' minds as they go about their everyday business of making a living.

It was an overcast and windy morning on the last day of the Chinese calendar. The wind was gusty when they left their apartment building. Shuk Fan, shivering with cold, decided to go back home to get a sweater. Tsz Ming looked at his watch—ten past nine. 'We're taking the ten o'clock hydrofoil,' he said. 'It's ten past nine already. If we miss it, we'll have to forget about our holiday.'

'The weather forecast on TV last night said a cold front would be reaching the South China coastal region in the New Year.'

'But it's ten past nine now,' Tsz Ming said. 'On other days, if we miss the ten o'clock hydrofoil, we can take the one at eleven. But it's New Year's Eve, the tickets are sold out. If we miss this one, we can't get to Macau for the holiday!'

'There's a strong northerly wind today and the temperature has dropped all of a sudden. It's safer to take an extra sweater. You just wait here. It won't take five minutes. We'll take a taxi to the ferry pier.'

Without waiting for Tsz Ming to say okay, Shuk Fan turned and ran towards the lift. By the time she was back with the woollen jacket in her hands, it was twenty past nine. They stood at the corner of the block trying to hail a taxi, but no taxi was in sight.

'We should've come out earlier.' Tsz Ming was a little anxious.

'Don't worry. We'll get to the pier in twenty minutes.'

No taxis came.

One mini-bus after another past them. Some were packed full and some had no passengers.

'Let's take a mini-bus.' Shuk Fan suggested.

'The mini-bus doesn't go to the waterfront. We'll have to walk all the way to the Hong Kong–Macau Ferry Pier after getting off. That'll take even more time.'

'What other choice is there when there's no taxi? We waste more time standing here waiting in vain. Let's take a mini-bus.'

A mini-bus arrived and stopped in front of them. Shuk Fan got on first; Tsz Ming could only follow.

'No need to worry. It's just half past nine. With a little luck, we'll get to the ferry pier at ten to ten. Mini-buses are as fast as taxis, though a bit of time will be lost with the passengers getting on and off.'

For all her reassurance, every time the mini-bus stopped at a red light, Tsz Ming would grumble—Shuk Fan shouldn't have insisted on having breakfast at home just to save a few dollars.

Shuk Fan ignored him.

When the mini-bus was in Causeway Bay, Tsz Ming started again. 'Getting that sweater wasted too much time!'

Shuk Fan acted as if she hadn't heard what Tsz Ming had said and turned to look out of the window. But Tsz Ming went on and on, 'It would be all right if wasn't a day like this. But losing one minute today may mean missing the hydrofoil.'

The mini-bus was now outside the entrance of the Hong Kong and Shanghai Bank building. Tsz Ming looked at his watch anxiously and said, 'We won't make it!'

'What time is it?' Shuk Fan asked.

'Nine forty.'

'We will. We've got another twenty minutes.'

'Traffic is heavy and there are too many traffic lights in Central. It's really a bit dicey. I think. . . .'

'Eh?'

'I think we should get off here.'

'Here? Why?' Shuk Fan was puzzled, 'You know very well it's a long walk to the Hong Kong–Macau Ferry Pier.'

'I don't mean we should walk.'

'What do you mean then?'

'We'll take a taxi.'

'A taxi?'

'Yes. Taxis are much faster than mini-buses. We'll be okay if we take a taxi.'

'But we may not be able to get one here. Wouldn't it be even worse then?'

The mini-bus started to move again. When it came to a tram stop, there was another red light. Tsz Ming was so anxious he kept looking at his watch. 'We'll miss the hydrofoil for sure,' he said.

Shuk Fan was worried too, but she did not show it. She did not say anything more.

The mini-bus passed the tram stop and turned into Ice House Street. There was a man boarding, and it stopped for another minute. On Queen's Road Central, the traffic was so heavy the entire street was jammed with vehicles, like a net full to the brim with caught fish.

'Oh dear!' Tsz Ming's voice trembled with anxiety. 'Let's get off here!'

'We can't. This is a prohibited area.'

'Hey, driver,' Tsz Ming yelled loudly, 'can we get off here?'

'No, this is a prohibited zone.' The driver replied. 'Wait till we get to On Lok Yuen.'

'But we're going to the Hong Kong–Macau Ferry Pier to take the ten o'clock hydrofoil. It's already nine forty-five. If this traffic jam goes on for a few more minutes, we'll miss the boat.'

Upon hearing Tsz Ming's words, the kind driver poked his head outside the window, looked left and right and, seeing no sign of a policeman, decided to risk a fine and opened the door for them. Tsz Ming immediately gave him a dollar and got off swiftly with Shuk Fan.

After getting off the mini-bus, they climbed over the railings on to the pavement. Then they started to run, their legs moving like rolling wheels. Shuk Fan could not tell where they were heading, all she could do was keep up with Tsz Ming.

At King's Theatre, Tsz Ming pointed at a taxi stand on the opposite side of the road and said, 'We'll cross over.'

To save time, they ignored the oncoming traffic and crossed the street at once, skirting their way around moving vehicles, stopping once on a traffic island and sprinting towards the taxi stand on the other side of the street. They were lucky the traffic was almost at a standstill and the cars were much slower than usual.

There were three taxis waiting.

It being morning, very few people would want to go to other places from Central. Tsz Ming and Shuk Fan did not have to queue. They opened the door of a taxi and jumped in.

'Where to?' asked the driver.

'Hong Kong–Macau Ferry Pier,' said Tsz Ming. 'We're in a hurry. We're catching the ten o'clock hydrofoil.'

The driver nodded and the taxi started moving. When it got to a junction, it stopped. There was traffic in front; there was traffic behind. They were stuck again. Tsz Ming was so desperate, beads of sweat began to form on his forehead.

'What's happening?' Tsz Ming asked.

The driver leaned his head out of the window to get a better view. He answered in a low voice, 'There's a car accident ahead.'

'What?' Tsz Ming was flabbergasted. 'A car accident?' He looked at his watch. 'Oh Christ! Nine fifty already. The hydrofoil leaves in ten minutes.'

'The way things look, you'll probably miss the hydrofoil. Take the one at eleven!' The driver suggested.

As though jabbed by a needle, Shuk Fan yelled in a shrill voice. 'Take the one at eleven? Impossible! It's New Year's Eve today, the tickets are all gone!'

Tsz Ming frowned, turned to Shuk Fan and said, 'What's the point of saying all that now?'

Reproach was clear in his voice. Normally, Shuk Fan would have been angry with him. Right now, however, she knew very well how Tsz Ming felt. She shared his mood.

Tsz Ming also leant his head out of the window to gauge the situation. Just ahead of them there was a cross-roads, a major point of intersection for traffic in Central. Right now, it was dense with vehicles of different shapes and sizes. 'What can we do?' Tsz Ming was shaking with worry and anxiety. 'We won't make it!'

'We'll get off and walk!' Shuk Fan said in a loud voice.

The driver couldn't agree more. He said, 'Yes, if you want to catch the ten o'clock hydrofoil. Walk fast and you might make it. The traffic being what it is, I think it's faster walking.'

Tsz Ming looked at his watch again and shook his head. 'Just eight more minutes. Even if we run, we can't get to the pier in time.'

At this very moment, the cars ahead began to move. Tsz Ming, on the verge of despair, suddenly saw a glimmer of hope.

'Looks like the traffic ahead is back to normal. This is the heart of Central, the police won't allow a car accident to hold up the traffic for too long. Now, we might just be able to make it!'

The taxi went into Connaught Road. Tsz Ming felt relieved and said to Shuk Fan, 'We'll make it.'

But things were not as simple as he thought, the taxi stopped again at Whitelaw's.

'What now?' Tsz Ming was all tensed up again.

'Traffic jam!' The driver said in an almost matter-of-fact voice.

'Traffic jam?' Tsz Ming uttered the words like an excitable child.

The driver explained: 'Connaught Road Central is like this almost every day, bumper to bumper for most of the morning.'

Just as Tsz Ming opened his mouth to talk, the cars in front moved. The taxi went forward ten yards, and stopped.

'What can we do?' He looked at his watch. 'Five minutes, and the hydrofoil will be gone!'

'You'd better get out and walk!' The driver suggested.

'No, we can't.' Shuk Fan said. 'There's still such a long way, how can we make it in five minutes?'

'Why didn't you come out earlier if you wanted to catch the hydrofoil?' The driver asked.

'No point talking about it now!' Tsz Ming was annoyed. And now the cars in the other lane started to move. Tsz Ming could not but burst out in complaint. 'We're in the wrong lane. If we were in the right lane, we might. . . .'

Before he finished, the cars in front moved again. Tsz Ming looked outside. The cars in the other lane were all stationary. He knew he shouldn't have complained, and shut up at once. The cars inched forward like snails. They stopped after about twenty yards.

'What should we do?' Shuk Fan asked. 'At this pace, it will take us another half an hour to get to the pier.'

'There's nothing to be done,' the driver said. 'Connaught Road Central is like this every morning. Traffic jams all the way through. Your best bet is to walk.'

'What do you think?' Shuk Fan asked Tsz Ming.

'If we get off now, we'd have to be world-class sprinters to get to the ferry pier in four minutes!' Tsz Ming almost yelled.

Shuk Fan didn't go on. She told herself this year she'd have to spend the New Year in Hong Kong again, they'd as good as thrown a few hundred dollars into the sea.

The cars moved again.

This time, they actually went a long way. The taxi did not have to stop until it reached the traffic lights at the Yaumatei Ferry Pier. Tsz Ming looked at his watch: nine fifty-eight.

'We've got two more minutes!' He shouted.

The driver did not say anything. He was waiting anxiously for the lights to change. There was a tense look on his face and he was waiting like an eager warrior about to go into battle. Shuk Fan, too, stared ahead wide-eyed, as if driven by a burning torch inside.

The lights turned from red to yellow. The driver sped ahead even though he knew it was illegal to go at such a high speed. He himself was not late for anything but a sense of responsibility told him he should get Tsz Ming and Shuk Fan to the ferry pier before ten o'clock.

When the taxi arrived at the Hong Kong–Macau Ferry Pier it was ten o'clock. Tsz Ming handed the fare to the taxi driver and dashed towards the Immigration checkpoint.

They were the last two passengers to go through Immigration for the ten o'clock hydrofoil. After passing through customs they raced to the boat. They got in just as it was about to set off. The hydrofoil was two minutes late departing.

Chinese original published in Liu Yichang: *Inside the Temple*, Hong Kong: You Shi Wenhua Shiye Gongsi, 1977.

If Things Could Only Be This Way

By **SHI RAN**

Translated by Roberta Raine

For over a decade, from the mid-1980s until recently, fear has been one of the prevailing moods of the people of Hong Kong. The now disgraced Chinese Communist Party leader, Zhao Ziyang, once asked the reporters of Hong Kong, 'What are you [Hong Kong people] afraid of?' This story gains an added dimension of significance when read against such a background.

The Gecko

I just happened to look up, not on my guard or anything, when I saw a gecko climbing the thin wall between the kitchen and the bathroom.

If my line of vision had not left the television screen, perhaps I wouldn't have seen it. But it was too late. A shudder suddenly passed over me like a wave. My body was bathed in a cold sweat, goosepimples covered me from head to foot, and I was overcome with fear. My scalp felt numb as I fixed my gaze on the gecko's unmoving stance. I have been terrified of geckos ever since I was a little girl, and that terror has not diminished one bit with the passing of time.

We lived in a timber house when I was young. The geckos that I remember from my childhood would appear in our home anywhere, anytime. That was one of the everyday fears I had to live with. They liked to climb up on to the beams between the rooms, and would sometimes stay put for hours in one corner. They rarely lost their balance and fell down, but every time I walked past the beam that they were crawling on, my heart would still thump wildly and I would quicken my pace. At night I would lie in bed watching one long, fat gecko as it crawled on the ceiling, and would wrap the quilt over my cold, shivering body. All I could do was cover my head with the quilt and cuddle up next to my little sister. In my childhood nightmares, gigantic pale-grey geckos would drop down from the ceiling and squash my defenceless body, and before I was able to scream I would wake up, terrified. Those nights were very long. I didn't want to wake my parents, so with wide eyes I would scan the blurred shadows of the four walls of my bedroom. Tense and anxious, my eyes would finally get so tired that I would drop off into a dazed sleep.

My memories of childhood come in fragments. The tracks left by those geckos inhabited the darkest corners of my memory, and after I grew up I tried hard not to remind myself of them. I used to say that if I could choose any period of time in my life to return to, I definitely would not choose childhood. Children make so few demands on life, but then their choices are also very limited. Childhood is a one-way track, a road down which we are dragged by time, pushed and pulled towards the future.

During the summer vacation of my fifth year in primary school my family moved into the city, into a newly built eight-storey *tong lau*—a kind of apartment building typical of Hong Kong at the time. Ever since then, a *tong lau* to me has always been a building with stairs, no elevator, and two flats on each floor. We lived on the seventh floor, and as a child running up and down the stairs was no problem. Many of my memories of life as a young woman in the late '60s and early '70s are of going up and down those flights of stairs, entering and leaving the building. So many things happened in those days, things related to this city and to my own life. I started to take moody walks, pondering and questioning life. The lights on the stairways were always too dim, which was why I never saw geckos or other insects there. But the geckos did not leave me along with my childhood. Wherever I lived, the places that they haunted most frequently were the kitchen and the bathroom.

The strongest gecko-related memory I have from my girlhood was the time when I came face to face with one in the bathroom. I had never before seen a gecko's eyes so close up. I was in our tiny bathroom and had half taken off my clothes. I was bending down when, to my horror, I saw the gecko, its flesh-coloured body not more than half an inch away from my nose, its evil-looking eyes flashing as it watched me. I felt so sick I screamed, then opened the bathroom door and fled. Everyone in my family knew I was absolutely terrified of geckos. Still, these creatures kept coming and going, and I could no more stop them than I could stop all the people and events that came into my life in the days that followed.

———

Later on I left Hong Kong. That was at the end of the 1970s, and when I left, I also said goodbye to my youth. The years are like a vase holding a rich variety of experience: the neck of the vase is long and narrow, and each time I reach down into it my hand can only grab hold of a few things. But time has taught me hope. When I left this city all I wanted was to live in a different place for a while, where I could experience another way of life.

I never imagined that living abroad 'for a while' would turn into more than ten years. The vase was still full of variety, and if I ever felt uneasy or scared it was never because of a gecko. For more than ten years I never once saw a gecko in my home. Now and then I would see a group of reptiles outside in the bushes. Close kin of the geckos, they were usually dark green in colour and had larger, uglier bodies than geckos. I would still flee in terror, but the appearance of these reptiles didn't create such negative imprints in my mind.

I didn't view the city where I lived as foreign territory. If you live somewhere for more than ten years, if you are sincere and participate in that community, that place becomes your home for that period of time. Throughout the 1980s I lived very far from my birthplace, in a city where I studied and worked and loved and made friends and spoke a language that was not my mother tongue. Thinking back, that phase of my life was also filled with achievements and disappointments. In the interstices of that time, I experienced doubts about life, hesitations and indecisions.

My friends who stayed in Hong Kong said that I missed an entire glorious decade. But just as different planets are home to different forms of life, each of which evolves at its own rate, so we all have our own path to follow. Living in a far-off land, I learnt to be grateful just knowing that the people I missed were living a good life. And I shared with them the marvels of this wonderful city by thinking of it fondly.

Every now and again I would come back here, to this place so full of gecko-memories. Even though I would stay for just a short time, still I could see and feel the changes which swept the city like running water. On the faces of some of my childhood friends I could see both worry and complacency—they were like fire and water, and yet they co-existed and accommodated one another. This is a society that offers people great material comfort, and my friends have learnt to demand an ever higher standard of living. But beyond that, beyond those material objects that could be held on to, I could sense a deep anxiety pervading the whole city, an anxiety my friends were unable to shake off, try as they might.

'This city,' they said. 'We can't stay here much longer.'

I felt like a lost child here. I returned to the streets that I thought were familiar, and yet I couldn't find the roads that existed in my memory, although now and then vague traces of my old life would stir up disturbing emotions lurking just beneath the surface of my mind. I seldom saw any geckos, and I thought I was no longer afraid of them.

———

Just as people were rushing to leave this city in droves, I returned.

And now there was a new term in Hong Kong: 'returnee', and that was what they called me. Oh well, they could call me what they liked. My past is part of my life, and in future it will still be so. There is no need for explanation in matters to do with an individual's choice. If you call a rose by any other name, that doesn't change its shape. The reasons that I left Hong Kong so many years ago were different from those of the people who are leaving today, and the reasons why I decided to return now are probably also different from those of other people who are returning.

When I chose to return, my friends and relatives in the city where I had lived for over ten years could not understand my decision. When I quit my job, my boss said that he was very sorry to see me go. If only I would stay, my career prospects would be so wonderful. That I already knew. For many years, while working in the same field I had moved from one company to another and the outcome was always the same: every year I got a promotion and a raise. All this gradually became the norm and there was no surprise to speak of. I wasn't even afraid of the tumultuous environment of office politics, where so many people stepped on others in order to get to the top. Because I knew how to play the game, no one could easily walk all over me, but I've always maintained that I would never do the same to others.

In nature there are many creatures that are always doing senseless things: fish that struggle to swim against the current to lay their eggs and then die, completely exhausted; birds that leave their familiar environment, even flying at night, to go to another place where they don't even know if the climate will be suitable for them or not; plants that like to stay facing the sun's rays so much that their branches and trunks become deformed and twisted. Despite all these strange phenomena, people still say that if water doesn't flow downhill, it is violating the laws of gravity.

———

The only thing I have in common with other people who have lived abroad and then returned is that sometimes, walking in the streets that have changed so much, I find myself trying to look for familiar traces. Actually, soon after my return I had stopped trying to search out the streets of my past. The city was still changing, and I too, was still changing. Sorrow at what was no more and shock at what had taken over would sometimes soar like birds and wheel back and forth in the sky of my fragile mind, but I would never think to drive them away: everything in life has its cause. Thus I learnt to adopt a calm and equanimous attitude, and would just watch them hover in the air, wings fluttering.

———

After I had been living in this apartment for six months, the gecko appeared without a sign of warning. When I was looking for an apartment and chose this one, what I liked best was its simple style and white walls. Before moving in I carefully swept it clean, and then sprayed insect repellent in every corner of every room, in every closet and every wardrobe. After I moved in I made sure to always keep it spick and span, and didn't once see an ant or a cockroach.

This gecko was an outsider—one who ran in by accident, not following its usual route.

His sudden arrival took me by surprise. The skinny little gecko was only as long as my little finger, and I only saw it stay on the wall for a few seconds. By the time my shocked body reacted, the gecko had already fled and was hiding behind the dark kitchen door.

How I wished I hadn't lifted my head—then perhaps I wouldn't have seen it. I sat weakly on the sofa, staring blankly at the gleaming white wall. From the television in the other corner of the living-room came the sound of people shouting and laughing, but that did not draw my gaze to the screen. My nerves were like a tightly drawn bow, ready to let fly but checked somehow.

I recalled once again a horrible childhood scene of some grown-ups killing a gecko: first they picked up wooden sticks and brooms to knock the gecko off the wall, then they grabbed any hard object they could find and beat the gecko, who was scrambling away for cover, until it lay on the floor in a pulpy mash. Blood and guts were indistinguishable, and its little tail, which had separated from its body, was still twitching. I hid in one corner, eyes half shut, my heart pounding wildly to the rhythm of the tail on the floor, my hands tightly covering my ears—grandma had told me that geckos' tails get revenge by digging into your ears in the middle of the night.

I've always been an independent person, and have never feared anyone, not even when I was travelling alone in a strange city and staying in a dark room by myself. But the thought of a little stray insect thrashing about inside my ear and scrambling for a way out is enough to drive me mad.

It had been a long time since I had had the experience of terror settling upon me for an entire evening and occupying my mind completely; I couldn't sit down, couldn't relax. The gecko hiding behind the kitchen door had turned into a shadow a thousand times bigger than its actual size, totally enveloping my living space. I reduced the number of my movements in the room to their absolute minimum, and purposely made loud noises to warn the gecko, who was possibly hiding in some corner, of my approach. When I had to go into the kitchen or the bathroom, I even acted like a thief. Before entering I turned on the lights and searched the ceiling and walls, and only then tiptoed in. After quickly finishing what I had to do, I escaped in terror.

Exhausted, I lay down on my bed, considering whether or not I wanted to close the door. The reality of the situation was pathetic: my fear of these horrid reptiles, I now realized, had not subsided with the passage of time, nor with changes in circumstances, and not even with the approach of an entirely new era; on the contrary, my defencelessness and vulnerability had exacerbated my fear, making it even more awesome and overpowering.

The next day I fled from my home like a refugee, and I didn't want to go back even after a whole day at work. My home used to be the place where I most enjoyed spending time, but with the appearance of the gecko, my daily routine was disrupted and I was reduced to a bundle of nerves. All day long I felt panicky, and when I thought about going home I just didn't want to. If I told anyone else that I didn't want to go home because there was one gecko in my flat, wouldn't they think that I was wildly exaggerating and laugh at me?

Finally I dragged my tired body home. As I opened the door I exaggerated every sound I made, and in a replay of the night before, I sneaked in like a thief, trembling with fear. This home that I had spent so much time and effort setting up, bit by bit, seemed to have been destroyed overnight because of my irreconcilable fear.

The Battlefield

The gecko wasn't there.

My mind, worn out by continual fear, started to become somewhat numb.

Maybe the gecko didn't care for the unfriendly atmosphere of my flat and had left?

By the time I got settled down in my study and started to work it was nearly midnight. Midnight passed. I was sitting beside the fax machine, watching it swallow up the paper as I sent documents one by one across the seas. Then, as the machine made its low, grumbling sound, I saw—with the shock of one being struck by lightning—that skinny little ghost-like gecko climbing up the wall beside the fax machine. It flashed its blinking, rotating eyes and looked at me.

All at once I leapt up out of my chair and retreated behind the door, barely able to stop my body from shaking. Perhaps it was this series of rapid movements that scared it, for in a flash the gecko had escaped behind the curtain.

I leant against the door and surveyed the tiny room. This was intolerable. I could not imagine myself able to bear sitting there and concentrating on my work, only to look up and see that ugly, flesh-coloured reptile arrogantly crawling past my line of vision. It was no longer a question of being intimidated by fear. What was at stake was my personal space, which I needed in order to think and to work, and I had to defend it. I retreated to the bathroom and picked up a can of insect spray from the corner. I pulled out the long thin nozzle and returned to the study.

My left hand shook as I grabbed hold of the curtain. The gecko was cowering behind the curtain in one corner, not moving. With a shout I half-closed my eyes and raised the spray in my right hand, pressing down as hard as I could with my forefinger. A puff of white smoke shot like an arrow on to the gecko's body. I didn't see blood splatter everywhere, but then geckos are cold-blooded animals. The sprays of white smoke came one after the other and the gecko still didn't move. I did not release my finger, but continued to press firmly on the nozzle as I attacked with the spray. Then it started to climb upward. I raised my right hand and kept the long, narrow nozzle about three inches from the gecko, going after it with the killer spray. Because this type of insect repellent has a long, thin nozzle attachment, one can take accurate aim, so it's impossible to miss. It's something no home should be without.

At long last, the gecko struggled up to the ceiling, and I stayed the hand holding the insect spray. If I tried to follow it upwards with my attack, the spray would only fall back down on to me, and I had no intention of joining the gecko in death. The terrified reptile was still running for its life, trying to reach the corner at the top of the door, hoping to make its escape from the room. But just as it was about to reach the door, it dropped to the floor with a soft thud. I rushed forward, taking aim with the spray in my right hand, and pressed with my forefinger once more, sending forth an arrow of white fog. If there had been a mirror next to me at that moment, I would have been able to see the murderous expression on my face, my eyes flashing with bloodlust, no different from a crazed soldier on a battlefield raising his sword, or an angry madman with a gun chasing after his enemy.

The gecko stumbled its way out of the study, its movements getting slower and slower. If I had been more ruthless, I would have crushed it to certain death with one step, but I didn't dare. The memory of that gecko in the past, whose tail had separated from his body but wouldn't stop twitching, tore at my already overwrought nerves. The gecko, more desperate than ever, started to crawl in the direction of my bedroom. I stepped forward to block its way and shouted: 'Don't you *dare* go into my bedroom!' It seemed to understand me, because it then crawled, as if drunk, first underneath the tea table in the living-room and then escaped under the sofa. I followed it and squatted there, held my breath, and in a fit of hysterical anger sprayed under the sofa in one wild burst.

At last all was quiet.

The battle was over. I collapsed on to the other sofa, staring hard at the dark corner just opposite where the gecko was hiding. The room was filled with the smell of the insect repellent, but heavier still was the feeling of resentment in my heart.

At the office, when the news spread that I was planning to leave and return to Hong Kong, what touched me most was the way people urged me to stay—with words and with the expressions on their faces. The younger colleagues said quietly to me: without you by our side, this place is going to seem even more like a jungle.

But the law of the jungle—survival of the fittest—does apply to office politics. You can either be a wolf who goes after the fattest calf, or a bird that flies above the jungle and yet also lives in it: which one you are depends on your own choices and on your staying power. In the last three or four years, I had spent quite a lot of time counselling several fresh university graduates who were hired as administrative trainees in my office. Sometimes I felt that the effort I was putting in went way beyond the call of duty, but I know that I did it because I could see in them a vague silhouette of myself at that particular stage in life. Sometimes when one of those young people got upset because of internal power struggles, or became the victim of other people's rivalries, I comforted them—the often arbitrary and malicious attacks of the other side were actually the result of their own fear and insecurity.

In the jungle, most animals will only kill weaker animals out of hunger, or will only fight when being attacked; the world of humans, however, is much more complicated.

I've always demanded of myself that I be a woman of strong moral integrity. For this reason, when I found myself in situations that would normally make one lose one's nerve, I would stick to my principles, and this always enabled me to ride the storms with dignity. And yet now, the deep resentment in my heart makes me feel sad and sorry for myself. To think that one tiny gecko could unleash in me such a strong wave of panic and fear that I had to resort to violence! I felt completely deflated. I feared that in the long run, I would not be able to retain a sense of compassion as I went through life's even darker and gloomier valleys.

The reptile underneath the sofa could be dead or still alive—in any case, I no longer needed to worry about it.

Agreeing on Some Ground Rules

I woke up as the sky was brightening. It was a subtle feeling that roused me from sleep. I sat up in bed, and following the early morning light that shone through the curtains behind me, I scanned the floor in front of the bedroom door. The gecko was lying there quietly, head raised, looking right up at me.

The gentle, fresh fragrance that belongs only to the early morning hours circulated in the air. The smell of insect spray was gone. In the morning light the gecko cast a long, thin shadow on the gleaming surface of the polished floor.

'I don't want to keep trying to kill you. Let's agree on a few ground rules, all right?'

It lifted its head and listened.

'Originally I lived alone in this flat. You can stay here now, but you must follow a few rules: You mustn't come into the bedroom, and you mustn't go into the study either—these two rooms are off-limits to you. When I go out, you can move freely about the living-room, but please don't hide in the bookshelves. I don't want to pull out a book and accidentally squash your tail. As for the bathroom, there aren't many concealed crevices there, so don't let me see you crawling up a corner while I'm washing my face or taking a shower. I'm sorry if this hurts your feelings. Please understand that I'm sincerely trying to find a way for us to live together.'

The gecko continued to listen, patiently keeping its head raised.

'When I'm home, it's best if you stay in the kitchen, okay? There's lots of space for you on top of the kitchen cupboard and I can't easily reach up there. In short, you can stay, but I definitely don't want to see you. If you agree, please raise your front leg.'

The gecko, which had been lying there on the floor all along with its head raised, now gently lifted its right leg. I let out a satisfied breath.

'Good. May we live together happily. Now feel free to move about.'

It put its front leg down and slowly retreated from the bedroom, then disappeared in the direction of the kitchen. In that instant, the air in the room was filled with a feeling of forgiveness and tolerance. I lay back down on the bed and wrapped the quilt around me. My whole body happy and at ease, I fell into a deep sleep.

After this my life began to change almost imperceptibly. Little by little. Silence and harmony. I didn't see the gecko after that, but I could feel its continual presence in the flat. This was an extremely obedient and trustworthy gecko—never once appearing before my eyes. Every time before I left home, I always opened one window in the kitchen and one in the bathroom so that the gecko could go in and out. On rainy days, I would still leave the windows slightly open so that the gecko wouldn't get stuck outdoors. The insect spray was no longer needed, and if there were mosquitoes, well, they would be food for the gecko.

I had always kept a few plants in the flat. If I observed them carefully I could see the buds sprouting at the tips of the branches, and the leaves changing direction to face the sun every morning and evening. Through these things, I could appreciate the simple joy of living. I also liked to keep cut flowers, and would watch the colours as they blossomed, as well as their tired postures as they withered. Many a time, as I sat reading in the corner of a room, I would hear the sound of flowers dropping on to the table. When I raised my head the fallen flowers would be there on the table, their smell still permeating the room. We existed together, sharing the same space and time, but the flowers' lives passed even more rapidly than my own. Slowly I learnt that the withered leaves of potted plants didn't have to be thrown away— I could leave them on top of the soil in the pot and they would dry up and blend in with the soil. Just because their form of existence was different, who could say that they had completely disappeared?

Ever since the gecko started living here, I had the feeling of another type of life inhabiting the flat. Every time I came home I could sense, on opening the door, an expectant bustle inside. In the flat, in the corners where I didn't have to look, there was always a silent life waiting for me to return, breathing the same air as me. There was a feeling of affection in the air that you could almost touch.

Just one occasion, when I was in the kitchen cooking, I turned around to open the door of the cupboard and caught a glimpse of the gecko's tail as it quickly darted away.

In a cheerful tone of voice I teased the gecko on top of the cupboard: 'I almost saw you! Better be more careful next time.' As I spoke, I thought I saw the embarrassed face of the gecko in the corner. It was this belief, cherished so tenderly, that slowly smoothed away my fear.

As time went on I began to enjoy more and more the kind of subtle and harmonious living arrangement that we shared. The gecko's existence gradually seemed to take on a similarity to certain religious beliefs: if you have faith that something exists, then it does. Countless religious followers have never once seen the gods they believe in, but that doesn't shake their faith one bit.

———

Yet another stretch of time had passed since I came back to this city. I had not, however, brought my lifestyle from abroad back with me. I knew that each place had its own rhythm. Anyway, I didn't mind starting anew. But some of the attitudes and value judgements that surrounded me here made me feel like a stranger, and I wasn't sure if I could take everything on board. If I really had faith in myself, then these concerns could not be groundless. Would it be possible not to give up the standards I'd so painstakingly established for myself over the years, whilst at the same time adapt to the rapid changes of these times? This was something I often thought about when I was alone.

Time passed. There were still those who wanted to leave, and those who wanted to return. Amongst the waves of people coming and going, there were always some faces that seemed familiar, wearing expressions of joy or fear—countless numbers of people. I only knew that each one of us had to go along life's complicated and winding road until we reached the end.

———

One day several friends and I got together. Because we were very close, when we were together we never held back anything—our successes, failures, and doubts. As we were chatting away, I saw that it was raining outside, and for a moment thought about the gecko and whether it was caught out in the rain.

And then I heard N saying close to my ear: 'I just said, you're wearing a smile that only women in love have. Tell us, have you finally met a kind and responsible man that you can rely on?'

How could I tell my friends? If I said that the sweet smile on my face was because I was thinking of the gecko I was living with, could they accept that? Would they believe me?

Then there was another night when I was in the bathroom and had just finished my bath. I had turned off the tap and the gurgling water was disappearing down the drain when I heard the clear song of the gecko in the next room. There was a note of happiness that could only come from a creature full of love and joy for life. I too was extremely happy, because it was a sound that could only be heard if you listened with your heart.

What Really Happened

I awoke. Sun filled the room. The recurring nightmare I had been having for several nights in a row made me very tired, and I tossed and turned in my bed for a long time before finally getting up and leaving the bedroom.

In the living-room I opened all the curtains. The heavy smell of insect spray from the night before that still permeated the room made me catch my breath, and in so doing I sucked in the remains of the spray. I stood in the middle of the living-room, hesitating for a while. I pulled the tea-table away from the sofa, then slowly pulled out the sofa one, then two inches.

The grey remains of the gecko's body lay on the wooden floor where the sofa had been. I narrowed my eyes and inched forward, then bent down to look at the unmoving but slightly bent torso of the reptile, which was lying on its back. I didn't dare check for certain whether it was completely dead. The room was very quiet, and I could almost hear the sound of my heart beating. Although it was just a corpse, it still disgusted me. For a while neither of us moved. I turned around, went into the kitchen and picked up the broom in my right hand, while my left hand held the can of insect repellent. I cautiously returned to the corner where the gecko lay and used the broom to gently nudge its body. There was no response. I put down the can, bent down to pick up a fairly thin magazine, and in one movement swept the gecko on to the magazine. With my arm fully outstretched, I carried the corpse on the magazine and walked quickly to the bathroom. The gecko's dead, grey body slid down the magazine and with a tiny splash dropped into the toilet. I flushed the toilet and the water gurgled loudly as it spiralled downward. All went quiet and there was no more sign of the gecko in the toilet, but still, just to be sure, I flushed it again.

I returned to the living-room and put the sofa back to its original position. After moving back the tea-table as well, I bent down and picked up the can of insect spray. The sun that shone in through the window allowed me to see with an almost exquisite clarity my reflection on the polished floor: spray in hand, my posture looked just like that of someone holding a gun.

Chinese original published in *Su Ye Literature Monthly*, No. 3, 1992.

Red Rose and
Bastard Horse

By **XIN YUAN**
Translated by Jane C. C. Lai

This is a chapter from Xin Yuan's novel, Crazy Horse in a Frenzied
City—*a mock-epic spy story-cum-satirical political farce. The novel
is set in the years before the return of Hong Kong to Chinese
sovereignty. The protagonist, surnamed Ma (which means 'horse'
and is translated into English to avoid association of the word 'ma'
with 'mother'), is a Hongkonger who works as a photographer on a
newspaper. Much against his will, he finds himself running errands
for a man whom he believes to be the illegitimate son of a prominent
Chinese leader and who is supposedly in Hong Kong on an important
mission to do with the future of Hong Kong. In this chapter, Crazy
Horse, after one of his narrow escapes, wanders to the boutique run
by his former girlfriend, Red Rose. Questions of identity, of how
history should be presented and represented, of the status which
English as a language should be accorded in Hong Kong, and the
notion of hybridity—examined by other writers in this collection
as well—all surface in this story, but with a marked difference in
tone.*

Young Horse wandered about in the street, feeling ill at ease. He
needed some sort of disguise to save his skin. Threading his way
through Central, he came upon that boutique again. Was it a
conscious move? He wasn't sure.

He went up the endless winding stairs and got to the door. He saw the character for 'heart' painted in red, and held back from ringing the bell.

He hesitated a moment and turned to go down the stairs. But ill-fortune had it that gyrating her way up towards him was Red Rose.

'I've come to see if you have some old clothes that I might borrow,' he mumbled.

Red Rose radiated fragrance, her eyes peering into the depth of his heart. 'Not to see me, eh?' She smiled and let him off.

She unlocked the door. The red heart clicked open.

Young Horse went inside. A familiar place. He had lived there a few months, and then . . . well, then.

Red Rose was not nostalgic about the past either, and had done up the place in bright reds and greens. Not bad. Very postmodern. Not a trace of him left.

He sipped his coffee. Nice aroma.

He looked at the street scene. A familiar street scene.

He opened the wardrobe. Any old rags he could put on?

A cap, perhaps?

Or a bowler?

Or go with the trend at Chinese art exhibition receptions these days—don a long Chinese robe and chew on a cigar?

'Oh! Yes! Good idea. Try it on!' Red Rose urged.

Foolish Horse took off his shirt and slipped on the long robe. Then he took off his trousers. Red Rose helped him to straighten the sleeves, pull at the waist. Her fingers were everywhere. 'Wonderful! It suits you!' She said.

Occidental Horse transformed into Oriental Horse. A glance at the mirror told him he was neither Chinese nor Western, neither man nor foreign devil. That was problematic. But Red Rose kept saying it was nice. They never did meet on grounds of taste.

Besides, he didn't know whether there was any irony intended in what she said. He could never be sure.

'It suits you' could mean many things: 'You're such a weirdo, it becomes you to be odd', 'You are a camera-freak, carting your camera around all day pretending to be an artist and never buckling down to make a living', 'You act as if you're above it all—a poverty-stricken Chinese artist above it all?'

He didn't understand why she had this complicated hang-up over art. As a matter of fact, she had come to the Community Centre to learn photography, and that was how they had met. But then, she complained that he only had time for his photography, and complained about his being an artist. When they went to the theatre, she'd leave half-way, complaining of a headache. When they went to the cinema, she'd lose her temper unprovoked and demand, 'Are you too scared to eat pickled ginger in public just because you are an artist?'

It was ridiculous. He, the Young Horse, would have dared to swallow a whole pony. But that was not the point. The point was why so much resentment against art? Why blame everything on art?

She'd told him that when she was a typist she fell in love with a gweilo boss, because he would bring her to Swiss restaurants, he knew how to choose wines, and would give her nice Italian woollen pullovers with famous brand names. What was more, he played the piano and would go home with her and teach her how to play—her husband did buy her a piano but he didn't know how to play it. Had she fallen for the foreigner and become his mistress just because he could play the piano? Young Horse was beginning to think there was more to it than just art.

He could never fathom Red Rose. After her divorce, she set up a boutique and dressed herself to the teeth like a red rose. He couldn't stand the way she hugged and clung to foreign men, and that had turned him into a despicable, jealous Chinese male. Why was it that whenever she saw a foreigner in sight, she seemed to switch entirely, to run on another sort of battery? And that happened even with Indians, with Singaporeans, or Taiwanese. She just livened up. This gave him, a Hongkonger, a dose of inferiority.

No. It wasn't at that time that he started to read Fanon. He hadn't yet registered for that damned course on 'post-colonialism' at the Arts Centre. He was fidelity itself (a fortune-teller said there would be three major setbacks in affairs of the heart in his life, and so he thought each time that that was the last), but there was just no way he could hold her affection! He didn't know if it was just chance or what, but when she hopped over to the Philippines for a holiday, she got mixed up with a foreigner; when she went for a haircut, she picked up a foreigner, even when she signed up for a beginners' class in sketching, she picked up a foreigner.

Then, for a while, there was no keeping track of her. She stopped turning up for dates, reneged on her promises to turn up, and disappeared for whole nights. He went berserk with anxiety like a crazy horse in a hot frying pan, his guts on fire, his hooves in the air, his days anxious and long like centuries. . . .

'Hey, why are you staring at me like that!'

Well, it is all over. Water under the bridge. No recriminations, no regrets now. Red Rose was just a noble rose, appearing before him for the first time, rich with a strange fragrance.

'No! This outfit won't do! Haven't you got something a little low-key, not so eye-catching? I'm going to work, a bit more casual. . . . Oh, yes, I'd like to use your phone to make a call to the newspaper office.'

Red Rose rummaged among a heap of fabrics and pulled out a miniature sewing machine, which was in fact a phone. He cranked the pedal, put a spool against one ear and another spool in front of his lips.

'Yes, sir, what do you want photographed this week? Okay, the Legislative Council. The Steamed, Braised, and Double-boiled? Oh, that restaurant! And who? Rip-the-Fan. Patriot Liu. Ex-husband. . . . Chris Patten going to the TVB studio? . . . They're going to hook him to a wire? Can't they do it with dark-room effects? The sanctification ceremony of the Big Buddha statue . . . ? Okay. Okay. New-York-Wat—. No, I mean, has Siu Sin given you the pictures yesterday? Yes, I sprained my ankle, quite badly. No, it's not okay yet. That's right, yes. I need crutches. I'm trying . . .'

Red Rose was not listening. Where had she gone?

Good thing she wasn't around, or she would think him undignified. He never seemed to do anything right when she was around.

For a time, after leaving her, he felt as if he would never hold his head up high again. And, for a very long time, he lost all confidence in himself, doing jobs in which he seemed always to be taken advantage of. He even felt that he deserved no more.

He made another call.

Ring. No one answered. New-York-Water* was neither at the office nor at home. Where could she be? And what had happened

---

* New-York-Water is the nickname Crazy Horse gives to the reporter, Siu Sin, who works on the same newspaper and who unwittingly gets involved in Crazy Horse's plight.

to the little fat guy from the Mainland who was taking refuge in her place? Like New-York-Water, Crazy Horse could not go back to the office nor home.

Neither he nor New-York-Water carried a mobile phone. Now that they had lost touch, it seemed almost impossible to locate each other again.

Red Rose brought him a cup of tea, rose-scented. Her place was always scented, and soft as silk. He began to unwind to vagrant thoughts.

'Well? Still shooting pictures in the street, are you? Shot any pretty girls lately?'

He remembered that it was she who asked him (or was it the other way round?) to do a photo session for her—to promote the fashion collection she designed—and she served as the model.

She was vivacious in front of the camera. She had style.

Her designs were tantalizing. She didn't mind probing eyes: through the narrow slits, round the twirling strands, through the thin gossamer, the lingering glance was held, its appreciative warmth rewarded with a soothing caress.

She didn't mind men gazing at her, rather she seemed to reel and revel in their attention.

Behind his camera viewfinder, his eyes followed her as she moved around.

After a little rest, she took off her black blouse, showing her white shoulders. Just so, and she bent down to pick up the lethargic silk from the floor.

He smelt her scent, an indescribable scent, which sent his senses reeling.

Was he a hunter straining after the elusive scent? Or was he, rather, the hunted—confused, lost, tripped off his balance, intoxicated?

No! Go back to reality. Don't look back! That way danger lies!

In an instant, Drunken Horse went back to reality and became Alert Horse. No. He mustn't dive into it again as he used to do—it almost cost him his life!

No, no. He had work to do, take pictures, even write short reports. He had to edit his own work, erase a few words here, a few dozen words there, and delete all the motion verbs.

What sort of verbs? Meet, touch, clash, confront, mix, oppress, tolerate, possess, submit, endure ... and all the possibilities which arise when people meet. Arrayed like grocery upon the shelves. No. Horse was not in the 7-Eleven, he was in Red Rose's boudoir, his mind a riot, his senses rebellious, and he was trying to pull himself together. What more dangerous terrain for his state than the boudoir of an old flame? He decided to take himself out of here.

No more emotional entanglement. He'd rather leave and find himself a 7-Eleven.

Just as he was looking round for his trousers, the doorbell rang.

Damn. A big, tall Australian man came in. Obviously Red Rose's new lover.

When the two met, they embraced and kissed. Who was he? What was he doing there?

But he couldn't very well sneak off. That would give away too much of the game. Why not take it as it comes? Well, it had come, but how to take it, that was the problem.

The guy worked at a TV station, his name was Kadoorie, a producer or something.

Said he like Zhang Yimou's films. They had some sort of power in them.

Red Sorghum, for instance. One could imagine that. The big gweilo probably saw himself as a daring sedan-bearer who pissed into a wine vat and carried off a girl in one arm. How invigorating, exciting, and romantic.

They tried to tell him a story: about how romantic it was to drive to a deserted beach—he thought they were talking about another film, but they were telling him their own story—keep the headlights on, and then—he thought they were going to say they made love under the stars—have a barbecue by the headlights!

Yeah, very romantic. Old Horse didn't know what was so romantic about it. The smoke blackening the air, you'd call it pollution. Then they said they drank red wine and they drank white wine.

'Oh,' Young Horse said. 'Oh, white wine. Then you must have brought an ice-box with you then?' He was being deliberately sarcastic, but he really fed them the right line. Red Rose smiled sweet as rose-syrup or honey: 'Oh, yes, he did, you know. He thought of everything, never missed a thing.'

Well, bully for him. Rotten Horse lost that round.

Restive Horse tried to figure out how to get away.

Now the gweilo was blabbering about the programme he had put together. It was a programme about Hong Kong history, and he had to do it because the Hong Kong Museum of History had such a blinkered vision and dealt only with the history of the locals. He, Kadoorie, would go in for the history of the early Indian settlers. After all, wasn't it true that there were many rich Indian businessmen here even today?

That might be so. Many rich Indians. But the Aussie then rambled on to grouse about why there wasn't a single white face in the historical photographs? Well, that was a strange way of looking at it! From the way he talked you would have thought that he was fighting tooth and nail for a fair deal for some poor discriminated minority tribe!

But, hang on! The Aussie was just like some of the gweilos you saw these days! They jumped at any mention of local history! They jumped up and down wherever they heard any talk about cultural identity here, and they screamed: 'Discrimination!'

Young Horse humbly (as humbly as any Hongkonger) explained: 'There is a history in the telling of history. In the old colonial days we were not allowed to talk about history, it is only now that we have begun. . . .'

The Aussie had wrapped his arms around Red Rose, and his hands had disappeared from sight. Dejected Horse was very dejected.

'Here, it is said, 98 per cent of the population is Chinese. Why should the official organizations for the School Arts Festival insist on using English? Why should I have to talk to you in English? What's so great about you that the media have to propagate the gweilo perspective on history to prove that you have more right to live in Hong Kong than us Hongkongers?'

The gweilo didn't listen to him at all, nor did Red Rose. Her eyes were all aglow, her lips murmuring, 'Yeah, I know, I know.' The Boxer Rebellion mentality in Young Horse began to stir.

He saw his reflection in the glass of a framed Andy Warhol picture hanging askew on the wall across the room: he was dressed in a Chinese costume, and for some strange reason was forced into taking a Chinese stand.

Crazy Horse was a master of disguises, he looked the part whatever costume he was in, and he did better than that Japanese animation character Ranma Saotome* whose transformation could only be effected when splashed with hot or cold water.

The gweilo turned round to him and began to demolish his Chinese position: 'I'm tired of all this interest in traditional Chinese culture that Hong Kong intellectuals talk about these days: the Peking opera classes, the traditional Cantonese operas, the tea culture, and *tai chi* . . . I think it's all a lot of junk!'

'Is it junk just because you say so?' Chinese Horse sneered.

But Photographic Horse was never one for rhetoric, and having to argue in English diminished something of the little rhetorical power he had in the first place. Besides, his old anglophile girlfriend was wrapped in the gweilo's embrace. These were grievous losses, defeat upon defeat, insult upon injury. He opened his mouth and out rushed the words, 'You, you, you . . . !'

But in his mind was a montage of many things: the struggles to get Chinese recognized as an official language; how smooth Rose's back was; the wonders of Peking opera (how could gweilos ever understand them?); the Pearl of the Orient; frogs at the bottom of the well, how much did they know of the richness and the splendour of this big wide world; how smooth Rose's back was; and Red Rose saying, 'Only foreigners have such drive. The Chinese are so conservative!'

Photographic Horse was furious, cursing and swearing under his breath, rearing for the kill. But he only had a camera with him and what could he do with that? If he bashed up the camera, he couldn't even make a living!

The gweilo found him speechless and proceeded to pontificate on his postmodernist theories. According to him there were no native Hong Kong people in the first place, everything here was a postmodernist hybrid, it was a joke to talk about Chinese culture, because it was all a sham, a put-on! There was a woman assistant in his company, he went on, and every time she mentioned Chinese customs and culture he'd say, 'What Chinese culture? Nothing but lion dances and dragon boat races. . . . Ha ha!'

'And what did she say?'

'Ah, she's wised up! She's now got the point. "Yes," she says, "why did I used to think I was Chinese? Like you said, scratch the surface, and there isn't a real Chinese underneath at all!"'

---

* Ranma Saotome is known as 'Crazy Horse' in Hong Kong.

The gweilo waxed in pride and swept Red Rose into his arms as if she was the embodiment of all those who had renounced their Chinese culture through the baptism of his ideas.

It was pathetic.

Horse could hardly keep from blurting out Yu Dafu's patriotic lament, 'Oh, China! Oh, China!' But he didn't. After all, what was he? In front of a real Chinese of today, he was a bastard who couldn't even speak Putonghua properly! He admired the West, was pleasant to foreigners, was Westernized in his way of life, and forgetful of the glories of his forefathers—and that included his using a Japanese camera rather than a Chinese Seagull brand! But face to face with these privileged foreigners who had for so long enjoyed advantages in Hong Kong, he suddenly found himself turned into a Chinese in a long robe, squaring himself against the oppressions from foreign devils like those who threatened the Qing dynasty with gunships and cannonballs.

The evil hand of the invader groped lower and lower. . . . Red Rose turned smilingly in response. Quintessential Chinese Horse died a death!

Bastard Horse did have friends who were interested in traditional art. He did know people who knew all about Peking opera. It was true, though, that some of those who promoted the return to Chinese culture did it for political reasons that did not meet the eye. But *he* had no right to say that all interest in traditional Chinese culture was a sham! And *he* only a gweilo from a media company!

The couple before him were breathing more and more heavily, gazing more and more intently into each other's eyes, oblivious to the world. Red Rose, in an attitude of unbounded adoration, looked up at her man.

Vanquished Horse on his last legs saw his own blurred reflection in the dusty picture frame—in a long Chinese robe, wearing an un-Chinese and uncharitable expression, looking like a fool.

Chinese original published in Xin Yuan: *Crazy Horse in a Frenzied City*, Hong Kong: Youth Literary Bookstore, 1996.

PART V

Epilogue:
1997 and Beyond

The Case of Mary

By **XI XI**

Translated by Jane C. C. Lai

The idea that 'Hong Kong people do not care about politics' has been repeated so often it has almost acquired the status of a truth. Hong Kong people do express their views on politics—sensibly, vocally, insistently, or, as in this and other stories in this section, subtly, allegorically, even playfully or with irreverence.

Her name was Mary.

(Her surname I cannot remember. Those interested in people's names should read the novels of Fyodor Mikhailovich Dostoevsky or Ivan Sergeevich Turgenev, or Nikolai Vasilyevich Gogol. In their novels, the names of the characters are presented in as much detail as the authors' own.)

Mary was a Dutch child who had lived for a long time in Sweden.

(Nothing special about a Dutch child living for a long time in Sweden. Jorge Luis Borges, the Argentinean, when he was a child, lived for a long time in Switzerland; Italo Calvino, when he was a child, lived for a long time in Cuba. I know nothing of Mary as a child. Those who like stories about children should go and read Mark Twain's *Huckleberry Finn* or Lewis Carroll's *Alice in Wonderland*, or William Golding's *The Lord of the Flies*.)

Mary's mother had died.

(I don't know if Mary's mother was Swedish by nationality or just a resident in Sweden. I can only conjecture that Mary lived with her mother in Sweden. And now Mary's mother had suddenly died. The manner of her death? I don't know. Those who want to know all about the deaths of married women should perhaps read Tolstoy's *Anna Karenina*, or Flaubert's *Madam Bovary*, or *Oedipus Rex* by Sophocles.)

Mary's father became Mary's guardian.

(What kind of a man was Mary's father? I don't know. I only know he was Dutch by nationality. The Dutch Court, acceding to Mary's father's request, and according to the laws of the land, acknowledged him as Mary's legal guardian, and ruled that he had custody of Mary. The abandoned child is a not uncommon subject in literature. There are lots of novels on the subject: for instance, Fielding's *Tom Jones*, Dickens's *David Copperfield*, and Robert Louis Stevenson's *Treasure Island*.)

But Mary applied to the Court for a change of guardian.

(Now that is amazing. That a child should actually apply to the Court for a change of guardian. First, we can't help but ask: how could a child negotiate with the Court? Somebody must have helped her deal with all those complicated and tiresome legal procedures. But who? And then, why would a child want to make such a demand? Was she not satisfied with her own father? I know nothing about the emotional relationship between Mary's parents. Those who are curious about the intricacies of man and woman relationships must not miss out on Faulkner's *The Sound and the Fury*, or Hawthorne's *The Scarlet Letter*, or even Ibsen's *A Doll's House*.)

The Court, according to Mary's wish, appointed a woman as her guardian.

(The Court's ruling should not be taken lightly: it was made in accordance with the person's own wish. Such a judgement is a major breakthrough. Our society today is still a kind of patriarchal community with a small group of adults at its core. Children are given plenty of loving care, physically, but what they think hardly matters; and in legal matters, they have no right to speak at all. Well, not only are children not heard, sometimes even adults find no audience for what they have to say, and they cannot make known their innocence in court. There are examples of that in literature, in Kafka's *The Trial*, or Camus' *L'Etranger*, or the four gospels in the New Testament.)

So, the Netherlands and Sweden went to the International Court of Justice over little Mary.

(The Swedish authorities cited its own laws, turned down the request of the Netherlands government, and made Mary a ward under the protection of the state of Sweden. The Netherlands government objected to Sweden's decision as being a contravention of the 1902 Hague Convention, which stipulated that the custody of minors is to be decided according to the laws of the land. How many stories there are about struggles over the custody of a child! If you want to stress blood ties, there are, of course, the judgement of King Solomon in the Bible, and Li Xingdao's Yuan dynasty drama *The Judgement of the Chalk Circle*; but if you think love for the child is more important, then you would not have missed Bertolt Brecht's *Caucasian Chalk Circle*. So we pick what appeals to us, and attend to what we want to attend.)

28 December 1958. The International Court of Justice delivered its judgement: the Netherlands lost the case.

(The reason: the law that the Netherlands applied was a custodian law; that which Sweden applied was a protective law. The aims and the functions of the two are different. Both attempt to offer love and protection, but the former adds a level of monitoring and control. One could mark out a piece of land for the protection of wild animals, or one could catch the animals and put them in a zoo. But the two are vastly different. The year 1958 belongs to the 1960s of the twentieth century, a century that we claim to be a period of rule by law, an era when there should be respect for the individual's will. Perhaps we do not treat a child as an individual with a will of her own. But what if she does? The way I see it is: there are two countries, and one victim. Is there a work which shows a respect for the will of the child? I call upon you to assist me in my search.)

October 1986
Chinese original published in *Hong Kong Literature Monthly*, December 1986.

The Centaur of the East

By DUNG KAI CHEUNG
Translated by Dung Kai Cheung

This piece, also taken from The Atlas: Archaeology of an Imaginary City, *highlights the much-discussed question about Hong Kong—whether it is heterogeneous or hybrid in character. Is it the Centaur of the East or (as Xin Yuan would say) a 'bastard horse'? There is a touch of the apocalyptic in the implication that the centaur is a forerunner, perhaps, of the 'one country, two systems' policy by which Hong Kong will be governed for its first fifty years as a special administrative region of China.*

In *The Book of Imaginary Beings*, Borges made an astute observation. In what he calls the 'fantastic zoology' of the West, the centaur is the most harmonious of creatures, but its heterogeneous character has often been overlooked. The heterogeneity of the centaur lies in the fact that it is made up of two separate and distinct halves joined (or juxtaposed) together in seamless perfection, its human part possessing the pure and unadulterated qualities of a human body, and its animal part the perfect configuration of a horse. Examples of such heterogeneously combined creatures such as the centaur cannot be found in Chinese mythology. Although Chinese imaginary creatures are also often a mixture of pre-existing forms, they are usually a conglomeration of multiple individual parts rather than a simple dual attachment. For example, *xi wang mu* (mother queen of the west) in the ancient geographical and mythological work *Shan Hai Jing (The Routes of Mountains and Seas)* is a composite which 'looks like human, has a leopard's tail and a tiger's teeth, and howls'.

In studying the maps of the City of Victoria, disputes have long existed between those who adopted an interpretive model based on the theory of two distinct halves joined seamlessly together and those who adopted one based on the theory of multiple individual parts forming a composite whole. The former seems to be particularly suitable to reading the early maps of the city. For example, in an 1889 street map, the differences between the districts Central and Sheung Wan are already clearly discernible. Apart from a few east–west running streets which passed through both districts, such as Bonham Strand, Queen's Road, Hollywood Road, and Wellington Street, Central and Sheung Wan had features which were distinctly different from each other. The streets in Central were, without exception, all named after English dignitaries who had contributed to the founding of the City of Victoria. Pottinger Street, for example, was named after Sir Henry Pottinger, the first governor of the colony; D'Aguilar Street was named after Major General D'Aguilar, the early commander of the garrison army; and Aberdeen Street after Lord Aberdeen, Great Britain's Foreign Secretary in the 1840s. In sharp contrast, most of the streets to the west of Tai Ping Shan in Sheung Wan had indigeneous Chinese names, such as Po Hing Fong, Po Yan Street, Wing Lok Street, etc. According to existing documents, the architecture also divided the city into two halves, with Pottinger Street as the dividing line. To the side where Central District was, there were British-style buildings; to the side where Sheung Wan was, there were Chinese-style houses. Looked at from the harbour, the sight must have been one of heterogeneous coexistence.

The above view was later refuted. It was considered to be an oversimplification and not in keeping with facts. Citing the data based on various analyses of the quantity, positions, and density of a whole range of elements, cartographers tried to prove that Victoria had never shown any signs of existing in a state of dichotomy between east and west. Instead, they strove to establish the view of Victoria as a crossbreed or hybrid, the mixed elements of which could neither be retraced nor disentangled. This new model, based on the traditional *xi wang mu* paradigm, soon became fashionable. But the model which it aimed to supplant—that of two distinct halves joined seamlessly together— still retains a certain attraction among scholars. That is why some people still insist that Victoria was 'the Centaur of the East'.

Borges also makes a reference to Book V of Lucretius' poem *De rerum natura*. It carries this observation: 'The Centaur is an impossible creature, for the horse reaches maturity before the human, and at the age of three the horse would be full-grown and the human only a babbling child. Moreover, the horse would die fifty years before the man.'

Chinese original published in Dung Kai Cheung: *The Atlas: Archaeology of an Imaginary City*, Taipei: Lian He Wenxue Chubanshe, 1997.

22

Losing the City

By **WONG BIK WAN**
Translated by Martha P. Y. Cheung

Amid the many pessimistic stories about Hong Kong that have appeared in the West, this local piece stands tall. Here, rather than melodrama, is a quiet but harrowing depiction of people driven to desperation by a consciousness tormented with fear, eaten up with despair, and besieged with an imminent sense of loss. What is more, it offers a vision of the future that is unnervingly and provocatively ambivalent.

Now that I think about it, I realize that things had to be so. I had to be driving an ambulance through the streets, the blue light on top of the ambulance had to be flashing, and the man had to bleed and die. When someone died, Oi Yuk could not but feel pleased. And I had to come together with her.

It was the first time I saw anyone bleed to death, just two weeks after I started work. A dead body was really not the same as the rubber dummy used for training: there was the stench, the gurgle of the last gasps for breath, the weeping and wailing of the relatives.

The man was dead. My colleague had said behind me, 'No need to rush now. Switch off the siren, it's too noisy'.

So I took my time—stopping before the red light, moving on with the green, as if I was a learner driver at the driving school. As soon as the ambulance arrived at the hospital and the body was brought out, the family of the deceased was surrounded by a swarm of people, women as well as men.

'Coffin, shroud, burial service, all inclusive.'

'At 20 per cent discount now.'

'Shrouds, blankets, wreaths, minibus service to and from the crematorium—compliments of the establishment.'

'Call 11183888.'

I was shocked, and could not help shouting, 'Can't you just leave the family alone?'

A woman, slightly built, a baseball cap on her head, shouted back at me, 'People die, the dead have to be buried, we have to compete for business, that's the way it is!'

She was Oi Yuk.

We fell in love, we married. She got pregnant, her belly big with the living, and still she went about touting for business from the dead. I went on carrying the casualties in the ambulance, speeding through the midnight streets in the city. We bought a small house on the outskirts of the city, with a dismal mango tree and a miserable Chinese Wampee tree in the front of the house. I was on night shift, and I always watered the plants and cooked at dawn. Calmly and fearfully, I awaited the future—it had to be so.

Our new neighbour moved in at the crack of dawn—at five in the morning. My wife Oi Yuk was at the sewing machine working on a three-piece suit—the client had drowned and the body, bloated, had grown two sizes bigger, so some alteration work was necessary to make his suit fit for wear. I was sucking on some bitter sour Wampee fruit. A small black van drove up to the house next door, and a family got out quietly. They all looked scrawny. The man was scrawny and sallow-faced; the woman was scrawny, with dark rings under her eyes and thinning hair; the four children were like scrawny cats. Together they carried a table inside the house. Then they quietly took down from the van a few mattresses, pillows, and other bits and pieces of furniture. The smallest child also brought out a big rattan cage. In it was a white mouse, incredibly fat.

Later I saw the whole family in the sitting-room, all sleeping on the big dining-table. The fat white mouse squeaked loudly in the night.

Oi Yuk and I seldom ran into our neighbours. Sometimes when we looked in the direction of their house, we saw only the pathetic-looking dining table in the empty sitting-room. The sallow-faced man went to work in that small black van, the scrawny children often sat in their upstairs balcony watching the moon in the dead of night, while the scrawny woman stayed alone in the sitting-room watching television. In the dead of night the sallow-faced man would sometimes repair a wardrobe in the garden, and sometimes when I came home from work, he would now and then flash me a grin, showing a set of gleaming white teeth. Just a flash, and then no more. In the dark, I always wondered if that was not just a flash in a dark dream.

Oi Yuk had a minor haemorrhage and went into the hospital for a check-up. One night, I was in the garden eating a piece of bread, enjoying the tranquillity and the sweet fragrance of roses from the next street when suddenly I heard a knock on the door. It was the sallow-faced man. He broke somewhat nervously into a grin and I saw that same set of gleaming white teeth.

He said, 'I'm Chan Lo Yuen, I live next door.'

There was nothing I could do but open the door for him, 'It's almost midnight. You're up late.'

He smiled, 'Sorry to disturb you.'

I said, 'Would you like to come in for a cup of coffee?'

He hesitated a while before saying, 'Could you come over to my place? Something has happened.'

I finished off the piece of bread and said, 'Okay. Let me put something on.'

Chan stood at the door and waited for me, sometimes raising his head to look at the moon, sometimes looking down shyly and watching the glorious daisies at his feet. As we stepped into the moonlit street, I struck up a conversation with him, 'I'm Jim Hak Ming. I attend to casualty cases. My wife works as an agent for a funeral parlour.'

Chan said, 'H'm, I'm an architect. My wife stays at home to look after the kids. Four of them. We're returnees from Canada, just back.' We were already outside his house.

There was a long iron rod stained with blood outside his door.

I stopped. He just glanced at the rod and then led me into the garden, as if nothing had happened. Counting on the fact that at 175 centimetres I was taller than him by almost a head, and weighed a good 70 kilos, I wasn't to be put off, and I followed him inside.

The door was half closed; I was greeted with a familiar stench. He pushed open the door, behind it was a pool of blood.

'You want to come in? It's all right. They're all dead.'

The lights were still on in the sitting-room, the television was showing a Cantonese film with the sound turned off, the CD player was on—it was Bach's 'Suite for Unaccompanied Cello, No.1 in G'. Chan listened attentively to the music, a look of peace and radiance on his face, like that of a Christian, 'Such beautiful music. How close it is to religion! It's like a gothic church, like the pyramids in ancient Egypt. It lifts the spirit, higher and higher—life is over in a flash. Do you like Bach?'

I drew a deep breath. The scrawny woman's eyes were still open, as if she was watching television, and there was a child-like look of absorption on her face. She was sitting there prim and proper, her head had been smashed and the brains were trickling down her forehead; the track suit she had on was also drenched with blood, as if she was drenched with sweat.

'Sorry to have given you a fright. Would you like a cup of coffee?'

I stood there, cold all over. Then I took an involuntary step forward. The blood soaked my sneakers, my toes felt sticky and cold. I said, 'No, I think I'd better call the police.'

Chan smiled, 'There's no hurry. I've made some coffee, have a cup first. I'll be here anyway.' He looked down and said, 'Sorry to have bothered you. The kids are upstairs, you want to go and have a look?'

I said at once, 'No, no need.' All of a sudden, I felt flustered, and asked, 'What about the white mouse?'

Chan said, 'It had to be.'

I guessed he didn't know whether he was answering my question. Then he looked sideways and said, 'Listen. Bach's music twists and turns. Unbearably painful. But it had to be. Have you been to the new church in Amsterdam? I've been there to listen to the organ recitals of Bach. In Europe, there is permanence and peace. When I came back to Hong Kong . . . the apartment buildings I built only three years ago had already been torn down. You like Bach's music?'

I quickly replied, 'Eh! I like Kenny G. I'll be off now.'

Still standing in a pool of blood, he said politely, 'Sorry, I won't see you out, my feet are drenched in blood. I wonder if the kids have died. I'll go up and see.' Then he waved me away.

I ran like mad out of the house. At the door, I tripped on the iron rod and fell flat on the ground, my mouth was spattered with blood. I left a bloody trail of footprints behind me, like red lotuses in snow.

'Something's happened! Something . . . something. . . .'

———

The chap who reported the case was a bundle of nerves—probably still suffering from shock. I'd just heard that my colleague Lam Kwai had been promoted again. Not for me the post of District Commander, I guessed. Because of the localization policy, they said. Night had fallen. Alone, I watched the night scene of Victoria harbour, drawing deeply on my cigarette. The colony was going to vanish forever, like my wife Valerie. It had to be. Right now she was probably sitting beside a fire in a house in some meadow in Naples. It should be cold there already. Not so in Hong Kong, where the seasons are so indistinct you don't stop to look back and think. Now that I thought about it, it had been six years since Valerie left me, and in all those years I hadn't thought about her at all, not until tonight.

I arrived at the scene at thirty-one minutes past midnight. The forensic pathologist and the photographer had not arrived. According to the preliminary report of the ambulance people, the five casualties were all dead. A neighbour, his eyes all red, had reported the case.

The uniformed inspector said to him, 'This is Chief Inspector Evans. Tell him the details.'

The young man then said to me, 'He just said something had happened. He didn't say, "I've done something". It was as if the whole thing had nothing to do with him.' He looked sad and distraught.

The inspector told me the suspect was still in the kitchen. When the police first arrived, he was making coffee, and now he was drinking it, 'as if the whole thing had nothing to do with him', the inspector said. He hadn't been handcuffed, because he was not armed and was very quiet. I frowned, and went upstairs to inspect the scene.

'The children were aged three, four, six, and seven. The two girls, aged six and seven, are in this room.'

The inspector opened the door. The eldest girl was slumped over her desk. She had been drawing when the back of her head was smashed open by a hard object, leaving a wound the shape of a star. The younger girl was lying on the bed, a blood-stained teddy bear in her arms, but her head was almost severed from her body. In the middle of the room was a large pool of blood with a severed finger. It was clear that she had been killed before her body was lifted on to the bed.

'The two boys, aged three and four, are here. I thought at first they were asleep.'

The inspector opened the door to another room. And now the forensic pathologist and photographer had arrived and the camera was flashing and clicking. The two boys were lying prone in bed and still covered with a blanket. But the wall was splattered with blood. The backs of their heads also had star-shaped wounds, and their skulls were fractured.

'The murder weapons?'

The inspector replied, 'The suspect has wrapped them up in a plastic bag. He has even marked it with a sticker which says, "Weapons: one iron rod, one knife".'

'Take him to the psychiatric unit for an examination first, then take his statements.'

'Yes, Sir.'

I stood for a while in the blood-splattered room. In all my thirty-odd years as a cop, this was the first time I had been unnerved by the stench and the turgidity of blood. If only I could have had a double Scotch!

I saw flashes of blue light swirling outside the window and I yelled, 'Switch off the siren, bloody fools.'

Some officer replied from afar, 'Yes, Sir.'

I looked more carefully—it was the blue moon, its light ominous with murderous intentions. I felt old and tired, I shivered slightly. This startled me—I really was old. I had long forgotten what fear was. But at this moment, I was overcome with fear and apprehension, and I felt so lonely.

I guessed it was time for me to leave this colony. The colony will be no more.

———

The psychiatrist's preliminary diagnosis showed that the suspect was not suffering from any mental disorder, he just had a slight cold and exhibited some symptoms of depression. He refused to say a word in the police station. Under the law, he could only be held in custody for forty-eight hours, and now there were just ten hours left. The relatives of the suspect were all in Canada, only an elder brother of the dead woman was in Hong Kong. According to this man, two days before the murders took place, two hundred thousand dollars in cash had been transferred into his bank account, and he had received a letter from Chan the day after the murders, asking him to use the sum for funeral arrangements for his wife and four children. 'I'm afraid I won't be able to see you for a long, long time'—that was how the letter ended.

Chan was gaunt and haggard but calm. He watched me quietly. I asked, 'You were drinking Blue Mountain coffee in the kitchen after the incident. You like Blue Mountain?'

He just stared at me blankly, as if someone, or something, had died in him. I was stunned, and felt as if I saw myself in him. I sent a constable out to prepare some coffee, while I drew out the photo we found at the scene. A suburban house—probably in Canada—Chan and his family together with a big shepherd dog in the garden, all laughing; even the dog seemed to be laughing, sharing the fun. Chan looked down a little, glanced at the photo, and then his attention drifted. The constable brought in the coffee, as well as a CD player with earphones and amplifiers. The room was filled with the mellow aroma of coffee. From the CD player rose the music he had been listening when the murders took place—Bach's 'Suite for Unaccompanied Cello, No.1 in G'. I lit a cigarette, and then sank slowly into meditation and silence.

'Do you like Bach?'

Chan did not reply.

'I guess you don't want to say anything anymore. Good. You know, after I get off work, I don't say a word. Sometimes I go to Lan Kwai Fong and spend the whole evening drinking, listening to people yapping. Not to have to say a word is a luxury.'

Chan now looked at me. I had no idea whether he was listening or thinking.

'My wife, her name is Valerie. I brought her to Hong Kong soon after we'd got married in Dublin. Have you been to Ireland? It's a beautiful and sad place. There are horses in the meadows; in spring, the fields are full of daisies. Our son is called Davie. He has green-flecked eyes: beautiful, like the plains of Ireland.

211

'Valerie never liked Hong Kong, maybe because I had flings with one Chinese woman after another. There was once when I got really pissed, and I blurted out to her that I'd fallen for a Chinese woman with a phoenix tattooed on her back. The next day when I got home I found Valerie lying prone in bed, her face red with pain. I lifted the blanket, and saw a huge phoenix tattooed on her back. Christ! The blood was still wet! I knelt on the floor and begged her to forgive me.

'It was no use. You know, I'm a cop. I'm British. There's no way I could have resisted the temptations of this colony.

'She went back to Ireland. I took Davie with me and followed her to her sister's place. I didn't say a word, and she just held Davie in her arms and cried.

'Then she came back to Hong Kong. On and off for many years. Davie began to go to school by himself, and started to date teenage girlfriends. Valerie left me. From Milan she sent me a postcard asking for a divorce.

'Later on she lived with an Italian. Before she went to Italy, she made love with me for the last time. The phoenix on her back had been eradicated, and her beautiful back was a wasteland of ugly scars. I cried as we made love. She only said, "He's nice to me, much nicer than you are. I'll be a lot happier with him. Please forgive me, I can't carry this love-cross anymore."

'After she left me, I began to grow very quiet.

'There are many things in life which are so heavy and so intricate you just can't talk about them. I think you can understand, just as I think I can understand you.'

Then he fell silent. He was behaving as if I was the prosecutor and he was a cold-blooded murderer with many lives on his hands. The way of the human soul is so intricate, and its darkness so heavy you just can't talk about it; and morality is beside the point. His love for Valerie was no more and no less than mine for Chiu Mei, but he had ruined her beautiful back, her love, and the first half of her life; and I had killed Mei, Ming Ming, Siu Yi, Siu Yuen, and Siu Sze, as well as the big white mouse.

I couldn't carry this love-cross anymore.

The thought of killing Mei had kept flashing through my mind: the first time was when we were still in Calgary, Alberta. We had been there only a few months. She was pregnant with Siu Yi, I was unemployed, and the two of us were trapped inside the house all day because of the heavy snow. Mei liked counting money—she'd changed all our cash into coins, and was counting them one by one. 'Enough to keep us going for two years, four months and five days,' she said.

I was watching television and in the background was the monotonous sound of coins being counted. And then I heard what sounded almost like a sigh of contentment—'Another day is gone.'

When would these days end? It was at that moment that the thought of killing her suddenly flashed through my mind. It was no more than a flash: I'd smash her brain, slash open her belly with a knife to let out that dark purple foetus, then kill Ming Ming in her sleep. The police would treat me as a VIP, we'd hit the headlines in the Calgary newspapers. The thought terrified me and I could not help but shiver. Mei turned round; her face was purplish, her eyes greyish black. She seemed to have seen through me, 'Chan Lo Yuen, I know you hate me. You hate me for forcing you to leave Hong Kong. But who knows? We have jumped out of the frying pan into the fire, and in the end we may jump from the fire back into the frying pan. Who knows?'

I was eaten up with pain and sadness, I couldn't say a word and just held her in my arms.

I never knew that winter was so interminable in Canada. Snow started to fall as early as November. Mei grew more and more reticent, and kept busying herself in the kitchen preparing food: cereal, fresh fruit, cheese, smoked salmon, spaghetti, chocolate mousse, apple pie, walnut cookies, lobster bisque, goose liver, roast duck. . . . The two of us sat there staring at a table full of food as the television droned on and on—it was no different from the life we had led in our Hong Kong apartment.

Then Mei decided to keep a shepherd dog. She'd feed the dog first, then Ming Ming, and finally me. The food we couldn't finish we threw into the rubbish bin. I only existed somewhere along the line formed by the dog, Ming Ming, and the rubbish bin. I put on a coat and went out, into the world of wind and snow. A few maple trees stood in desolation in the garden, shivering and shaking in the wind. The night was snow white, the moon clear and beautiful. I walked blindly, on and on. My legs got so numb I could hardly take another step. But I wanted to get away from this prison of sumptuous food. We'd thought we'd find freedom in Canada, only to be trapped in a prison bounded on all sides by snow. Had the Basic Law been promulgated? What they were drafting were ordinances of a prison. We had run away from one prison, only to find ourselves in another.

I sat resting in the soft cold snow. I was tired.

In a dark purple dream, I heard the light sobbing and the faint sound of breathing in Mei's womb.

I woke to find myself in a snow-white room in a hospital. The nurse greeted me kindly: 'Mr Chan.' Mei was looking at me from afar, her face purple, bloated, like a flower tainted with bad luck and smeared with dirt.

'You shouldn't give birth to the child. Get rid of it.'

Mei burst into tears.

After the child was born we moved to Toronto. It was crowded and the air was polluted. The people liked to go out for dim sum meals, read gossip weeklies from Hong Kong, and speculate in the property market—more like the people of Hong Kong, and more reassuring for us. We bought an apartment in a high-rise block and a Japanese car, and I found a job as a clerk—an architect working as a clerk. My colleagues were ever so friendly and kind to me, and the manager was ever so polite—'Mr Chan, do you mind sorting out these bills for me?' The days passed quietly and slowly. At five past five in the afternoon, the entire office would be deserted. Sometimes I would stay behind, and stand before the window looking at the snow and the grey dark evening sky. Soon, I'd be lost in thought and sometimes I'd see Mei's purple face and the two scrawny babies—their faces also purple, like cherries. I wanted to crush them, crush them hard, and splash the ground of snow with the purple red juice.

Siu Yi cried all the time, and would wake Ming Ming, and the two would cry in turn throughout the night. Mei and I suffered badly from lack of sleep. She started to lose her hair—locks and locks of it littering the floor—she even lost her eyelashes. I couldn't keep my hands steady when I was driving. Even when I was in the office, I kept feeling that someone was watching me outside the window, quietly and smugly—watching the fun. I looked up: nothing was there. My mind rang with the crying of the babies in the depths of my pitch-black soul.

Mei couldn't sleep with the babies crying, so she went into the kitchen and started to cook. At five in the morning, the two of us sat staring at a table of food, and the dark firmament of snow outside. I glared at the squeaking white mouse before me, and suddenly realized that it had given birth to hundreds and thousands of white mice. They were everywhere—scuttling about in the kitchen, the bedrooms, the attic, even my driver's seat. I jumped up, dashed into the babies' room, and swooped up Ming Ming and Siu Yi in my arms, lest they should be attacked by the mice. They wailed. I turned round. Mei was standing at the door, weak and frail; her feet were bare, her shabby nightdress crumpled, her arms crossed over her chest. She said miserably, 'Let's go back to Hong Kong.'

In the end we moved to San Francisco, and found an old house in the Bay Area. I bought a second-hand Ford that rattled hopelessly, and found a job as a draughtsman in an architect's firm.

The children were still frail and scrawny, and they were very touchy and given to crying. One night Ming Ming had another crying fit, but I was exhausted, and I was beginning to get used to the noise; I just turned over and went on sleeping. Suddenly, I was woken by a blue light. It was lightning without thunder, a familiar sight in the summer sky of San Francisco. The house seemed unusually dark and quiet. There didn't seem to be any sound of the children crying. I felt as delightfully surprised and frightened as Cinderella, and wandered freely into this strange kingdom of blissful silence. In this kingdom of silence Mei had vanished. It was mine alone. As the lightning continued to flash, noiselessly, I laughed, noiselessly too.

How I wished Mei and the children would all vanish!

But I started to grope about in the dark. I turned on the lights, and went looking for the kids and Mei in the babies' room. Siu Yi was sleeping soundly, but Ming Ming's bed was empty, with signs of her having lain here. My heart started to pound.

Finally I found Mei in the kitchen sipping a cup of hot chocolate. She looked at me, and broke into a faint smile. I hadn't seen her smile for a long time. Ming Ming was sitting on the floor, leaning against the gas cooker. Her face was purplish blue, a banana was jammed fully into her mouth. Mei said, 'She won't cry anymore.'

I nearly fainted. I took Ming Ming in my arms at once, removed the banana from her mouth, then rang for an ambulance. Ming Ming was still breathing, but barely. I patted her face and felt such a sharp pang in my heart I nearly burst into tears. Mei just sat there quietly sipping her hot chocolate, an innocent and peaceful expression on her face. Standing here in this kitchen rich with the aroma of hot chocolate, in this apartment criss-crossed with flashing blue lights, supported by a hard-working wife and an angel of a daughter, and a middle-class background that enabled me to be one of those fortunate enough to run away from Hong Kong—the ambulance should be here any minute—I felt the overpowering irony of a happy life. Looking at Mei, I once again laughed, in distraction and dismay.

———

Ming Ming recovered quickly. But her parents, Mei and I, had to go and see a psychiatrist, and Ming Ming and Siu Yi were put into a child-care centre. A heavy drain on our limited savings.

The situation became stable again. Except that I would have dreams of killing Mei, and wake up in a cold sweat. Then I would hold her tightly, call her 'My precious', say I loved her, apologize for putting her through hell, and make love to her.

Mei brought the two children home to save some money. She also went back to her old job and worked as a substitute nurse at weekends. I stuck at my boring job as a draughtsman, feeling all the time that I was a first-year architecture student who would never be promoted to year two. Since she had had that banana jammed into her throat, Ming Ming had stopped crying altogether. But she had a sorrowful look, her large eyes blinked in sorrow too. Once we discovered some blood in the potty she used, but she just bit her lip, there was not a tear in her eyes and no expression on her face. We examined her and found that her private parts were red and swollen with infection. It suddenly dawned on me that because of our frailty and weakness, she had been ruined.

Quietly and with my heart in my mouth—as if in anticipation of misfortune—we nevertheless managed to settle down in San Francisco, until winter arrived.

Autumn had given way to winter in the space of a few days. Evening came early, and I hadn't yet turned on the lights. Ming Ming was playing on her rocking horse in the darkening playroom. Siu Yi was sound asleep in the cot. Mei was out. Sitting alone in the sitting-room having a can of beer, I dozed off.

It was completely dark when I woke up. No sign of Mei yet. Her car was still outside. So she hadn't gone out in her car. I opened the wardrobe and saw that she hadn't taken her coat either. All of a sudden, I caught a faint whiff of the pungent smell of disaster. Like in a dream, images floated before my eyes—of Mei sitting on the sofa watching TV, her head smashed, brains trickling down her forehead; of Ming Ming sitting slumped over her desk, the back of her skull fractured, like a star, and dripping blood. Like someone who had gone mad, I took Ming Ming into my arms and shook her, 'Where's Mommy? Where is Mommy?' But she kept shaking her head.

Had Mei really left me for good? Panic-stricken, I kissed Ming Ming again and again—what a spitting image she was of Mei! But Ming Ming was frightened and turned her face away.

I ran along the tree-lined street calling Mei's name. The neighbours turned on the lights and leant their heads out, then they closed their windows.

At the top end of the street where Mr Kim—a Korean—lived, I saw him arriving home in his car. He stopped and said, 'I saw your wife, she was sitting alone in the park.'

I found her under a withered maple tree. She was sitting on a white bench. Her face was purplish white and a little sallow; she hadn't put on a coat, just wrapped a big, purple-red scarf round her neck. I sat down quietly beside her. Ming Ming struggled away and went playing on the grass.

It was a cold starry night.

After a long while, Mei asked me, 'Do you like living here?'

'Well, it's not a matter of liking or not liking.'

'How does it compare to life in Hong Kong?'

'Even in Hong Kong, it's not a matter of liking or not liking. Besides, there was no time to think.'

A meteor suddenly flashed across the sky.

'Remember the lawn outside the Chemistry Building at the University of Hong Kong? We used to sit there, wondering when we would have a home of our own, fitted with lights, bright like stars.'

'H'm.'

The Mei I remembered always had on the elegant cap of a student nurse. And she was always reciting softly the motto of her profession: 'Love, care, and concern.'

'I've always yearned for a stable life. My demands on life are actually very simple.'

And my hope at that time was that the high-rise buildings in Hong Kong would, like human civilization, go all the way to heaven, I had thought that my buildings were the Tower of Babel. When was it that we had had those thoughts? In those days, when we were young.

Mei leant gently against my shoulder. In just a year or so, we had moved house three times, had two children. She was now very frail, and flabby, her body a deflated balloon.

'Shall we go back to Hong Kong?'

———

But things had really scared Mei in those days. The Sino-British negotiations had broken down, the Hong Kong dollar was suffering a sharp decline, and people were rushing to supermarkets to stock up on food. Mei came straight from the hospital looking for me, not bothering to change out of her uniform, and burst into tears in my arms, 'I can't stay here anymore. Let's get married and leave Hong Kong.' Her white cap shook before me like a fluttering butterfly. I saw that what kept it in place were dozens of hairpins—they seemed to have grown there, like spikes.

She wanted to marry me, and so I said yes. I never thought about saying no, I loved her.

———

'Chan Lo Yuen.' She always called me by my full name, and now she reached out her hand and held mine.

'It's strange. Lately I seem always to be looking for things, I keep feeling as if I've lost something.' She smiled nervously. 'When you've gone to work, I keep feeling that I'll never see you again.'

'It's as if I've lost something. As if you're already in the grave, and I'm walking over your grave, calling your name.'

I kept quiet all this time. Darkness was everywhere; the lights in the apartment block in the distance were far away and beyond our reach. Yes, something had been lost, there was no turning back, ever.

'Let's not think about going back to Hong Kong.' Mei gave up the idea and said, 'Because I'm pregnant again.'

'I see.'

'A child is a new hope for us. Let's do our best and give our child love, care, and concern.'

She laid my hand gently on her belly. All of a sudden, I felt my hand burning. Terrified by the unknown future awaiting a new life, I said haltingly, 'Must we . . . must we have the baby?' And the image gradually rose in my mind of a bleeding baby half buried in the earth while Mei and I groped in the dark trying to find it, calling its name.

'Yes, we must, we must have this baby.' Mei replied slowly but firmly. I knew she had made up her mind.

———

We had thought we could really settle down after the birth of the baby. He was healthy and strong. We called him Siu Yuen. He had a sweet temper, better than his two sisters. And he slept well and seldom cried at night. Even if he did, a little attention on our part would quiet him down. He also seemed more open and easy-going than his sisters.

But things still kept happening, one after another. Ming Ming was nearly four now, and had started going to nursery school. But suddenly she refused to go, no matter how Mei coaxed her or warned her with harsh words. One day she even threw a tantrum and wet herself. As Mei helped her change, she saw that there were ugly bruises on Ming Ming's legs. Only then did Ming Ming say, 'They beat me at school. I talked Chinese with Yau Sang, and they beat me.' Yau Sang was the only other Chinese pupil in her class. Mei stood there as if she had been struck by thunder. Frowning, she said to me, 'Lo Yuen, I'm afraid disaster is bound to hit us.'

Then I lost my job. I went home with the cheque and the politely phrased redundancy letter, and, after closing the door, I leant back against it and sank slowly to the floor. Evening came particularly early in winter. I was unnerved by what I saw before me: another snow-bound world; the baby crying non-stop every night; I and they hurting and destroying one another; blood splashing, gathering into a small pool, with perhaps a white, icy-cold lily rising from it and blooming, who could tell? Then I found Mei in the kitchen; I could only hold her tightly in my arms and said, 'I have nothing now but you, Mei.'

Mei was always a tower of strength when I was weak. She made me some coffee and said, 'We still have enough savings to last us one-and-a-half years. Besides, we can apply for unemployment benefits.'

She tipped her head to one side, thought for a while, and then broke into a faint smile, 'It's lucky it doesn't snow in San Francisco. Or else, I would probably die . . . and so would the kids. . . .'

Suddenly she looked at me, almost savagely. I was so shaken my coffee mug dropped from my hand and smashed on the floor.

I suspected that in some corner of our hearts, memory and passion had been lost, and it was snowing—an unbroken snow. In San Francisco, in Hong Kong.

Mei would not let Ming Ming go to school anymore. She kept Ming Ming in the house, held the two babies in her arms, and kept saying, 'They want to kill Ming Ming.' Then she went and bought a hundred metres of black cloth, and spent days at the sewing machine. When the curtains were made, she hung them up, enshrouding the house in black. 'They are spying on us, they want to kill Ming Ming.' Even at home she would put on her raincoat and rubber boots, and a pair of transparent plastic gloves—the type used by doctors. 'I'm scared, Chan Lo Yuen. When will the rain stop?' Actually, winter days in San Francisco were as sunny as in Barcelona.

I couldn't stand it anymore. I took Ming Ming back to school. When I came back, I held Mei firmly in my arms, and tore away her raincoat, gloves, and rubber boots. 'Mei, you're not well. What should I do to give you and the kids peace and plenty?'

She looked down and said slowly, 'There probably is nothing you can do, Chan Lo Yuen.'

Silently she picked up the raincoat and other plastic items on the floor, drew back the black curtains enshrouding the house, and went into the kitchen to cook. She went about her business slowly and quietly, like a psychiatric patient just back from shock therapy. I stood in the sitting-room—now bright and tidy—while the music which Mei had put on—Bach's 'Suite for Unaccompanied Cello, No.1 in G'—rang faintly in my ears. All of a sudden, I felt very old and tired. I'd long forgotten what fear was like, but at this moment, I was overcome with confusion, and fear.

To my own surprise, I actually hit Mei. Ming Ming had come back from school, and Siu Yi and Siu Yuen were both hungry, so Ming Ming took them into the kitchen. Mei was still very dejected, I heard her pottering about in the kitchen, leaving the kids to look after themselves. A while later, they started to cry. I went in. The kids' mouths were all spattered with blood, and in their hands they were holding some meat, also covered with blood. Mei was shouting orders to them in a low voice, 'Eat it. Eat it. Eat it to drive away the evil! The curse of death is upon us!' She, too, scooped up a spoonful of raw meat and blood to put it into her own mouth.

I seized her hair and flung away the spoon, 'What's this?'

She replied, 'Chicken heart, cow spleen, pig's liver.'

I pointed a finger at her face, 'You want the kids to eat this?'

And then, to my surprise, I started to hit her, slap her face again and again. The kids cried even louder; she didn't cry, and didn't hit back, just narrowed her eyes and looked at me. I stopped; she turned round, snatched up a kitchen knife, and pointed it straight at my throat. I could feel it, cold and glinting.

'Have you forgotten, Chan Lo Yuen? Love, care, and concern.'

Why had things come to such a state? All I wanted was to give her love and concern, give her a caring home!

Ming Ming came up to us quietly, and clutched Mei by her leg. Tears began to stream down Mei's cheeks. She put down the knife, knelt down and said, 'Ming Ming, your parents have done wrong. Out of the frying pan into the fire, and out of the fire back into the frying pan. And we don't know what wrong we have done.'

And we thought in our wisdom we had created the Tower of Babel, believing it would lead us straight to heaven.

But in the end destruction was all.

I went alone to Europe, and then back to Hong Kong. I could not go on carrying the love-cross.

But I couldn't recognize Hong Kong anymore. I walked too slowly, people kept treading on my heels. The teller at the bank said, 'Your identity card number, please.' I tried to remember it, and heard the teller say, 'Next, please.' I wanted to walk down memory lane and have a cup of coffee at the Honolulu Coffee Shop, only to find that it was there no more. The phone numbers now were all seven digits. And Hong Kong English bewildered me. Sam Hui's films still made me laugh, but the young people in the cinema were all so impatient with him, some swore aloud, others booed and yelled, 'Go home, grandad!' The elected Legislative councillors were only in their twenties. I aged quickly in Hong Kong.

I rented a small but tidy apartment in Eastern District. Like Alice in Wonderland, I returned to my bachelor life of loneliness and silence. When I was free, I sat on the window ledge watching the planes take off and land, staring at the huge metal flying objects that swept past my window, and at the gleaming strip of land that was the runway lying between the city and the ocean. What an amazing city. Truly unique!

I teamed up with my partner from the old days and worked until ten in the evening every day. Life was all right. But I slept lightly, and would wake up hearing the crying of children. I didn't know if I was just imagining things.

But Mei and Ming Ming managed to track me down. Siu Yuen was crying, Mei was heavily pregnant. I hung my head thinking, 'It's Rosemary's baby—the Rosemary in our hearts.'

'Smack!' Mei slapped me hard on the face without a word. I nursed my burning cheek lightly.

Silently I took Ming Ming in one arm and the sleeping baby from Mei in another. She picked up the luggage and silently followed me into the house.

I even made love with her that night, pressing against that weird and evil knoll that was her belly.

The decision could have been made that night.

After they came back to Hong Kong, Mei, Ming Ming, Siu Yi, and Siu Yuen fell ill frequently and they infected one another. Air pollution put Ming Ming under the recurrent attack of colds and influenza. Food contamination made Mei prone to diarrhoea. And noise pollution made even the good-tempered Siu Yuen frown and cry all the time. To bring back our memories of Canada, I bought them a big white mouse. The mouse and I were the healthiest in the family. It grew quickly like cancerous cells. And my decision, conceived in the dark, was taking shape and waiting to be born.

I didn't know how to explain things clearly. Had I ruined them? Or had they ruined me? Or had we all been victims? Siu Sze, our fourth child, was healthy and growing well, and kicked and cried like all babies would. Six of us in the family now, and like every family in Hong Kong, we lived in peace—temporarily, fearfully. Like every housewife too, Mei took the kids to school, remembered the price of food, and dressed herself up for parent-teacher day. Ming Ming grew more garrulous, and she'd use triad jargon in the melodramatic manner of TV soap opera stars. Siu Yi broke all the glasses in the house, and Siu Yuen never grew tired of falling ill—diarrhoea, fever, rashes. Life became an impossibly complicated prescription—two doses of this, three spoonfuls of that. Meanwhile, the design plans piled high on my desk, and at weekends I still had to go to karaoke bars with the developers and contractors, eat seafood contaminated with heavy metal and all sorts of poisons, spend money like crazy and earn money like crazy. All of a sudden, I began to miss my life in Canada and America—that solid sense of loneliness and fear—because I was then sober and clear-headed. But I had no other choice.

Out the frying pan into the fire, and out of the fire back into the frying pan.

Emigration is no more than a false hope. But then hope is never something just out there, or not there.

Mei no longer talked to me about love, care, and concern. She was completely worn out—running with me up and down the wrong roads of life. But then like hope, the bright and right road is never something just out there, or not there.

I believed that my decision was absolutely correct, the brightest decision.

I loved my family, so I made the decision for them.

I found in Sai Kung a quiet and out-of-the-way house, with a dismal mango tree in the garden. Our next-door neighbours were a couple. They were like a pair of clowns, cheerful and always laughing. After we had moved in, the kids learnt to like watching the moon; Mei loved watching TV in the middle of the night; I grew fond of music, and the silence in the music.

That night, the moon had certainly been very bright—a blue and glamorous night. Everyone at home was relaxed and quiet. Ming Ming was drawing, Siu Yi playing with her teddy bear, Siu Yuen and Siu Sze were already in bed, Mei was watching TV. And I was listening to Bach's 'Suite for Unaccompanied Cello, No.1 in G' from beginning to end, paying full attention to the intricacies of the composition—no matter how abstract, there had to be an internal logic in things, nothing would happen without a cause. The equipment was a knife and an iron rod.

I never knew there could be so much blood in a person. Mei simply didn't recognize it was me, she was still crying 'Help! Help!' before she died. Ming Ming's painting was splashed with blood. Siu Yi was too small to know anything, she thought I was playing with her, and called 'Daddy!' Siu Sze didn't even wake from his dream. Siu Yuen half-opened his eyes and fell at once into the abyss of eternal darkness and unconsciousness.

The last to go was the big white mouse.

———

Taking action was not difficult. Giving an explanation was. I had always wanted to be an honest and sincere person—and because I was sincere, an explanation was that much more difficult.

It was so heavy and so intricate I just couldn't talk about it. Therefore silence.

But my point was: there had to be an internal logic to everything, that was why nothing was incomprehensible.

I wondered if the Chief Inspector before me had got my point. He was a lonely man, lonely souls could understand each other a lot more easily.

Because of loneliness, one could be more sober and clear-headed.

———

He put his signature to the statements prepared by the police. Before he left, he just shook my hand firmly. His hand was warm. The handshake was sincere.

Chan Lo Yuen refused to answer any questions when he was brought to trial. The defence counsel questioned Jim Hak Ming, the witness, over and over again.

'At fifteen minutes past midnight on the sixteenth of September, you reported to the police that the accused had killed some people. When you first saw the accused, was he on your left side or your right side? You said there was an iron rod stained with blood: was it outside the door or inside? You said you saw the dead woman Chiu Mei: were her eyes open or closed?'

The witness grew impatient, and said to the judge, 'Your honour, when it rains, it rains, when a mother wants to marry off her daughter, she marries off her daughter, when this guy wants to kill his folks, kill them all, he kills them all. There's no stopping it. What will be, will be!'

The whole courtroom burst into laughter. The judge glared at him and said, 'The witness is perverse, he shows no respect. He treats life as a joke, the court as a playground, a market! The court is adjourned.'

Chan Lo Yuen was found guilty on five charges of premeditated murder, and given the death sentence. In a few days, his case would be reviewed by the Governor and the Executive Council, and his sentence would be commuted to life imprisonment.

Outside the Supreme Court I ran into Lam Kwai. He'd been promoted to Deputy District Commander. He was very pleased when he saw me, and complained laughingly that his new job was too demanding and he wanted early retirement. But I could see that he was proud of himself. He was almost ten years my junior, and had worked under me when he was at the Triad Society Division. During the riots of 1967, we worked side by side dealing with the strike at the plastic flower factory in San Po Kong, and together we forced our way into the Wah Fung Apartment Building in North Point. Once a bomb exploded within a metre from us, and we pulled each other on to the ground to take cover. . . .

'Will you be coming to the club for a drink tonight?'

I only said, 'I've stopped drinking. Stomach trouble.' Then I left.

I felt empty and light-headed, as if a little drunk, even though I hadn't had a drink at all. So I stood for a while beside the railing in front of the Supreme Court, looking out at Victoria harbour. Hong Kong was still very prosperous. When the court was dismissed, lawyers and family members who had been attending the trials walked past me in groups—it was like the end of a film show at a cinema. But I suddenly thought about Chan Lo Yuen, and myself. He would never ever see this beautiful harbour again, and the world would soon forget him. But that was his own conscious decision. As for me, I had no choice, I would lose this city.

When I left Ireland I was still a young lad with green-flecked eyes, like Davie. When I went back, I would still have my big frame, but the rest of me would hang loose on it like a large outfit that had lost its shape.

—

Not long afterwards Davie was arrested. The year before last when he came back to Hong Kong, he had been arrested at Lan Kwai Fong, having been found with twenty grams of 'ice' on him. The charges were dropped only after a lot of hard work on my part. But this time, he was caught with twenty kilos of heroin—with an estimated market value of about ten million Hong Kong dollars—in the boot of his BMW sports car. Only now did it suddenly occur to me that he was just a college student, and yet he was driving a BMW sports car—and I'd never even asked.

Lots of things had changed drastically, and yet I'd never noticed.

I went with a lawyer to see him. As soon as Davie saw me, he broke down and cried. It reminded me of when he was a kid and he fed some insecticide to the cat while giving it a bath, killing it. Then as now, he just cried and yelled, 'Daddy.'

He was still my Davie, my angel, my darling, the apple of my eye. A big frame, green-flecked eyes, panic-stricken—the spitting image of me.

'Daddy, help me!'

How could it be that I'd no idea when he'd changed from a mechanical engineering student to a drug dealer out to make big money? Was it when I was having a drunken brawl? Was it when I was making love at dawn to a woman I'd picked up on the street? Was it when I was at the races? Or when I was firing a gun, beating up a suspect? Was it when 1997 was looming and the whole of Hong Kong was jittery and neurotic? Or was it when the tanks and artilleries started to roar in Tiananmen in 1989?

'Daddy, get me out, quick!'

He thought he'd simply stolen an apple from his neighbour! Furious, I leapt up, clutched the iron grille and shouted, 'What else do you want me to do, you little bastard!'

I banged my fist on the wall, 'What else do you want me to do?'

Standing outside the door of Lam Kwai's spacious office, I felt embarrassed, I couldn't take another step. Someone was inside taking orders from him, 'Yes, Sir.' I didn't know what to do.

Lam Kwai had already heard the noise: 'Yes, come in.'

Then he said in a low voice, 'You go out first.'

The other one replied, 'Yes, Sir.' and came out.

It was Inspector Ma from the Serious Crimes Division. He greeted me, 'Good morning, Sir.'

I explained to Lam Kwai why I had come to see him. He was still in good form, strong and sturdy, his eyes sharp as a knife, a deep scar on the back of his hand—he got it when he and I were attacked and injured by a bank robber.

He thought for a while and said, 'Look, Evans, this is not robbery or assault. Even if I said yes, others won't.'

He let out a long sigh, stood up and went before the window, fading into a shadow. Outside there were officers on marching drills. Such familiar and reassuring sounds—Att-ent-ion. Eyes Front. In those days we were young.

'Besides, the Attorney General's Chambers has decided to press charges.'

He slowly took off his jacket, probably because of the heat. I saw his strong, well-developed muscles tighten and then relax before he said, 'Evans, the times are really different now. The power of the Brits is on the wane. Their days are numbered, they won't run any risk to do someone a favour. The Chinese are not up to it yet. So, there really isn't much hope with the AGC.'

I said in a soft voice, 'I can use money.'

He turned around; he was as handsome as ever: 'If you need money, I can lend you some. But. . . .'

His looks still charmed me, I loved him no less than I loved Davie.

'Evans, you'd better not take this risk. And it'll be better for you to leave the Force sooner rather than later. If you stay, you'll only find out that sooner or later things and people you know change, for better or for worse I don't know. But it's sad to have to witness all this. I'm only forty-one. It's too early for me to chuck it in, emigrate, and live in retirement: I'm stuck. But you're different. You'll have an easier time if you go back home.'

Suddenly I saw Davie holding up my heart and slashing it with a knife.

'And why not? The world won't stop moving. You've aged a lot these few years. I bet you if we had a long-distance race now, you'd lose.'

With that, I lost Davie, and I lost him.

'Thanks.' I said. 'I understand.'

I didn't know why, but suddenly I wanted very much to have a hat, a good hat, to protect myself. Since I came to Hong Kong, because of the heat, and because it was too easy, I'd forgotten Ireland's harsh and difficult winters.

———

After Davie was put on trial, I handed in my application for early retirement. With a pension of over a million Hong Kong dollars, I could start a corner shop in Dublin, or get a franchise to run a petrol station. In Hong Kong, things moved at high speed. Less than a week after I handed in my application, none of my men bothered to buy any cigarettes for me or bring me an ashtray. They even cancelled the newspaper subscription for my office.

Later on, I went to the psychiatric detention centre to visit Chan Lo Yuen. Even though a number of doctors were unanimous in their diagnosis that Chan was not suffering from a mental disorder, he was still sent to the psychiatric detention centre, for reasons of greater safety. I went to see him, probably because I wanted to say goodbye to him—although he wouldn't have understood. He had had a crew cut, was scrawny, but seemed in good spirits. The correctional officer said he never spoke, but just spent his time sitting alone in his room reading the *Encyclopaedia Britannica*, and in the evenings he'd play the violin—'very boring music, full of repetitions. Is it called Bach?' He also said that Chan always carried in his pocket a photo of his family, including a shepherd dog. 'Chan won't talk to you,' the young officer explained kindly, as if it was his duty to save me from disappointment.

Chan was happy to see me, and a little awkward, like a son on meeting his father, and sat there respectfully. I had nothing to say to him either, and just gave him a few CDs, a CD player with earphones, and a small amplifier, like the set we had used when we took his statements that day. 'Try it.' This time it was Handel. His music ran like a cool soothing hand over tortured souls. We didn't speak, but we grew closer in the music.

Suddenly I understood Beethoven in his deafness. Music is the language of the lonely.

Halfway through Handel's 'Messiah', time was up and I had to go. We shook hands. Chan's hand was still warm, and it was a sincere handshake.

I said to him, 'Take care. Who knows, things being what they are, chaotic and all, who knows if there won't be a replay of the fall of the Bastille! Or maybe they'll let you out. But that will have to be many years after 1997. By then, the world won't know you, and you won't know it either. That's good, like a rebirth.'

He was amused, and laughed. Then I said, 'Be a good chap. Be good.'

When I came back from visiting Chan, I seemed to have sorted out all my affairs in Hong Kong, I didn't know why. Later on, Lam lent me two hundred thousand dollars, strictly for bailing Davie out.

I met Lam in the club and before I opened my mouth, he handed me the cheque: 'Take your time to pay me back. This is the first time and also the last.'

I had never have to worry about money in my life. This was the first time I had felt hard-up, and also the first time I had felt the burden and pain of money. That evening Lam Kwai drank fiercely, cursing and swearing all the time—'The mother fucker, the fat asshole.' Not until two in the morning when the club closed did he stagger off to get his car. Outside the club, a sea breeze was blowing, the pleasure boats were rocking gently in the Causeway Bay typhoon shelter, the neon lights were still on, dazzling as ever.

Suddenly he embraced me tightly and said, 'Evans, you're old, and weak. I've always thought of you as tall and strong. How cruel!'

I pushed him away, 'You're drunk. Go now.'

He laughed, staggered a few steps, and said, 'I'm off. We won't see each other again. I shall remember you, because you've taught me so much. When I grow old, I'll be like you too. But I shall always remember you as young, brave, and strong, as I shall remember myself.'

A patter of footsteps, and he disappeared somewhere in the carpark. Door opened, door closed. Headlights on, the engine roared. He was off.

A long time afterwards I would remember how I felt that night.

When things went back to normal, fear turned into fun. Later on, Oi Yuk and I started this game of blood pool. We'd fill the tub with warm water, open a bottle of red wine, play a card game—the loser would pour a glass of red wine into the water, turning it into blood—and we'd make love there. Oi Yuk was heavily pregnant now, she looked like a blood spider. We also played Chief Inspector and Murderer, Judge and Counsellor. I'd put on Oi Yuk's pyjamas, she'd don my three-piece suit to play the murderer of the baby's doll. Then winter came, and we were rushed off our feet. People died in droves, I was busy rushing people to hospital, Oi Yuk was busy arranging burial services for her clients, and when we were home, we'd be busy preparing for the arrival of the baby—cot, toys, education fund for the baby.

The day that Oi Yuk went into labour, I met that gweilo—the Chief Inspector. He'd grown a beard, it was streaked with white, and his clothes were a little shabby. He was smoking under the 'No Smoking' sign.

I greeted him, 'Remember me? Remember that murder case—five in the family wiped out?'

People turned to look at us. I laughed.

He said, 'Oh yes, I remember you.'

I lit up a cigarette too—to hell with the warning. 'How are you? Another guy bumped off?'

He just shook his head. I chattered on. 'My wife's in hospital. Premature labour, bacterial infection. Doctor said the baby might be mentally retarded.'

He just said, 'Oh,' and went on smoking.

An orderly came up to us—a little late, but here he was. He didn't say a word, but just pointed at the sign 'No Smoking. Penalty 500 dollars'. I dragged the Inspector by the arm to the garden outside the hospital.

As we were standing under the sun, he suddenly asked, 'What's to be done?'

'They won't fine us. I know the chap.'

'No, I mean what will you do, if you have a mentally retarded baby.'

'It will be okay; it will still be a lovely baby.'

He lit another cigarette. I watched two sparrows on a tree twittering and chattering.

'My son . . . caught red-handed with drugs. He jumped bail, was arrested at the airport. More charges, no bail. He tried to commit suicide.'

I was all attention. 'Is he dead?'

He shook his head.

I was disappointed, naturally, so I just said, 'Good. It's good to be alive, better to be dead.'

He smiled grimly, 'It's strange.'

I nipped off a rose from behind me, and with a flourishing of my arm, I presented it to him as if I was playing a magician's trick. 'Hey there, don't look so glum. Your son was caught napping, he went on the run, tried to kill himself, but there's no stopping him, is there?'

He said, amazed, 'You're such a smart crazy chap. What do you say I should do?'

I replied, 'Nothing. What can you do? You don't grow any roses, you don't get any roses. What to do? Nothing. Just get on, get on with it.'

It all came out muddled and confused, and the gweilo was confused and puzzled. Another orderly was walking up to us from afar. I looked down; we were standing on the grass, beside the sign 'No stepping on the grass. Penalty 500 dollars'. I pulled him by the arm and said, 'Let's go. No point talking about it anymore.'

He didn't say anything either, just looked down, mumbled 'goodbye', and went off, his hands stuck deep into his pockets. In the bright light of the winter sun, his big frame stood out prominently, but his body seemed lifeless, like a puppet.

231

Our baby does turn out to be mentally retarded. He doesn't cry much. Oi Yuk and I are still overjoyed. At night, we take turns to play with him, tease him, hold him, kiss him—life is wonderful. At night, I still drive the ambulance up and down the streets, the blue light flashing, taking casualties to the way of recovery, or death. My wife Oi Yuk is still gleeful when she learns that someone has died. She has designed a new outfit for the dead—a coat trimmed with artificial fur or sheepskin. Our baby is growing bigger by the day, and is very happy. He has rosy cheeks, it's just that he can't turn his head, and his eyes are constantly fixed on a person or object—a very attentive baby, he'll grow up to be a boy who gives life his full attention. There is a huge fire in the city, there are huge political rows. There are people who emigrate, people who are worried and confused. But Oi Yuk and I will live our life to the full. The owner of the house next door to us soon has the house painted a cheerful pink, and the garden is planted with new rose bushes and jasmine, and a gardenia tree. Another family has moved in, the man loves to cook while the woman works in the garden and repairs electrical appliances. Come what may, we shall live on, and be full of hope, love, care, and concern. For hope is never something just out there, or not there. It's like what God did to light and air. Let there be hope, and there is hope.

Chinese original published in Wong Bik Wan: *Tenderness and Violence*, Hong Kong: Cosmos Books Ltd, 1994.

23

The Hazards of Daily Life

By **XIN YUAN**
Translated by Jane C. C. Lai

This is another chapter from the novel, Crazy Horse in a Frenzied
City. *In this chapter, Crazy Horse, the reluctant agent, is in a bar in
Lan Kwai Fong. Disguised as a woman, he has to pass a message to
an Englishman whom the Chinese leader's illegitimate son wants
to meet. 'One country, two systems'—supposed to guarantee the
stability and prosperity of Hong Kong after 1997—receives here a
linguistic treatment as dazzling in effect as a fireworks extravaganza.*

Bam! The bartender slammed down a mug of beer before Crazy
Horse, breaking his dream.

He glanced at the Englishman opposite, and found that the man
was looking at him.

From the look of it, he was like a weakling eyeing somebody
weaker, a bullied child looking for a smaller kid to bully. Crazy
Horse didn't like that look.

He put down the beer mug with a thud—the Englishman was
startled, as if from a dream, and rubbed his eyes. Then Crazy
Horse took it out.

He held it in his hands a while, then handed it to the man.

The Englishman seemed puzzled, but he held out his hand and
took it. He touched its hard surface. You couldn't tell whether or
not he had seen it before.

'It's a personal seal with a name on it. Don't you recognize it?'

The man's answer was enigmatic. He dipped the thing into his drink, then stamped it on a coaster, leaving the imprint of a name. Then he looked up, and smiled.

'It's a name, it identifies you like your name,' Young Horse explained. 'It's your identity!'

'It's like your sex,' the gweilo said, and winked at him.

Old Horse sensed that the conversation was moving to dangerous ground.

For one thing, gweilos use a lot of innuendos in their language. The man could be using the word 'sex' to refer to Crazy Horse's gender, or he could mean the thing itself. One reason why he didn't like those devils was that they brought sex into everything!

Besides, dressed as he was, in drag, he was going about the business of his nation—at least the business of the future Special Administrative Region. ('Who do you think you are? Qiu Jin the revolutionary heroine?' he asked himself.) But he became aware at the same time that women compatriots of his (all the girlfriends he had had, whether of long standing or passing fancy, for instance), might have had such experience of sexual harassment. Sexual harassment east and west—depending on whether you joined the Chinese orchestra or the ballet company. (Although if you joined the Chinese Repertory Theatre, you might have more time to spend boning up on racing tips on horse and hound.)

But let's go back to the question of sexual harassment, or back to the question of sex, back to the impending danger, impending threat, in the situation confronting Old Horse.

'Do you know this guy?' Old Horse pointed at the seal, hoping to move from sex to politics, using the ambiguity of political language to replace the ambiguity of the language of sex.

'What if I do? And what if I don't?' the Englishman leered. Hell. He was moving the ambiguity from politics back to sex!

Old Horse was going to say, 'He wants to see you!' But somehow he just couldn't come out with it.

Perhaps he couldn't simply say it without it sounding like the solicitation of a pimp. How could he persuade himself that this was going to be a major contribution to the Sino-British negotiations and to the common good of the populace?

He felt as if he were sitting at the corner of a long conference table, strenuously going through documents and memoranda, trying to recall some forgotten detail in the minutes of some meeting, chasing after the flood of verbiage which flowed from the offices of bureaucrats, and trying to make out whether, in the ongoing discussion, people were referring to Appendix AB or CD.

Then the long arguments, each side defending his own position, circuitously, directly; the exchanges forwards and backwards like swords, like rapiers. . . .

But no. It wasn't like that.

The present situation was: sitting in this circus of a bar, uncomfortably crammed into a tight-fitting dress, the high-heeled shoes pinching his feet, the make-up sticky on his face, he was being forced over and over again into playing a role he didn't want to play. And this Englishman before him—whom he could not figure out—was this man playing an inconsequential prank, or was he serious? Or was there some conspiracy?

He could not get to the bottom of it.

(But the conspiracy theory was everywhere. The papers, for example, had a photograph of a senior official curling his lip as he told the public not to treat the new system of pensions as a conspiracy.)

What the hell was he doing here?

Crazy Horse hummed and hawed, hesitated, and at last came out with it: 'He . . . he wants to see you.'

The pale face (like the desolate emptiness in the sky after the glory of a resplendent sunset) was almost expressionless, the raised glass having hidden much of the face.

He really couldn't tell whether he was acting as a pimp or a go-between for a secret political negotiation.

'Hello, honey!'

Another gweilo who had squeezed close to him in the crowd a moment ago was now by his side, and was affectionately clasping him by the shoulder, saying, 'A riddle for you. I'll give you a big prize if you get the answer right!'

He wagged an index finger before Old Horse's eyes. It looked as if it had an insinuating life of its own as it headed for the bridge of Old Horse's nose. 'Take a good look!'

Old Horse turned away in disgust.

235

He was annoyed, the possibility of a Sino-British dialogue was interrupted. Behind him, he heard two gweilos talking about the Sino-British negotiations and commenting naively on Hong Kong politics.

And in front of him this one was pushing a face, mouth open, towards his, 'You know why Beethoven never used this finger to play piano?' The finger came at him like a guided missile.

Old Horse got up and backed away. The gweilo lunged into empty air and fell down in the booth seat.

The two gweilos behind him were still engaged in their elementary thinking process: 'D'you know why Hong Kong people don't express their views in the Sino-British talks?'

The riddle-man was crawling up, and the guided missile was on the move again, curving and circling through the air. Trailing behind it was the free bonus of a gigantic grin, backed by myriad fireworks on the pimpled face, fireworks that whistled and flared to exuberant brass-band music to spray the sky with colour and then fall through the dark night to sprinkle the waves of the ever beautiful harbour of Victoria.

'Don't you point your finger at me!' Young Horse shouted.

'Right! Bingo! You've got it! Because the finger is *mine*, not Beethoven's! Ha ha ha! I'll give you a big prize for this!' the gweilo shouted.

He pursed his lips and dashed forward like a bear making for honey. Old Horse was quick to rise to the occasion. He whipped the table cloth off the table, waved it beside him, turned matador-fashion, and the prize-giving Santa Claus dived straight past him.

One of the two gweilo commentators was saying, 'Why don't the people of Hong Kong use their—'

Santa Claus Descending could not brake, and his pointed finger went straight into the commentator's mouth.

Then *smack*, the big fat lips of Santa Claus kissed the commentator's face.

This newly arrived journalist for the *South China Morning Post* or the *Far Eastern Economic Review* never thought that discussing the crisis in Hong Kong with such detachment would bring him this grievous bodily kiss, and he choked. Something had jammed his mouth.

His companion, an Aussie, somewhat slow on the uptake, did not notice the drama around him. He was looking down, reading the wine list or something, and mumbling to himself (because nobody could hear what he was saying), repeating what his friend was saying, 'You were saying why the people of Hong Kong don't use their . . .' He looked up, saw the latest development, and added in amazement, '. . . finger?'

Santa Claus Descending's finger was trapped; he was a captive wolf. The journalist commentator was speechless, waving frantically for help. Had you not known that he was choking, you might have thought that he was sobbing and shuddering in the ecstasy of a deep-throat climax—an experience he had never had back home, and was discovering for the first time in this colonial territory. He writhed and turned in mortal agony in his booth seat, energy drained from his limbs, delirious.

The slow-on-the-uptake Aussie stood up. He was a real marvel, if a trifle slow, like a mechanical Arnold Schwarzenegger someone had forgotten to wind up. The giant genie slowly raised his left hand and then his right to pull apart the Siamese twins. But they were stuck, and nothing worked.

Old Horse saw that this impasse was just the right moment for a getaway. (Typical Hong Kong mentality!) But he had some unfinished business to finish with this pale, almost osteocarcinomatic Englishman.

He took an address from his pocket and held it in front of the man's eyes.

'In three days at 7 p.m. he'll be waiting for you.'

Were they going to meet him in that Stanley villa which sometimes made it into the news? Many high-ranking Chinese officials had probably stayed there. After reading the address, the man took out a lighter and burnt it, then dropped it into the ashtray.

Such swift action was conducive to confidence.

It was obvious that the man had come to Hong Kong not just to go to Edward Lam's gay film festival. The barmaid served Old Horse a mug of beer. He took a mouthful, and suddenly realized that he hadn't ordered one! He checked the table: the ashtray had disappeared. When was it taken away?

Damn! All was discovered! At the very least they had been watched. He had forgotten to check whether the entire address had been rendered into ashes. His eyes panned like a camera in search of the barmaid. But he couldn't find her. He tried to ascertain whether there were any suspicious characters about. No one from last night's crowd seemed to be there, but then everyone looked suspicious. He was in disguise, others were too perhaps?

The best move was probably to make for the door. But before he even stood up, the man across the table had vanished. In times of crisis, look after Number One. That's the way it is now in Hong Kong. He made as if to go to the toilet, and left a signal for New-York-Water to say they would meet up in her flat that night. He dared not talk to her for fear of bringing her trouble. He didn't even know who was tailing whom, and whether he was a target for the other side.

He was just about to push open the door of the men's room when he saw a man coming out of it and suddenly remembered the way he was dressed. As he went into the ladies', he felt the man was glaring at him. Was he one of them? Crazy Horse couldn't be sure. He hurriedly shut the door, and looked to see if there was a bolt to secure it. In the mirror he saw a dishevelled face, flaking make-up over pallid cheeks. He was a man with a job and an apartment: why had he fallen to this sorry state, like a frightened mongrel without a home?

There was a knocking on the door. Knock, knock, knock. Who was there? They were after him. What should he do? He looked around. Was there a way out? He saw a square of a window at the back. He pushed with difficulty and it opened. The knocking came again. Knock, knock, knock. There was no time for hesitation. He poked his head out. There was a laundry rack outside. He caught hold of it and pulled himself up, easing his body out of the window. Half of him got out, and then he was stuck. He twisted and turned and yanked. He felt as if he were a cork that would not be pulled out of a bottle. Knock, knock, knock. The knocking started again.

Somebody was pushing at the door. He turned and twisted, heaved himself in and out of the bottle. He could not spend the rest of his life like this. There he was, one body in two places, one country, two systems, one will in two minds; the top half of him was in the air bathing in the light of the new moon, the bottom half was in the loo. He tried again, hoping for a smooth transition, when body and soul would unite. In the moment of desperation, an idea was born, the fire of inspiration flared, giving him unbounded strength, and he pushed. Rip! The sound of cloth torn asunder. His long skirt was rent.

His legs took him to freedom, but he lost his balance. Quickly he grabbed hold of the laundry rack and dangled from it like a swing, like a pendulum, like a high-ranking colonial civil servant being courted into the embrace of the new regime, swaying forwards and backwards, attracting at once the attention of the potted plants on the window sills and the tatty brooms in the back alley—a scene so moving that the fat curled-up pussy cat waiting for his master's consoling caresses wept.

Old Horse felt his feet cold, his skirt trailing in the breeze. He was walking on air, his legs now soothed by, now free from, the frail gossamer that might at any moment be gone with the wind.

He saw clearly now that he was only one floor up from the ground. From a television set in a flat nearby came the news broadcast—the talks had broken down and Chris Patten was taking part of the political reform package to the Legislative Council. And meanwhile the Chinese and the British accused each other of playing the economy card.

Then on the screen came a portrait of Mao—probably from a Western magazine—with a bright red lipstick mark on his left cheek which caught the eye more quickly then the mole on his chin.

Two naked legs passed to and fro in front of the TV set and got in the way. He gave up watching, closed his eyes, and let go of the rack.

The great hard earth rushed at him and slapped him in the face. He felt as if his bones were dispersing in all directions. He blacked out and fainted dead away.

After the impact, he thought he had had it. He lay there thinking back on the folly of half a lifetime, of too much drinking, too little exercise, of never having any success in love, never having taken the arty photos he had wanted to take, never having been director of a film, and then ending his life in a back alley like this. Shame!

He yearned for the sound of police-car sirens, for a running gunfight sequence, for the heart-rending gut-twisting music that comes at the end of films, but there was nothing.

He heard only the muffled sound of television broadcast in the distance, of water dripping from a tap, and even the fat pussy cat which wandered past ignored him and walked on, in search of some young cats to miao with. He didn't know how long he lay there. Then he heard some noises up above. Perhaps someone had broken into the toilet and was looking down. He strained to turn over and rolled into the dark shadows under the verandah.

He could not understand why even though he was pursued to the death the whole thing was done with so little rhyme or reason, with so little pomp and circumstance, so very differently from what befell the familiar movie heroes he used to watch. Then the noise stopped, taking away even the thrill of danger in suspense.

He crawled under the stairway and curled up there.

Moments passed. Hurried footsteps, as if some heavies were running past.

He lay there, curled up like a newborn babe, or more like an abandoned newborn babe (Relax. I have no intention of asking Ye Luzun to film a few Category III sequences for insertion here as Yau Kong Kin did in his *Babe*.) without a past, without a future, just curled up there, motionless, cut, bruised, and exhausted.

Time passed. Night was sure to have fallen. The alley grew dark with shadows, things were blurred. The hustle and bustle of night revellers filtered through the distance to reach his ears.

The abandoned babe stirred, as if waking from a coma, and slowly lifted himself from the ground. Then, trailing fuzzy strands of light, looking this way and that, and clinging to the walls, he staggered to his feet.

He felt dizzy. He didn't know where to turn, didn't know whether there was anybody tailing him.

Not for him the bustle of life, but he still made his way out there clinging to the wall. He had to go down the slope out there before he could get to his 'vintage' car. Once in his car, even if his home was wrecked, he could still go to New-York-Water's place. He could at least find temporary shelter there.

His head felt cold. He touched it to find that his wig had gone, he didn't know where or when. There was no way he could find it now. He pressed ahead and got out of the alley.

He tried to minimize his bulk, to shrink into an insignificant target, to be like a mere stone on the slope.

Fortunately, on the slope, there were always endless parades, of guests attending the openings of new bars, dressed as variegated ladies in colourful period costumes, as Indian maharajas, as Robin

Hoods and highwaymen, as demented nuns, as armoured knights. If, in the midst of this carnival, there was a half-man half-woman with dishevelled hair, flaking make-up, and wrapped in a long shredded *petit fleur* skirt, no one would pay any attention.

Thanks to the mixture of cultures and the rupture of time and space.

But someone recognized him. . . .

Chinese original published in Xin Yuan: *Crazy Horse in a Frenzied City*, Hong Kong: Youth Literary Bookstore, 1996.

About the Editor

MARTHA P. Y. CHEUNG received her BA and M.Phil. in English Literature from the University of Hong Kong, and her Ph.D. in English and American Literature from the University of Kent at Canterbury. She has taught English Literature and Translation at the University of Hong Kong, and Translation at the Chinese University of Hong Kong. She is now Associate Professor of Translation and Associate Director of the Centre for Translation at the Hong Kong Baptist University. She has translated many works of Chinese literature into English, including those of Han Shaogong (*Homecoming? and Other Stories*, 1992), Liu Sola (*Blue Sky Green Sea and Other Stories*, 1993), Zhu Tianxin, Lai Shêng-ch'uan, and of Hong Kong poets such as P. K. Leung (*Foodscape*, 1997), Tsai Yim Pui, and Choi Ka Ping. She co-edited (with Jane C. C. Lai) *An Oxford Anthology of Contemporary Chinese Drama* (1997), and co-translated (with Jane C. C. Lai) *100 Excerpts from Zen Buddhist Texts* (1997).

About the Authors

CHAN PO CHUN 陳寶珍 was born in Hong Kong in 1953. She received her BA in Chinese Language and Literature and M.Phil. in Chinese Literature from the Chinese University of Hong Kong. In 1991 her collection of short stories *Looking for a House* 找房子 (1990) won an inaugural prize in the fiction section of the Hong Kong Biennial Award for Chinese Literature. A collection of her prose work, *Crazy Friends* 狂朋怪友, was published in 1994. She is now Associate Professor in Chinese at the Hong Kong Baptist University.

DUNG KAI CHEUNG 董啟章 was born in Hong Kong in 1967. He received his BA and M.Phil. in Comparative Literature from the University of Hong Kong. Since 1992, his works have been published in newspapers and magazines such as *Sing Tao Daily* 星島日報, *Su Ye Literature* 素葉文學, and *Hong Kong Literature Monthly* 香港文學. He has won several prestigious literary awards in Taiwan, including the Unitas Novel Writing Award for New Writers (1994), and the United Daily News Literary Award (1995). He is now a full-time writer, well-known for his experimentation with narrative forms and the play of genres. His major works include *Androgyny* 安卓珍尼 (fiction, 1996), *The Double Body* 雙身 (novel, 1997), *The Rose of the Name* 名字的玫瑰 (short stories, 1997), and *The Atlas: Archaeology of an Imaginary City* 地圖集：一個想像的城市的考古學 (fiction, 1997). He is also a literary critic and has co-written and edited *The Book Teller—Reading and Criticism* 說書人：閱讀與評論合集 (1996), *Speaking and Writing—Interviews and Readings of Ten Hong Kong Writers* 講話文章：訪問、閱讀十位香港作家 (1996), and *Speaking and Writing II—Interviews and Reviews of Hong Kong Young Writers* 講話文章：香港青年作家訪談與評介 (1997).

P. K. LEUNG 梁秉鈞 (pen-name for fictional works: Ye Si 也斯) was born in Hong Kong in 1949. He received his Ph.D. in Comparative

Literature from the University of California, San Diego. He taught at the University of Hong Kong, and is now Professor of Chinese at Lingnan College. He started writing in the late 1960s and has since established a reputation as a writer of amazing energy and diverse accomplishments. Not only is he a poet and a novelist, he is also a film critic, a literary cirtic, and a culture critic. His major works include *Shimen the Dragon-keeper* 養龍人師門 (fiction, 1979), *Thunder Rumbles and Cicada Chirps* 雷聲與蟬鳴 (poems, 1979), *Island and Mainland* 島和大陸 (short stories, 1987), *Journeys* 游詩 (poems, 1985), *Three Fish* 三魚集 (novella, 1988), *Postcards from Prague* 布拉格的明信片 (short stories, 1990), which won the first Hong Kong Biennial Literary Award for Chinese fiction in 1991, *Hong Kong Culture* 香港文化 (essays, 1995), *A Poetry of Floating Signs* 游離的詩 (1995), *Cultural Space and Literature in Hong Kong* 香港文化空間與文學 (essays, 1996), and *Foodscape* 食事地域誌 (poems, 1997).

LIU YICHANG 劉以鬯 was born in Shanghai in 1918. After graduating from St John's University in Shanghai in 1941, he worked variously as translator, leader-writer, and editor-in-chief on newspapers and magazines. He also founded a publishing house. In 1948, he came to Hong Kong. Since then, he has worked as the editor of a number of newspapers, while he devotes his spare time to literary writing and to the promotion of literature in Hong Kong. He founded *Hong Kong Literature Monthly* 香港文學 in 1985 and is still its chief editor. His representative works are collected in an anthology which he himself edited: *Selected Works of Liu Yichang* 劉以鬯卷 (1991). His novel *The Drunkard* 酒徒 (1963) has influenced a whole generation of Hong Kong writers and is still considered one of the best experimental novels to have appeared in Hong Kong in the 1960s.

LOK SIU PING 駱笑平 was born in Hong Kong in 1952. After graduating from the First Institute of Design in 1973, she worked as a freelance illustrator. She studied copperplate etching at the Ecole dés Arts Decoratif in Paris from 1979 to 1982, and came back to Hong Kong in 1984. She is now a freelance illustrator and prints designer. She writes fiction and prose from time to time.

NG HUI BUN 吳煦斌 was born in Hong Kong in 1949. She studied Biology in Hong Kong and received her master's degree in Ecology from the San Diego State University. She has translated into Chinese Jean-Paul Sartre's *La Nausée* and short stories by Gabriel Garcia Marquez and other Latin-American writers. Her translations have been published in periodicals such as *Seasons* 四季 and *The Thumb Weekly* 大拇指周報. She has also published a collection of prose, *Remembrances and Thoughts* 看牛集 (1991), and two volumes of short stories, *Cows* 牛 (1980) and *A Collection of Short Stories by Ng Hui Bun* 吳煦斌小説集 (1987).

SHI RAN 適然, real name Lok Sik Yin 駱適然, was born in Hong Kong in 1955. After finishing her secondary school, she worked as a reporter and an editor for a number of magazines and co-founded *The Thumb Weekly* 大拇指周報 in 1975. In the following year, she emigrated to Los Angeles and received her BA from the University of California, Los Angeles. In 1990, she returned to Hong Kong and is now a newspaper columnist. Her fictional works and prose were published in *Sing Tao Daily* 星島日報 and *Su Ye Literature* 素葉文學.

SONG MU 松木, real name Choi Chun Hing 蔡振興, was born in Hong Kong in 1953. He read Philosophy and English Language and Literature at the Chinese University of Hong Kong and devoted his spare time to literary pursuits. He is now a secondary school teacher. Apart from fiction, he also writes prose, film reviews, and literary critiques. He has published a collection of prose entitled *Nighttime Bicycle* 夜行單車 (1995).

WONG BIK WAN 黃碧雲 was born in Hong Kong in 1961. After graduating from the Chinese University of Hong Kong, she took a course in French language and culture at the Université Paris 1. She now works as a freelance writer for a number of newspapers and magazines. She has published three volumes of short stories—*After that* 其後 (1991), *Tenderness and Violence* 温柔與暴烈 (1994), *Seven Types of Silence* 七種靜默 (1997)—and a volume of prose, *It's Good—the Way We Are* 我們如此很好 (1996).

XI XI 西西, real name Zhang Yan 張彥, was born in Shanghai in 1938 and moved to Hong Kong with her parents in 1950. After graduating from Grantham College of Education she worked as a primary-school teacher until 1979, when she decided to take up writing full time. Her first story 'Maria' was published in 1965, and since then she has established herself as one of the most enchanting writers in Hong Kong, adept at genres ranging from short stories, novellas, prose, poems, reading notes, to novels. Her best-known works are *My City* 我城 (novel, 1979), *Cross Currents* 交河 (short stories and essays, 1981), *Stone Chimes* 石磬 (poetry, 1982), *Deer Hunt* 哨鹿 (novel, 1982), *Spring Prospects* 春望 (short stories, 1982), *A Girl Like Me* 像我這樣的一個女子 (short stories, 1984, the title story of which won the prestigious Taiwan United Daily Prize for Fiction in 1982), *Beard with a Face* 鬍子有臉 (short stories, 1986), *Manuscript* 手卷 (fiction, 1988), *Elegy for a Breast* 哀悼乳房 (novel, 1992), and *Flying Carpet* 飛氈 (novel, 1996).

XIAO SI 小思, real name Lo Wai Luen 盧瑋鑾, was born in Hong Kong. She read Chinese Language and Literature at New Asia College, Chinese University of Hong Kong. After graduating in 1964, she received her Diploma in Education from the Northcote Training College. In 1973, she went to Japan to study Chinese Literature at Kyoto University and received a master's degree in 1981. She is now Senior Lecturer in the Chinese Department of the Chinese University of Hong Kong. She has published several volumes of prose, and is a well-respected researcher in the field of Hong Kong Literature.

XIN QISHI 辛其氏, real name Kan Mo Han 簡慕嫻, was born in Hong Kong in 1950. She has published a collection of prose entitled *At Holiday Time* 每逢佳節 (1985), and two collections of short stories: *The Blue Crescent Moon* 青色的月牙 (1986), and *The Red Chequers Pub* 紅格子酒鋪 (1994). She works in the education sector and writes in her spare time.

XIN YUAN 心猿, real name Yeung Siu Lin 楊少蓮, was born in Hong Kong in 1970. She read Fine Arts and Comparative Literature at the University of Hong Kong and has worked in the mass media. She is now pursuing postgraduate studies in Britain. *Crazy Horse in a Frenzied City* 狂城亂馬 (1996), first serialized in *Hong Kong Today* 現代日報, is her first novel.

YAN CHUNGOU 顏純鈎 was born in China in 1948 and received his primary and secondary education in Fujian Province. During the Cultural Revolution, he was sent to settle in the countryside as a member of the production team of the Yongfu Commune in Fujian. He came to Hong Kong in 1978 and worked as a typesetter and a proof-reader before becoming the editor of a newspaper supplement. He now works as an editor in a publishing house. He began writing after arriving in Hong Kong and has won a number of local literary awards. His fictional works include *Traffic Lights* 紅綠燈 (1984) and *Divine Retribution* 天譴 (1992).

YU FENG 俞風, real name Yu Hon Kong 余漢江, was born in Hong Kong in 1958 and graduated from the Hong Kong Polytechnic. A surveyor now, he has published a collection of prose entitled *Sunshine on the Wall* 牆上的陽光 (1994), and a volume of poems entitled *Watching the River* 看河集 (1994). He is also editor of *Su Ye Literature* 素葉文學, a literary magazine that has been a major nourishing ground for many local writers.

About the
Translators

CHAN NGA TING completed her BA in Chinese and Translation at the Chinese University of Hong Kong. She is currently studying at the City University of Hong Kong for her MA in Language and Law.

MARTHA P. Y. CHEUNG (see About the Editor)

DUNG KAI CHEUNG (see About the Authors)

KWOK HONG LOK received his education in Hong Kong and Canada, and teaches Translation at the Hong Kong Baptist University. His English translation of Anthony Chan's play *American House* is included in *An Oxford Anthology of Contemporary Chinese Drama* (1997).

JANE C. C. LAI studied at the University of Hong Kong and the University of Bristol. She taught English Literature and Translation at the University of Hong Kong for many years, and is now Chair Professor of Translation, Director of the Centre for Translation, and Dean of the Arts Faculty at the Hong Kong Baptist University. She has a long association with the Hong Kong theatre scene, mainly in the area of translation of playscripts for performance. Plays translated include those by Shakespeare, Harold Pinter, Tom Stoppard, Eugene O'Neill, Arthur Miller, Edward Albee, Samuel Beckett, Bertolt Brecht, and Jean Genet. She is the co-editor (with Martha P. Y. Cheung) of *An Oxford Anthology of Contemporary Chinese Drama* (1997) and the co-translator (with Martha P. Y. Cheung) of *100 Excepts from Zen Buddhist Texts* (1997).

P. K. LEUNG has, since the late 1960s, devoted much time to the translation and introduction of contemporary Latin American,

French, and American short stories to the Chinese reader. One of his recent works is a collection of poems and essays by Gary Snyder, *The Mountain is the Mind* (1990), which he co-edited and co-translated. He also co-edited and co-translated into English (with the American poet Gordon Osing) his own volume of poetry, *City at the End of Time* (1992). Some of his translations of modern Chinese poetry are collected in the anthology, *Lyrics from the Shelters: Modern Chinese Poetry* (1992).

DAVID PATTINSON is an Assistant Professor in the Department of Translation, Lingnan College, Hong Kong. He works on Ming and Qing dynasty informal literature, and has published translations of contemporary Chinese fiction and late Ming letters.

CATHY POON, a freelance translator, studied translation at the University of Hong Kong and received her MA from the Chinese University of Hong Kong. She has translated into English *Chinese Ceramic Pillows* (1993), *Chinese Archaic Jades from the Kwan Collection* (1994), *A Child's First Library of Values* (1997), and other books.

ROBERTA RAINE began studying Chinese language in 1986. She is due to complete her Ph.D. in Translation at the City University of Hong Kong in the summer of 1998.

JANICE WICKERI studied Chinese at Middlebury College and Princeton University, and has lived in Taiwan, Hong Kong, and the People's Republic of China. She is Editor of *The Chinese Theological Review*, an annual volume of translations, and Managing Editor of *Renditions*. She has also edited *Explosions and Other Stories* by Mo Yan (1991), and is co-editor of *May Fourth Women Writers: Memoirs* (1996). Her English translation of Ma Zhongjun's play, *The Legend of Old Bawdy Town*, is included in *An Oxford Anthology of Contemporary Chinese Drama* (1997).